WORF THREW HIMSELF FORWARD.

He slammed Technician Tarses into the side of the tube and was jolted away. With one easy motion, Worf grabbed Tarses. The technician let out a loud cry as he hit the floor of the tube, twisting to get out of Worf's hands.

Worf looked down at the panel. Only one more command was left before the shuttlebay doors would open and the bay would depressurize, destroying the helpless alien Sli—and Worf and Tarses as well.

"They have to die!" Tarses shouted. "They're killing us all!"

Look for STAR TREK Fiction from Pocket Books

Star Trek: The Original Series

Sarek
Best Destiny
Shadows on the Sun
Probe
Prime Directive
The Lost Years
Star Trek VI: The Undiscovered Country
Star Trek V: The Final Frontier
Star Trek IV: The Voyage Home
Spock's World
Enterprise
Strangers from the Sky
Final Frontier

#1 Star Trek: The Motion Picture
#2 The Entropy Effect
#3 The Klingon Gambit
#4 The Covenant of the Crown
#5 The Prometheus Design
#6 The Abode of Life
#7 Star Trek II: The Wrath of Khan
#8 Black Fire
#9 Triangle
#10 Web of the Romulans
#11 Yesterday's Son
#12 Mutiny on the Enterprise
#13 The Wounded Sky
#14 The Trellisane Confrontation
#15 Corona
#16 The Final Reflection
#17 Star Trek III: The Search for Spock
#18 My Enemy, My Ally
#19 The Tears of the Singers
#20 The Vulcan Academy Murders
#21 Uhura's Song
#22 Shadow Lord
#23 Ishmael
#24 Killing Time
#25 Dwellers in the Crucible
#26 Pawns and Symbols
#27 Mindshadow

#28 Crisis on Centaurus
#29 Dreadnought!
#30 Demons
#31 Battlestations!
#32 Chain of Attack
#33 Deep Domain
#34 Dreams of the Raven
#35 The Romulan Way
#36 How Much for Just the Planet?
#37 Bloodthirst
#38 The IDIC Epidemic
#39 Time for Yesterday
#40 Timetrap
#41 The Three-Minute Universe
#42 Memory Prime
#43 The Final Nexus
#44 Vulcan's Glory
#45 Double, Double
#46 The Cry of the Onlies
#47 The Kobayashi Maru
#48 Rules of Engagement
#49 The Pandora Principle
#50 Doctor's Orders
#51 Enemy Unseen
#52 Home Is the Hunter
#53 Ghost Walker
#54 A Flag Full of Stars
#55 Renegade
#56 Legacy
#57 The Rift
#58 Faces of Fire
#59 The Disinherited
#60 Ice Trap
#61 Sanctuary
#62 Death Count
#63 Shell Game
#64 The Starship Trap
#65 Windows on a Lost World
#66 From the Depths
#67 The Great Starship Race
#68 Firestorm

Star Trek: The Next Generation

Dark Mirror
Descent
The Devil's Heart
Imzadi
Relics
Reunion
Unification
Metamorphosis
Vendetta
Encounter at Farpoint

#1 Ghost Ship
#2 The Peacekeepers
#3 The Children of Hamlin
#4 Survivors
#5 Strike Zone
#6 Power Hungry
#7 Masks
#8 The Captains' Honor
#9 A Call to Darkness

#10 A Rock and a Hard Place
#11 Gulliver's Fugitives
#12 Doomsday World
#13 The Eyes of the Beholders
#14 Exiles
#15 Fortune's Light
#16 Contamination
#17 Boogeymen
#18 Q-in-Law
#19 Perchance to Dream
#20 Spartacus
#21 Chains of Command
#22 Imbalance
#23 War Drums
#24 Nightshade
#25 Grounded
#26 The Romulan Prize
#27 Guises of the Mind
#28 Here There Be Dragons
#29 Sins of Commission

Star Trek: Deep Space Nine

#1 Emissary
#2 The Siege
#3 Bloodletter
#4 The Big Game
#5 Fallen Heroes

STAR TREK
THE NEXT GENERATION ®

SINS OF COMMISSION

SUSAN WRIGHT

POCKET BOOKS

New York   London   Toronto   Sydney   Tokyo   Singapore

An *Original* Publication of POCKET BOOKS

POCKET BOOKS, a division of Simon & Schuster Inc.
1230 Avenue of the Americas, New York, NY 10020

STAR TREK is a Registered Trademark of Paramount Pictures.

This book is published by Pocket Books, a division of Simon & Schuster Inc., under exclusive license from Paramount Pictures.

ISBN: 978-1-4516-4171-4

First Pocket Books printing March 1994

10 9 8 7 6 5 4 3 2 1

POCKET and colophon are registered trademarks of Simon & Schuster Inc.

Printed in the U.S.A.

Acknowledgments

Thanks and appreciation go to Jeff Artemis-Gomez for helping me get it right;

To Jerry Schneiderman, Jonathan Frater, and Keith A.D. Post for technical support and encouragement;

And to my ST:TNG experts, Kevin Ryan and John Ordover.

SINS OF COMMISSION

Chapter One

"BEGIN PROGRAM," Captain Picard ordered.

Murmurs rose, excited yet subdued, as if anticipation had taken a form of its own.

The sound engulfed him, sweeping him out into the enormous room as his eyes followed the ascent of the silver chandeliers, slowly soaring toward the ceiling, incandescent with the fire of hundreds of slender yellow candles.

Picard walked forward, his hands lifting slightly from his sides as if to embrace it all. The curved wooden stage stood before him, mostly hidden by long curtains of crinkled crimson velvet. All around, back, behind, and above him, were the tiers of boxes, shadowed and draped with shimmering gold and red in the finest theatrical tradition. Yet there was also a grace of architecture more reminiscent of the organic revival of the twenty-third century than the boxy wooden amphitheaters this structure was patterned on.

That was the way of improvement—someone took an idea and reinterpreted it using innovations that had been developed, whether it was stronger materials or a new way of presenting a story. The difficulty was maintaining the integrity of the original while enhancing it with the new. In Picard's opinion, that's exactly what Barclay had done with this play, *Cyrano de Bergerac*. Even the clothing of the cast wasn't quite seventeenth century but a mélange of synthetic fibers combined with classical restraints and ornamented by dark glowing jewels. Strands of sparkling gold and pearls were laced through the women's hair and hung around their throats on intricate chains, while the men wore embroidered scabbards, with the filigree handguards often held by a deceptively casual hand.

The program was running—Picard could see the thief and Christian over to one side. He could have chosen to view the scene from a box or the top of the stairs, but instead he moved among the crowd of men who mingled on the bare floor of the theater. Known as the pit, the floor didn't have seats like the boxes that surrounded them.

Picard quickly scanned the boxes and located the holographic image of Dr. Beverly Crusher, dressed in the palest of sea green gowns that shimmered like ice when she moved. Her vibrant red hair was pulled up to one side and back, with a cascade of large curls falling down to brush one bare shoulder as she turned her head to speak to du Guiche. Unlike the other women, she wore small white flowers in her hair, not jewels. Barclay had designed her costume as well as the set.

Picard took a deep breath, clasping his hands behind him, smiling and at ease for a rare moment. Barclay had become more than a genius when his brain was enhanced by the alien probe they encountered at the Argus Array. Picard considered it fortunate that Barclay had been involved in a production of *Cyrano de Bergerac* when the contact had been made. Picard agreed with most critics that the essence of Rostand's French verse had never been fully captured in English. Yet Barclay had translated it offhandedly one night, complete with the production notes and set design. When Beverly read it, she had insisted his version be performed right then and there.

This was a recording of that performance. Ensign Barclay and Dr. Crusher had been the only two actors in the midst of computer-generated simulations.

As Picard mingled among the men in the pit, he listened to the progress of the play. Barclay as Cyrano called out his challenge from above, and various voices around him responded, "Oh, is it Cyrano?" "Sh! The play! The play!"

Picard didn't listen to the words so much as Barclay's assured, measured tones. And he didn't see Barclay. It was Cyrano de Bergerac.

Suddenly Cyrano leaped from a box above, landing with a subtle flourish as if to say such a deed was no effort to him. A young blood sitting behind Beverly jumped up and swaggered down the stairs to face Cyrano, his nose tilted as if he smelled something not quite to his liking. He challenged, "Sir! I do say, your . . . nose is rather large."

"Rather." Cyrano lifted a brow slightly. "Is that all?"
"All?"

Picard walked closer as Cyrano gravely removed his gloves. "My dear boy, you've squandered an opportunity! Here among the expectant crowd, what more perfect place to display your wit and style?" He shrugged, addressing his friends who were standing near. "Why, the possibilities abound. . . . This young man could have expressed his disgust—if that is what he intended to convey—with a sneer, ''Tis a misfortune indeed to be born with a nose like that, but if it were I, then I would have it no longer!' "

A laugh rose around them at the double entendre. Cyrano swept his hand in the air, stilling the sound. "But perhaps he is not so bold? A more timid soul would slyly suggest, 'Need you a wider glass for your wine, sir?' But then again, one could simply describe the monstrosity, as if it were separate from the human within it—'Look!' " Cyrano exclaimed in mock horror, pointing one finger as the other attempted to hide his large, uptilted nose. " 'Tis a deformed—' "

Picard's communicator chittered.

He tapped his comm badge, allowing the program to continue. "Picard here."

"Captain," came the softly accented voice of his ship's counselor. "May I join you on the holodeck?"

"Certainly, Counselor."

Picard turned to the rear of the theater in time to see the huge door materialize. Deanna Troi smiled as she stepped inside. Even relaxed, she held her back perfectly straight, and every long curl was immaculately in place.

"Ah! *Cyrano de Bergerac.*" Her smile deepened. "Again? I thought you viewed this play just a few weeks ago."

Picard raised his brows, but the counselor apparently knew him well enough to make light of the professional edge to her question.

"Barclay's interpretation is a remarkable achievement," Picard said, excusing his interest. "This play has traditionally been considered more artifice than art— theatrics rather than poetry. But what Barclay has done here," he said, glancing up at the theater again, caught once more by the candle flames and tiny flashes of light that danced off the chandeliers, "is show us it is our own limitations that shape us, with Cyrano the embodiment of the superficial—a man so concerned with his appearance that he won't tell a woman he loves her, so concerned with independence that he seeks out enemies to prove he's no man's lackey. This polishes perversity until it rings a tone as pure as church bells."

Troi clasped her hands behind her back as she looked around the holodeck theater. Cyrano was finishing his monologue, his voice rising and falling as he built to his denouement.

"I remember the first time I saw Barclay's version. It was breathtaking." She looked back at Picard. "But I'm sorry to interrupt, Captain. I thought you would be through by now."

Picard nodded shortly. "I've seen it once already. Computer end—"

"This is your second viewing today?" she interrupted, a considering glint in her eyes.

Right in front of them, Cyrano began the "Ballade of the Duel between Monsieur de Bergerac and an Idiot in the Theatre de Bourgogne." As he composed the first stanza, he threw back his cloak and drew his sword.

Picard gestured. "This is the scene I wanted to see."

The blades of the foils met with a light clash, then began to etch intricate silver arcs in the air as the two men fenced.

"He's very good," Troi said, with a nod at Barclay.

"Yes, the choreography is superb. But it's in the way he concentrates on the composition of the poem—see there?—rather than the actual duel that makes this scene so powerful. It reveals an even deeper mastery of the blade."

"I think I understand." She nodded, as if fitting a puzzle together. "For you, Cyrano de Bergerac embodies the Gallic temperament with all its refinements and accomplishments."

"Panache," Picard said, more to himself than Troi.

"Yes, the perfect Frenchman, isn't he? Forceful, flamboyant, and lively, yet tender when it's called for. Expert at fencing with both swords and words. And you find that fascinating because this is your ancestry—"

"End program," Picard said.

The theater dissolved into a large black cube, bisected by a glowing yellow grid. The transition was startling—Barclay's Theatre de Bourgogne had become that real.

Troi sighed in disappointment. "I was enjoying that."

"Yes, well," Picard said with a slight smile, glad there was such a thing as captain's prerogative so he could end discussions if he wished. "You wanted to see me, Counselor?"

Troi immediately returned to business. "Yes, sir. I'd like to give you my report now, if I could."

He nodded. "Certainly. We're not due to arrive at Lessenar for another hour."

As they started toward the door, Troi added, "I'm going to try to talk to Worf during our regularly scheduled time. He's been hard to get hold of lately."

Picard examined her more carefully. "Is there a problem with our security chief, Counselor?"

The holodeck doors opened with a reverberating clang. Two crew members in gray coveralls were passing by.

Troi smiled and nodded at them. But her smile faded as she joined the captain by his side, pacing silently down the corridor to the turbolift.

"I'm not certain," she said, finally looking up again. "He's a little like our friend Cyrano. Brave, confident, proud . . ."

Picard nodded. "There's nothing of concern in that."

Troi waited until the doors closed on them and Picard gave the order for the bridge.

"No," she said, impatience creeping into her tone. "It's the other qualities—oh, like being stubborn and compulsive—that cause problems."

Picard nodded thoughtfully, remembering Worf's latest security report. It had been much longer than usual, and had included a number of rather insignificant incidents to support Worf's contention that security procedures were too lax on board the *Enterprise*. Yet Picard hadn't completely discounted the report when he read it, thinking that Worf's intuition could be telling him something that the facts had not conveyed.

Now, as he silently waited out the turbolift ride,

preferring to discuss the matter in private, Picard acknowledged that anything concerning the ship's security was worth an in-depth inquiry. He straightened his shoulders, his rare hour of relaxation over. It was back to being the captain of a Galaxy-class starship, responsible for over a thousand crew members and their families.

Chapter Two

"IS THERE ANYTHING in particular that has you worried?" the captain asked her.

Deanna accepted the hot cup of tea, tucking one leg under her. The sofa in the ready room was surprisingly comfortable.

"No," she said slowly, taking a sip of her tea. "It's just that a lot of little things seem to be adding up lately."

"Little things?" The captain sat down across from her, holding his own clear cup.

"Yes. I accessed Worf's latest security report." She wondered how many of the section heads knew that in addition to periodic consultations and her Betazoid empathic talents, she used their reports as a barometer of their emotional state. Counseling wasn't all just empathic sensations—she needed background, too. Without realizing it, she sat up straighter, confident of her assessment of Worf.

Picard cleared his throat, surprising her by agreeing. "Worf's report did seem odd."

Deanna gave him a quick look. She should have known

8

the captain wouldn't have let something like this slip by him.

"Then you see what I mean," she said. "Lately he's been hard on his security crew, more severe than necessary, I think. People need positive reinforcement, but Worf seems to have forgotten that."

"Do you know what might be causing this?"

Deanna sighed. "I hate to say it, but I think Alexander's presence in his life is making Worf question himself. Worf grew up thinking he was pure Klingon—remember when he first came on board? He constantly denied there was any trace of human influence in his behavior. But now he's had the chance to see how different he is from other Klingons, and his son leans even more toward human values."

The captain frowned thoughtfully. "I thought Worf had come to accept his unique upbringing."

"It's an ongoing process. When new things challenge our concept of who and what we are, it can raise new questions. Or," she told him with a shrug, "Worf could simply be experiencing some sort of backlash from the sudden change of Alexander coming into his life. You know, Worf didn't choose this lifetime commitment—it was handed to him." She ducked her head slightly, wishing she understood Worf better. But she tried to suppress the desire, aware that it was only her exaggerated sense of professional perfectionism that was bothering her. "I can't be sure until he talks to me. His aggressive reactions sometimes distort the empathic signals I receive from him."

A note of curiosity crept into the captain's voice. "What about Alexander?"

"He trusts me, so it's not difficult to sense how he feels." She shook her head. "And Alexander is confused. On the one hand, Worf is doing everything he can to encourage him to be a little warrior. But he won't let

Alexander challenge his authority on anything. Nothing. Worf thinks his word should be law, and he's always talking about discipline and self-control. Alexander sees the other children are encouraged to just have fun."

"You seriously think the root of all this lies in his son?"

"Worf is watching Alexander growing up and having to choose between two very disparate cultures. The echoes could be distressing to Worf."

The captain clinked his cup against the saucer as he shifted, reminding Deanna how much he disliked anything that seemed to be prying into his crew's private lives.

"I wouldn't bring this to your attention, Captain, unless I believed it was affecting Worf's performance as security chief."

"Yes, I'll keep in mind that he may be more on edge than usual. But I don't see a real danger to *Enterprise* security in this."

"At this point, I'm more worried about his security officers than him." Deanna smiled at him. "And Alexander."

"Yes, he's filed dozens of reprimands in his last report. I'm sure morale in security is very low." Picard set down his cup and picked up his padd, making a notation. "I'll speak to Worf about pending some of the more minor ones. Have you any other suggestions?"

"I'll continue to try to talk to him informally. You know that Worf discontinued Alexander's counseling sessions. We barely managed to work out a preliminary communication process between them, and not much more than that, I'm afraid." She tightened her lips, again working to keep the self-reproach out of her voice. "If Alexander's erratic behavior continues, the teachers will eventually log a request that he and Worf return to therapy. But therapy won't be productive if Worf doesn't actively cooperate, and putting a request on permanent file will make him resent it even more."

"So we'll keep it unofficial for now. Very good. If it makes him rein in harder on his staff for a time, well, that may be beneficial in the long run."

Deanna consulted her own padd. "The rest of my weekly report is fairly routine. I've put it on file for you to read later. But there is one matter we need to discuss about Medical Technician Tarses."

The captain nodded slightly. "Our half-Romulan, uncovered during the drumhead session with Admiral Satie. His probation recently ended, did it not?"

"It's one quarter, really." Deanna knew the captain had had a special interest in Simon Tarses ever since they both had been accused of treason by Admiral Satie, and Simon's lie about his Vulcan ancestry had been discovered. "Yes, your recommendation for probation rather than dismissal from Starfleet has helped him come to terms with this. But now that his probation is over, he's requesting a transfer off the *Enterprise.*"

Picard looked up, his forehead creased. "Where would he like to go?"

"Almost anywhere. His main concern seems to be to get off this ship." Deanna considered her words carefully. Empathic knowledge was such an intangible quality that it was sometimes difficult to convey without going too deeply into specifics. "I think he's trying to run from something in himself."

"You'd like me to deny his transfer request?"

"Yes, sir. It would give me another quarter to work with him."

The captain stood up, thoughtfully walking over to the tall window next to his desk. He gazed out for a moment. "Are you certain you're not reading too much into his request, Counselor?"

"Tarses still feels isolated and distrusted, and it would confirm his worst fears if we let him go now. He has developed a few friendships—Guinan being one." Deanna paused, taking in the considering tilt of Picard's head. "And I think continuity is what he needs at this point, so he can deal with the real issues at hand."

The captain met her eyes again. "Agreed, then. I'll deny the transfer request, but"—he raised a hand—"you'll be the one to inform him of why."

"Yes, sir." She went to the dispenser, setting down her cup and absently watching it disappear. "I'll go right now."

"Thank you for your report, Counselor."

Deanna nodded as she left the ready room, stepping out onto the bridge.

Immediately she was hit by the increased air of anticipation. There was always this feeling at the start of a mission, and for the Lessenar project, Picard had put Commander Riker in charge. Riker was sitting stiffly upright in the captain's chair—taking his command seriously. He was reading the tactical console in the armrest.

Deanna glanced up at the viewscreen, but they still weren't in range of the planet. That explained why she felt Will's tension so clearly. He wasn't comfortable with inactivity.

As she walked toward the ramp, Riker glanced up. Neither smiled, but their eyes met and held for a moment.

Deanna paused when she reached the top of the ramp. Worf was still at his station, and he barely nodded a greeting to her before looking back down at his tactical panel.

"Isn't your shift over, Worf?" she quietly asked, trying not to disturb the hushed atmosphere.

Worf's rumbling voice seemed deeper than usual. "We arrive at Lessenar in thirty-two minutes."

"But you've already completed your shift, Worf. I'm sure this mission isn't that delicate." She stepped closer, noting the other officers' interest. "Why don't you let Ensign de Groodt take over?"

Worf's jaw moved as if he was clenching his teeth. "I will remain at my station."

Deanna hesitated, but she had to say, "You have other obligations, Worf."

"I am on duty, Counselor!" Worf didn't look at her, and his lips barely moved.

Deanna tried to control a surge of exasperation as Worf returned to his readouts, ignoring her. She took a deep, calming breath, shaking her head as she walked toward the turbolift. She turned, facing back out at the busy bridge crew as the doors closed in front of her. She hoped her talk with Technician Tarses would be a little more successful.

"Come in."

The silver door slid aside to reveal Tarses in his austere blue-and-gray rooms. His quarters were on Deck 13, on the underside of the saucer section, so he had only two windows in the main room. They were slanted out from the floor, in the opposite direction of those in Deanna's quarters. Deanna liked looking down onto the starfield for a change, though it made some people uncomfortable, as if they were falling into space. Other than the stars, there wasn't much else to look at in Tarses' quarters. There was a thick glass bowl on the table and a similar glass vase resting on the ledge. She reminded herself that Tarses had been on probation practically since he joined Starfleet, and hadn't had a chance to go on shore leaves and acquire souvenirs like the other crew members. But the barren, impersonal quality of his rooms still bothered her.

When he saw her, Tarses sat forward in his low, comfortable chair, holding his Vulcan lyrette in one hand and a small plectrum in the other. "Counselor Troi, I thought it would be you."

"Don't get up," she said with a smile. "I'd like to hear one of your songs."

13

Tarses glanced away. A deep line appeared between his brows. "That's all right. You don't have to."

"I'd be honored." Deanna sat down on the sofa, rubbing her palms across the rough, nubby weave.

His shoulders moved uneasily under his blue tunic, and he passed the triangular plectrum from one hand to the other. He didn't quite meet her eyes. "You're just being nice."

"So humor me." Deanna leaned forward with her elbows on her knees. She'd sit there all night if she had to.

Tarses pressed his lips together, bending his head over his lyrette. A chord and a few notes began a stumbling melody, as erratic and fanciful as a sun-shower.

Deanna watched Tarses carefully. He was a good-looking young man with dark hair and slightly pointed ears, hunching protectively over the lyrette. He hasn't quite mastered his instrument yet, Deanna thought, but he certainly has a passion for music.

When the song trailed off uncertainly, Tarses lifted his head. "I'm not done with it yet."

"That was quite pretty. The harmonies are influenced by Vulcan meters, aren't they?"

"Yes." He blinked up at her, nervously passing the plectrum from hand to hand. "You're going to make me ask, aren't you?"

Deanna drew in her breath, trying not to let him see that she was steeling herself. She liked him, and he took things so hard. "Yes."

He bit his lip, making himself meet her eyes. "Did the captain approve my transfer request?"

"No, I'm sorry. He didn't."

His eyes widened, and the waves of desperate hurt that he tried to control were almost more than she could block. Sometimes it was difficult to look beyond the immediate pain to the ultimate good that would come, and she had to swallow before saying, "I asked him not to."

"Y-You?" He leaned forward. "Why? You know I wanted it. You know how important it is to me."

"When you asked for the transfer, I told you I didn't think it was a good idea."

"*You* don't think it is!" Tarses got up from his chair, distracted. He placed the lyrette on the table, rubbing a hand over his head, then letting his fingers trail for just a moment on his pointed ears. His hair was longer than usual, just covering the tips. "What about me? I need a fresh start, and I can't have it here."

"Simon, the hearing was a long time ago. Nobody holds it against you." Deanna gestured with both hands, encompassing the *Enterprise.* "And you're off probation now. You have your new start on the best ship in Starfleet."

Tarses quickly shook his head, his hands clasped together. "It was too big a mess. On another ship I could meet people and they wouldn't know."

Deanna stood up, deliberately striding in front of him. "Everyone at your next posting would know that you're part Romulan, Simon."

"It's n-not that! It's because they accused me of being a spy." He tried to turn away. "And . . . and all those hearings. Then I was confined to quarters and put on probation. Everyone knows."

"That's what you've been saying all along." Deanna crossed her arms. "But I know you're smarter than that. In those hearings you were made a victim, just as Captain Picard was. Neither of you were blamed for the admiral's instability. You went on probation because you lied on your application. Is that what you don't want people to know about?"

Tarses licked his lips as if to speak, but stopped himself.

She shook her hair back. "You don't think you can go back to telling people you have a Vulcan grandfather, do you?"

Tarses looked up abruptly. "Why not? I—I didn't know I was Romulan until I was sixteen. I studied the Vulcan culture thinking it was my own. I'm more truly Vulcan than Romulan!"

Silence hung between them as Deanna tried to absorb the pain held in such denial.

Then slowly she tilted her head. "You must find your own terms, Simon, but you won't be able to deny your Romulan heritage. At the very least, it's in your records now, and that fact will always be known about you."

Tarses clasped his hands together as if wanting to hold on to something. "I was going to ask you about that, too, Counselor. Can I request that . . . that information be put in a closed file? I don't think anyone with a viewscreen should be able to know that about me."

"Tarses, your grandfather was Romulan. It's nothing you need to hide. The Federation doesn't stand for prejudice, particularly in Starfleet."

He let out his breath. "That's easy for you to say! But you know what people think about Romulans. Nobody trusts them, and I don't want anyone to know I . . . well, that I have anything to do with them. Because I don't!"

"Your father was half Romulan."

Tarses abruptly turned and paced off. When he came back to her, his head was down and he was holding one finger between his eyes. His effort to steady his voice was clear. "You're not going to let me c-classify that information, are you?"

"Tarses, I think you'd be causing an even bigger mystery by doing that."

Tarses dropped back down in his chair, his forehead creased and his hair tousled by his nervous hands. "I guess that's it then!"

Deanna clasped her hands behind her back. This was a delicate moment. "What are you going to do now?"

He raised his eyes to the ceiling, turning one palm up. "Now? What can I do? I have to keep on living with everyone looking at me, remembering what happened. I—I see everyone, you know, being a medical technician. It's not like I can hide. And they all know how I was accused."

"Don't slip back into that, Tarses. It's not just the hearings you need to deal with. Did you read the files I sent you?"

"I know about Romulans. They have a common root with Vulcans, but in every way—morally, philosophically, and scientifically—Romulans are inferior. Not just inferior but warped into fanatical tyrants."

"Come now. You must be able to find something of interest in the Romulan culture."

"Really? Like how my mother was—" He broke off, struggling with his voice. "I—I wish she'd never told me. She had to, though, when she found out I was serious about going into Starfleet."

Deanna pressed her lips together, resisting her impulse to tell him what she thought of a mother who hid her son's heritage from him for so many years and then urged him to falsify his application instead of helping him accept who he was. "Have you spoken to her recently?"

"What? Oh, sure. She thinks my transfer is a good idea."

"I'm sure," Deanna said with a wry edge to her voice. Tarses's mother was in a great part responsible for this strong denial.

"She'll be disappointed, I suppose." Tarses absently rubbed the lyrette. "She thinks that's what's keeping me from promotions. I try to explain that there aren't many promotions among the support techs, but she's used to the union system in the Moonbase manufacturers."

"Have you asked her about your father again?"

His hands tightened into fists. "I can't d-do it, Counselor." He caught her eye as she started to say something, rushing on, "I tried, really I did, but it bothers her so

17

much when I even hint about it. I just can't. She's so old, and she's worked so hard to give me everything I have. She has such hopes for me. I can't hurt her like that."

"But you don't really know what happened."

"I know enough."

Deanna met his gaze. There was such a sad, pinched look in his eyes.

"If that's—" she started to say, but she suddenly felt something very strange. Like the scent of a flower as she raised it to her nose, that gradual envelopment of sweet perfume, a tingling of awareness washed across her empathic senses. It was delicate, yet more finely tuned and melodious than anything she'd ever experienced. She slowly turned her head, holding her breath as she tried to sense outward, beyond the bounds of the *Enterprise.*

"Counselor?" Tarses asked in concern. "Is something wrong?"

"I don't know," she said distantly, not certain what it was she was sensing. But it called to her. She tapped her communicator. "Captain Picard, this is Counselor Troi. Is everything all right?"

Chapter Three

COMMANDER RIKER couldn't help hearing Deanna confront Worf at the tactical station. Riker even managed to catch a glimpse of Deanna's face as the turbolift doors closed on her. She was making an effort to be expressionless, holding her chin high, but the corners of her mouth were drawn in and her fingers were plucking at the leg of her tight-fitting maroon jumper.

Riker suppressed a smile as he turned back to the viewscreen. He was probably the only one who knew how irritated Deanna was right now. What made it even funnier—what he hadn't been able to bring himself to tell her yet—was that without realizing it, Worf sparred with Troi in exactly the same way he had with K'Ehleyr. Riker had watched enough Klingons on board the *Pagh* fighting with the women they respected to know the signs of Klingon courtship when he saw them. It was their way of testing the strength of their prospective mates.

His smile deepened as he imagined what Deanna would have to say about that. He felt a little guilty about not telling her, but she was bound to figure it out on her own sooner or later. Or maybe Worf would, and then their little spats would become more self-consciously restrained and wouldn't be as interesting for anyone— including him.

Unbidden, he thought of Deanna's mother, Lwaxana, and the look on her face if she ever found out "Mr. Woof" was subliminally doing a Klingon mating dance around her daughter, heir to the Holy Rings of Betazed, holder of the Fifth Chalice of Riis. . . .

Riker didn't quite manage to smother a laugh. He quickly covered his mouth with his hand, pretending to smooth his beard as he glanced at the other bridge officers. No one had noticed. Not that it would be the first time the crew had caught him laughing to himself.

Still, this was no laughing matter. Deanna was doing her job, just as he should be. And that was something they had in common—neither would let personal desires interfere with his or her duty.

Riker consulted the arm console one more time. He was in charge of the current mission to clean the atmosphere of Lessenar. The preliminary research by the Lessenarian scientists was insufficient for analysis, so the *Enterprise* scientists hadn't had much on which to base the setup of the mission operations. Still, Lieutenant Chryso, in charge of Atmospheric Studies, already had her team working on it.

Riker glanced back at Chryso, posted at one of the aft stations to coordinate the sensor reports for her department. He could hear her low, measured voice, and when he turned, she was finishing the programming of her panel with a last few touches of her graceful hands. Her smooth skin glowed dark brown and her black, almond-shaped eyes were shining when she glanced up. She gave him a slight nod to acknowledge everything was under control.

Riker faced forward again, knowing they'd be able to get the job done once they reached the planet. The Lessenarians were a humanoid species; he expected a certain amount of frustration when dealing with other humanoids. Maybe it was because humanoids were just similar enough to one another that, without realizing it, both species started making assumptions until they hit a brick wall of incomprehension. Then they had to backtrack to find where their concepts diverged and set things on a clear path again before getting on with the mission. After a few tangles like that, it could get really exasperating for everyone involved.

In addition, this would be the first extensive contact between the Federation and Lessenar, so their mission had a dual purpose of diplomatic exchange as well as scientific investigation. Riker was pleased Picard had assigned him to coordinate the various aspects. He appreciated the challenge.

He glanced at the navigation officer. "Status, Ensign Ro."

The light shifted on her dark, glossy hair as she consulted her readings. "Three minutes until we reach the star system, sir."

Riker tapped the arm console, sending their ETA directly to Picard's computer. Since the captain wasn't needed on the bridge, Riker didn't want to interrupt him in his ready room with a verbal page.

From behind him, Worf announced, "Entering scanning range, sir!"

Activity picked up at the stations as the bridge crew received the scanner reports. He could hear the tense, quick movements as Lieutenant Chryso began to rapidly key her panel, processing the information.

After a slight pause Data looked back at Commander Riker, his eyes glowing brighter yellow than his pale gold-toned skin. "Readings indicate there is an unusual amount of solar activity in this system, sir. I recommend raising the shield output."

"Make it so."

"Aye, sir!" Worf immediately snapped back. "Generator power increased to fifty-four percent. All deflector generators on full standby."

Riker glanced back at Worf. He sounded like he'd been ready for this.

"On viewscreen," Riker ordered.

The stars shifted as the sensors tracked the planet. Just then, the door to the ready room hissed open, revealing Captain Picard.

"Magnify." Riker got up in deference to the captain, taking a couple of steps forward to stand behind Navigation and Ops.

The image of a planet, split between greenish blue seas and the usual brown continents, almost filled the screen. They approached along the northern axis, but the tiny, glittering ice cap looked like an afterthought. And where Earth, for instance, would have been swathed in gauzy white clouds, the surface of Lessenar was almost obscured by dense vertical bands of milky green. The glowing bands appeared edge-on to the *Enterprise* and they nested within one another, forming a tight circle over the ice cap and spiraling out in larger and larger circles around most of the northern hemisphere. In some places the walls of green were so tall that the depth of the atmosphere was a tangible sight.

"Magnificent," the captain murmured.

"What is it?" Riker asked.

"One moment, sir." Data finished tapping out a rapid-fire sequence. "It appears that the solar emissions are creating the influx of electrons into the atmosphere. The phenomenon is centered around the magnetic poles, where the electrons are reacting with airborne pollutants."

"What kind of pollutants?"

Lieutenant Chryso answered absently from her station, "The primary chemical reaction taking place is ionization."

At Riker's narrowed eyes, Data added helpfully, "The

solar electrons are reacting with ozone, releasing radiation, which we then see as color—"

"Thank you, Data. I understand ionization." Riker gazed up at the brilliant green ribbons. Their edges reached far out into space, causing a wavy distortion in the normal round outline of the planet. "How tall are those things?"

Data studied his console, touching an access node here and there. "The lower edge is located at a height of one hundred kilometers. The upper region is much less clearly defined and extends to heights of up to one thousand kilometers from the surface."

Riker considered this. "Take us into high polar orbit, Ensign."

"Aye, sir," Ensign Ro acknowledged.

Worf called out from behind, "Sir, shall I contact the Advisory Council?"

"Not yet, Mr. Worf. I want to find out a little more about their situation first." Riker braced his hand against the back of Ro's chair. "Chryso, what effect is this having on the planet?"

She didn't look up from her panel. "Unknown at this time, sir. I'm reading a marked concentration of fine solids in the atmosphere, such as carbon particles, fluorides, and sulfates, as well as nitrogen. These appear to be reacting with the solar particles, creating lethal secondary pollutants."

As they circled the planet, they surveyed a second set of wavy, iridescent banners ringing the southern hemisphere and reaching far out into space. Riker shook his head as the banners rippled and moved, sometimes merging to create spectacular dense plumes of green clouds.

From behind him, Captain Picard asked, "Would these conditions be dangerous to an away team?"

Chryso turned to answer and was caught by the sight on the viewscreen. Her eyes widened at the dense green bands. It took a moment before she collected herself. "Possibly, sir. Biofilters would be advised."

Riker was already nodding, deciding which officers he'd take with him on the away team.

Data cocked his head over his readings. "Sir, I do not recommend use of the transporters. The chemical interactions and heavy ionic influx will interfere with the integrity of the matter stream."

"No transporters." Riker rapidly reviewed his planned sequence of actions, noting the changes that would be caused by this complication. "Open a channel to the Advisory Council, Lieutenant Worf."

"Channel open, sir."

"Members of the Advisory Council of Lessenar, this is Commander William T. Riker of the Federation starship *Enterprise.*" Riker was careful about his tone. The opening exchange could be particularly tricky.

Worf announced, "There is a reply, sir."

"On screen."

The planet with its glowing green bands dissolved into the static-filled image of a humanoid sitting in what appeared to be a chair with a tall, curving back. It was hard to tell with the picture so broken up.

"Commander Riker, this is Wiccy Ron Micc, head of the Advisory Council. Welcome to Lessenar!"

"Thank you, Council Head." Riker smiled and tried to see past the static. "It seems we're having some trouble with our transmission. If you could wait for just a moment." Over his shoulder, Riker ordered, "Can't you clear that up, Worf?"

Worf was intent on his console, and he barely looked up as he rumbled deep in his throat, "I am attempting to recalibrate the transmission bursts."

Riker turned back to the council head, unable to see much of the man beneath the lines of sparkling static. He pressed forward anyway. "Council Head Wiccy, the *Enterprise* is at your service. We understand you requested aid from the Federation regarding the atmospheric conditions of your planet."

"Yes, and we are eager to receive you, Commander Riker. A reception has been prepared for you and your fellow officers."

Riker raised a hand, not sure the council head could see him. "Thank you for your generous offer, but we're currently unable to transport through your atmosphere."

"How unfortunate!" The man seemed distressed. Riker missed his next words in a burst of static that drowned out the picture.

"What's happening, Worf?"

Worf sounded defensive. "The radiation waves are interfering with subspace and radio frequencies."

Data was considering his control panel with an expression very close to a frown. "Sir, the fluctuations are directly related to solar activity. Communications efficiency has decreased by thirty-four percent."

Riker let out a controlled breath. "Council Head Wiccy, if you could coordinate the data burst transmission with my chief security officer, Lieutenant Worf, we'd like to get started on our scientific investigation."

A hiss of static blared, then, ". . . glad to. I'll have my comm . . . you. We appreciate . . . forward to . . . exchange . . ."

Riker rubbed his hand across his chin and mouth, then smoothed down his beard. Ensign Ro was looking up at him with a slight smile, watching his reaction.

"Thank you, Council Head Wiccy," Riker said, winding it up quickly. "I look forward to speaking with you later. Riker out." He turned, giving a tug to his uniform. "Data, try to get what you can from them. If they send it through enough times, the computer should be able to piece it together."

"Aye, sir." Data proceeded to monitor the matrix translation into the *Enterprise* computer.

Riker went and sat down in his usual seat to the right

of the captain's chair, gazing for a moment at his arm console without seeing it. All that formal politeness got on his nerves. The malfunctions didn't help any.

Finally, in a low voice, he told the captain, "At least I'm spared a 'reception' for the time being."

The captain returned his smile. "Better you than me, Number One."

"Is that why you put me in charge of this mission?" Riker stretched, feeling the tension starting to dissipate already. "Well, I'll have to take a shuttle down soon for face-to-face talks with Council Head Wiccy. And Lieutenant Chryso has already stated the necessity for ground-based tests."

"Agreed. In the meantime, let's see what we can find out about these unusual conditions."

Riker looked over at Ops. "Mr. Data, have you—"

"Sir!" Worf interrupted. "Long-range scanners report a vessel entering this system."

"Identify!" Riker ordered, glancing at Captain Picard.

Worf was already working on it. "They identify themselves as the . . ."

Worf seemed to hesitate a moment, and Data smoothly interjected, "The *Prospector,* sir. Passenger starliner B2004, registered under Peristroika, Inc., Moscow, Earth."

"A starliner?" Riker asked, beginning to smile. "Let's have a look at her."

From the main cylindrical body with a single warp nacelle projecting from the underside, it was immediately clear it was an older ship. The tiles were darkened around the access ports and the recessed loading docks, and several wide seams were visible near the front where major work had been done on the hull. Still, there was an excess of viewports and a sleek heaviness about the craft that seemed altogether different from the efficiency of Starfleet designs.

Suddenly Troi's voice came over the communicator.

"Captain Picard, this is Counselor Troi. Is everything all right?"

Picard exchanged a glance with Riker. "Everything's under control, Counselor. Is something wrong?"

There was an obvious hesitation. "I'm not sure. I'm sensing an unusual emanation."

Before Picard could answer, Worf announced, "Sir, we are being hailed."

"Counselor, join us on the bridge," Picard said, before standing up and nodding back to tactical. "Thank you, Lieutenant Worf. On screen."

Riker leaned forward as a robust older man appeared on the viewscreen. Dark bulkheads loomed just above and behind him in the confined space. The man had shoulder-length gray hair and a scraggly beard that rested on his barrel chest. His eyes were creased as he squinted down at them. Fine lines of static ran along the top and bottom of the screen, but the interference wasn't as bad as it had been during Riker's discussion with Council Head Wiccy.

Picard stepped closer. "Greetings, *Prospector,* I am Jean-Luc—"

The man cut him off in midsentence, turning to shout over his shoulder, "Marca! Do something about the static, will you?" He faced full into the screen for a moment, his blue eyes surprisingly intent. "Damn stuff'll drive you mad, won't it?"

Chapter Four

PICARD HARDLY BROKE STRIDE. Dealing with aliens gave one plenty of patience. "Apparently static is a natural feature of this solar system."

"That so? Come to think on it, I never had reason to test it out 'fore now." The man smiled, his cheeks rounding out above his white beard. "I'm Capt'n Jacob Walch. This here's the *Prospector*."

Picard shifted, clasping his hands in front of him. "I wasn't informed that Lessenar was a scheduled stop on a vacation tour."

"Sure enough!" Walch flung up a beefy arm. "Come see the Mummified Planet, Wrapped in Its Own Atmosphere. I'll send you our brochure. This ain't nothing right now. Them streamers change colors, getting more red on the bottom sometimes. And wait till the sparklers start coming on! You jus' can't see a purtier sight anywheres."

Picard blinked up at him a moment. "You come here simply to view this phenomenon, not to take on passengers?"

"This is jus' one of the many fine sight-seeing stops in

this sector. We'll leave come ship's morning." Walch leaned forward, suddenly conspiratorial, his eyes crinkled at the corners. "If you ask me, seems a waste not to drum up business since we come here anyhows. But my business partner says no go. This planet ain't a member of the Federation, so insurance won't cover us if we deal with them."

"Yes, well—"

"You-all sure picked the right orbit. Mind if we jus' fall in behind? The tourii—that's my tourists, you know," he said as if it were necessary to explain. "They'll get a big kick out of seeing Starfleet's *Enterprise*. The flagship of the Federation!"

"Yes, well . . ." Picard tried to begin again.

"It's a go! Move her on in, Paddy." Walch gestured to someone with a thick finger. "Make sure the front ports got a good view of the ship 'long with the planet."

Picard held up a hand. "Captain Walch, if you please." He waited until he had the man's attention. "The *Enterprise* is conducting tests of this planet's—"

"Whoa there!" Walch called out to his crew. "Heave her on back a little. Let's give these boys some room."

Data consulted his panel. "The *Prospector* has taken up a position at a distance of 11,402 kilometers, bearing 120 mark 35."

"Fine. Just fine." Picard tried to summon up a smile.

"Anything you need, you jus' let me know." Walch winked. "Got the best outfit in the galaxy here. Food, wine, luxury accommodations. Hey, maybe you'd like to sample some of our entertainments—we got plenty of room. Had to empty out two whole decks on account of them Sli." The last word sounded like a sneeze.

"Excuse me?" Picard asked, his expression fixed.

"Sli. You know—big jellyfish thingamabobs. I got five of 'em on board. Perform emotive concerts, they do," Walch said proudly.

Picard glanced at Riker. "Could that be what the counselor has been sensing?"

Riker shrugged, starting to answer when Walch twitched his shoulders back, raising his thick finger again. "Hey, I got an ideer! Join me for evening mess. That's the ticket! How 'bout it, Jean-Luc?"

Picard was already shaking his head. "No, no, really. Thank you. I don't think that's necessary."

"No bother t'all! Just throw a couple more cows on the fire. Bring everyone," he said, looking from one member of the bridge crew to another. "Y'all invited! We'll have us a real—" Walch broke off, peering intently past the captain.

Picard glanced over his shoulder to see Worf standing at attention, staring fixedly at the top of the viewscreen.

"Well, I'll be damned! If it itn't Worf!" Walch slapped his thigh, grinning openly at their security chief. "I knew you was on the *Enterprise!* Don't know where my mind was at. How are you, son?"

Picard stepped back toward the tactical station. "You and Captain Walch are acquainted, Mr. Worf?"

"Acquainted!" Walch repeated behind him, rocking forward with a hoot of laughter. "I known this boy since he was small enough to wrassle! Nobody'd tangle with him now—no, sir!"

Worf seemed to be clenching his jaw, but he nodded, "Aye, sir."

"Very well." Picard turned and sat down, leaving the matter to Worf's discretion.

Just then, Deanna Troi entered the bridge. She took in the grizzled man on the viewscreen and swept her eyes over Picard's relaxed posture. She must have sensed the lack of tension on the bridge, because she silently sat down next to Picard.

Meanwhile, Jacob Walch leaned forward, beaming for all he was worth. "Come on over, Worf! Bring Alex—I ain't seen the boy in a dog's age. Must be purt near his pa's size by now, heh?"

"If you'll excuse me, sir." Worf sounded quite self-conscious. "I am unable to speak with you now. However, I will contact you when my duty shift is over."

"Sure, Worf, sure. You and Alex give us a holler when you're done working. I'll be here." He clawed a hand through his beard, never taking his eyes off Worf.

"Sir?" Worf asked Picard.

"I have nothing further," the captain said.

"Enterprise out," Worf quickly announced, cutting off the next comment from Walch as the screen returned to a planetary view.

In the silence that followed, Picard glanced at Commander Riker and wasn't too surprised to see him struggling not to grin too openly. Counselor Troi seemed to be staying deliberately quiet.

"'Son'?" Riker said softly, when he caught Picard's eye on him. But he carefully pitched it loud enough for Worf to hear.

Worf shifted sharply, narrowing his eyes. "Walch is an old friend of my foster parents."

Picard crossed his legs. "He seems like a genial man to me. Wouldn't you say so, Number One?"

"I found him completely charming," Riker agreed, his poker face firmly in place.

Not long afterward, Worf entered his quarters, carrying a long, slim package. The lights were dimmed to a purple glow along the wall that held the replicator. The remains of a meal sat on the dining table. Mostly little mounds of green were left on the translucent plate.

Worf decided to ignore the uneaten portion. "Alexander, come clean the table."

His son appeared in the doorway to his room, startled, his mouth a round O. "You're home."

"Yes." Worf frowned at how vulnerable his son looked. "Close your mouth, Alexander!"

Alexander snapped his mouth shut, but now he looked confused. He shuffled his bare feet on the rug, tugging at the nappy blue pajama top he was wearing.

Worf sighed. "Clean the table, Alexander." He went into his room, hearing the sounds of Alexander clearing away his dinner and removing his paints and models from the main room.

Worf was unwrapping the package when Alexander reappeared. The boy idled by the door, digging his toes into the carpet without saying anything.

"Come here, Alexander." Worf held out a red and black scabbard. "I brought this for you. It's a replication of a samurai *miskazi* of the Kamakura period. When you become a warrior, you will receive the long sword." He pulled out a short sword, almost a meter long in all, with a blade that curved up slightly at the end.

Alexander eased back at the small hissing sound it made as Worf removed it.

"Don't you want to see it, Alexander?" Worf held it out to him. "Here."

His son took the short sword from him awkwardly, but his face lit up. "You got this for me?"

"Yes." Worf watched his son proudly. "The edge is blunted, so you may practice with this sword in holodeck simulations."

Alexander gripped the handle with both hands, making a few wobbly thrusts. "Instead of hand-to-hand combat?"

"No." Worf clenched his teeth together at the familiar argument. "Hand-to-hand combat is essential for a warrior. You know that, Alexander."

Alexander started examining the small hatched work on the grip. "This is pretty neat."

"This is part of your human ancestry, Alexander. The samurai warriors were a noble caste. They established an elaborate dueling cult—"

"I like the end knob with the swirly parts." He held the sword up to show his father.

"Alexander!" Worf had to work to restrain himself. "You must practice the art of silence."

"Why?"

Worf's eyes blazed. "Why must you always question me?"

Alexander considered it for a moment. "Teacher tells us to ask questions."

"At times, you must also listen to learn. Silence is the cradle of wisdom." He narrowed his eyes, thinking of other battles. "It can also be a powerful weapon."

Alexander sighed, rolling his eyes as if to say, *Another weapon?* But he took his new blade and slid it back into the scabbard. "Good night, Father. Thank you for the sword."

Chapter Five

ALPHA SHIFT WOULD BEGIN in a few hours, but for now Commander Data was in charge of the bridge. He was seated at Ops as usual, since the control panel gave him greater access to the computer library and sensor controls than the arm console of the captain's chair.

Per Captain Walch's statement that the phenomenon varied in intensity, Data noted that the situation had indeed changed since the *Enterprise* first arrived. Solar activity had increased by seventy-three percent. The visual scanners revealed that the layered green curtains were now laced by arcs and rays of moving silver light, and the entire atmospheric envelope was spangled with spectral chips of pure color.

In addition, the class-IV probes Lieutenant Chryso had planted in the atmosphere were reading a multitude of compounds polluting the air. These were interacting with one another as well as with the unusual influx of solar particles.

Based on Lieutenant Chryso's preliminary analysis and the ongoing work of Atmospheric Studies, Data confirmed that a large portion of the pollutants had been created by the inhabitants of the planet. The extent of their responsibility was more than had been reported by Lessenarian scientists, but Data noted that the discrepancy could be due to the primitive equipment used during their research.

Yet this discovery sparked an intriguing line of questioning. It was clear that the pollutants were destroying quantities of the flora, fauna, and even the inhabitants of the planet. Dozens of areas had requested immediate aid in the form of food and water. Commander Riker had already reported to Main Shuttlebay and was supervising the loading of relief supplies. Departure was scheduled for 0900 hours.

Though Data was involved in several scientific analyses, he scanned high-speed recordings of various broadcast channels the *Enterprise* had been monitoring. The static interfered, but he was able to determine that the arrival of the *Enterprise* was the cause of great excitement and optimism. Apparently the inhabitants had had little success trying to curtail the amount of pollutants they created—though they'd been actively trying for more than six generations.

As an incidental discovery to his monitoring, Data found that the view from the planet surface at night was just as spectacular as that from space. The Lessenarians took the sight for granted, with only the extremes of the condition acknowledged.

Data looked up to examine the main viewscreen again. It was spectacular by any species' standards. As per regulations when in formation with other vessels, the opticals included the passenger starliner *Prospector* along with the planet. Occasionally Data caught members of the bridge crew openly mesmerized by the sight of Lessenar—except for the navigation officer, Ensign Navarre. She didn't look up at the screen because "facing backwards always makes me feel nauseous." Data had heard other members of the bridge crew express similar sentiments, and he wondered if that was why Worf hadn't switched to the aft lateral sensors. But then Worf had left the bridge shortly after the *Prospector* arrived, leaving it to Data to perform that duty—

There was a sharp rise in energy readings from the aft scanners.

"Yellow alert!" Data announced, just as Ensign de Groodt called out, "Sir, there's been an explosion on board the *Prospector!*"

"Shields up." Data implemented defensive and offensive responses to a possible attack. His sensory processing speed automatically increased, and he took advantage of this to glance up at the main viewer every four seconds—optical surveys usually provided important information.

Sparkling fragments burst from the underside of the *Prospector* in a narrow stream. Immediately this was followed by an even bigger explosion. The *Prospector* was jolted up out of its orbit as the particles spun out, rapidly dispersing as the debris vaporized.

"Captain Picard here. Status, Mr. Data."

With his hands still moving quickly over his panel, Data replied, "Sir, the *Prospector* has suffered an eight-thousand-megawatt explosion in an area designated as a cargo hold. Currently there are no other vessels in this system."

"Understood, Mr. Data. I'll be there shortly."

"Sir," de Groodt interrupted. "We're being hailed by the *Prospector.*"

The last traces of the explosion were disappearing, and the *Prospector* was visibly canted to one side.

"On screen," Data ordered.

The static-filled image of Captain Walch appeared. His forehead was deeply creased, and they could hear the sound of shouting in the background.

"We had no warning!" Walch said without preamble.

"Two of our primary truss frames were blown to smithereens. Reroute gravity control through conduits 43 and 44!" he suddenly shouted. "And you better give us a simple field collapse, boys! I mean now!"

Data realized Walch was giving orders to one of his crew.

Ensign Navarre said, "Sir, the *Prospector* is decelerating."

"Maintain distance, Ensign. Do you require assistance, Captain Walch?"

"You bet I do, boy." He didn't even look up from his readouts. "Is there any way you can give us the inertial damping we need?" Without waiting for an answer, he turned away, ordering, "Evacuate decks A and B jus' to be sure. And get those generators back on line now! Where is Picard, anyway?"

Meanwhile, Data ran a series of computer simulations trying to reconfigure the inertial damping system of the *Enterprise* to cover the *Prospector*. "I am Commander Data, current commanding duty officer," he informed Walch. "Captain Picard has been informed of your situation."

"Sir, four emergency pods have jettisoned from the starliner," Ensign de Groodt informed him. "I've got locations from the subspace beacons."

"Continue monitoring," Data said evenly. Then to Captain Walch, "The *Enterprise* is unable to compensate for the structural field integrity without engaging a tractor beam."

"I don't know if she'll hold through that. And we got other problems." Walch was still working with his control panel. "The umbilical was severed and we're losing our gravitational stability. There's maybe thirty, forty minutes I can squeeze out of her." He stifled a shake of his head at the readout, obviously frustrated. "I'm gonna have to order evacuation."

Data tapped the transporter alert. "Transporter Chief, all transporters on line for possible evacuation of the *Prospector.*"

A crisp "Aye, sir!" returned instantly.

Data noted that life signs on board the *Prospector* were distorted by the wave fluctuations in the structural integrity field. "Captain, what is your current crew and passenger complement?"

"Sixty-four crew members and three hundred eight passengers," Walch answered, distracted. "Oh, and that mess of Sli in the other cargo hold."

The turbolift doors hissed open and both Captain Picard and Commander Riker came on the bridge.

"Eleven more emergency pods have jettisoned, sir!" de Groodt announced.

"Continue monitoring." Data addressed the screen, "Captain Walch, please stand by." Then he turned to the captain. He recognized the subtle signs of concern in Picard's expression. "You have the bridge, sir."

"Status, Mr. Data."

"Structural integrity field has been compromised on board the *Prospector,* bringing the ship to full stop. Failure of gravitational stability estimated in thirty-seven point eight minutes. The entire complement of the *Prospector* can be transported in twenty-eight point zero two seconds."

"Another three emergency pods ejected, sir," de Groodt put in.

"Twenty-seven point two five seconds," Data corrected.

Picard remained by Data's side. "Any indication of how this happened, Mr. Data?"

"There is an eighty-one percent possibility that the explosion originated on board the *Prospector,* sir. There are no signs of vessels in this star system, and there are no indications of additional incoming missiles on long-range sensors."

Riker's eyes were narrowed. "What about the planet as the point of origin?"

"Unlikely, sir. The site of the impact would necessitate an orbital trajectory. Our sensors would have detected such an attempt."

Picard nodded once sharply, making his decision. "Captain Walch, we can transport your personnel directly to the *Enterprise.*"

That caught Walch's attention. He stared into the viewscreen for a moment, relief mixed with the understandable reluctance of a captain faced with having to order abandon ship. His joking, genial mask was gone, and in its place was revealed a man who now met the captain's gaze with great dignity and composure. "Thank you," he said simply.

"Sir," Data said to Picard. "I recommend that the personnel on board the *Prospector* proceed to designated evacuation sites. The fluctuations of the field integrity within the ship, as well as that of the planet, may interfere with transporter modulation lock."

Picard looked to his counterpart on the *Prospector,* but Walch had a hand up to keep him from speaking. "Understood, Captain Picard." Activating a switch, he announced to his ship, "This is Captain Walch. All passengers please go to your designated emergency sector. There you'll be beamed on board the *Enterprise.* I repeat, all passengers are to proceed to their designated area for immediate transport to the *Enterprise.*"

In a subdued tone, de Groodt announced, "Another four emergency pods ejected, sir."

"Maintain contact, Ensign. We'll pick them up as soon as the transports are completed." Picard seemed to hesitate for a moment, as if he had something delicate to say. "Captain Walch, if you can give us access to your computer, perhaps we can determine a way to repair your life support system."

Walch instantly leaned over and keyed in a command.

"It's a mystery to me. Damage to that section of the ship—well, it just shouldn't've happened. Even if you fix it, there's nothing to be done about the structural integrity field. But you boys can sure give it a shot."

De Groodt informed the captain, "I have access to *Prospector* computer control."

"Acknowledged," Picard said.

Walch gave a final nod to the captain. "I'm gonna go set a fire under these folk. I'll see you on board the *Enterprise*. Walch out."

Picard seated himself in the captain's chair, settling his uniform. "Lower shields, Mr. Data. Begin emergency evacuation of the *Prospector.*"

"Aye, sir."

Data was kept busy for the next hour. He rerouted power from secondary systems to allow for continuous transportation without interfering with current mission operations. He also alerted sickbay of the arrival of the evacuees, and called up the personnel necessary to direct the passengers and crew of the *Prospector* to unoccupied quarters on Decks 9 and 11. Six transporter rooms with six evacuees arriving every minute and a half was the maximum influx of people for the *Enterprise,* but they could have easily housed ten times the number that were on board the *Prospector.* He continued yellow alert to minimize the activity in the corridors, and the captain sent Commander Riker down to personally oversee the dispersal of the evacuees.

The transporter evacuation didn't go as smoothly as Data had anticipated. Monitoring an open channel to facilitate the transports, he became fascinated by the reactions of the tourists. Despite the danger, many of them insisted on taking the time to bring their luggage over with them. The crew members of the *Prospector* were an immense help, and they moved the passengers along at a fairly rapid pace, treating them with a mixture of respect and what Data could only term as coddling, assuring the tourists that their belongings would be retrieved as soon as the life support malfunction was repaired. Still, a fair portion of the passengers were indignant over this "treatment," and Captain Walch became rather sharp with some of them, ordering them to the evacuation sites and reminding them that their lives were worth more than property. Data carefully filed away every comment and complaint for later study.

The transports would never have been completed before a total failure of the gravity system if the crew of the *Prospector* had not also continued loading emergency life support pods with passengers and ejecting them. By the time Captain Walch, the last man on board the *Prospector,* beamed to the *Enterprise,* dozens of the three-person pods were floating in the area. Due to the interference, they were unable to transport the occupants directly from the pods. Data plotted their positions and allocated tractor beam emitters to snare the pods and bring them in close enough to maneuver into the shuttlebays.

"I'm gonna sue!" one man yelled hoarsely over the closed radio wave bands of the pods. "My lawyers, T'Chal and Soloman, will take care of this. Starfleet is liable, you know!"

"Your complaint is logged, sir," Data responded patiently. This was the thirty-fourth time the man had repeated variations on this theme. "You must wait in your lifepod until the shuttlebay has been repressurized."

"Then do it!" he demanded. "What are you waiting for?"

Again Data explained, "The main forcefield has been lowered in order for the tractor beams to deposit the emergency pods within the shuttlebay. Without altitude jets and maneuverability, the pods would crash without the tractor—"

"You're torturing us!" Other voices agreed, clamoring

for release. The tone ranged from pleading to outraged, and they drowned out even the cries of pain from the few wounded evacuees.

"Fascinating," Data murmured, turning to glance at the captain. Picard was keeping a close eye on the evacuation procedures, but he left the details to Ops.

However, when the channel was closed, Picard told Data, "I'd say the tourists who rushed to escape in the pods are even more demanding than those who waited to beam over."

"I believe you are correct, sir." Data consulted his readings. "The main forcefield will be activated in twelve minutes."

"All that noise over a few minutes," Picard said thoughtfully. "Have La Forge download the information from the *Prospector*'s computers regarding the life support failure. I want an engineering team working on the problem."

"Aye, sir." Data wondered if the captain was already anxious to return the tourists to where they belonged. "The transporter in cargo bay four has been reset for quantum transport. The *Prospector* reports the hydrogen/nitrogen transport tank containing the Sli is prepared for transport."

"Acknowledged," Picard told him. "Proceed."

Data paged sickbay. "Dr. Crusher, please report to Deck 38 cargo bay."

"Now?" she asked. There was a disturbing hum behind her words. "I've got dozens of injured people in sickbay."

"The Sli will arrive in three minutes."

"I see." She knew as well as Data that the Federation had been able to find out very little about the Sli and their unusual emanations. The Ferengi had kept a close hold on those elusive beings. "I'll be right there."

It was exactly seventy-eight minutes after the first explosion when Data announced, "Evacuation complete, sir. Three hundred seventy-two evacuees are now on board the *Enterprise*. Aside from minor injuries, twenty-six individuals have been taken to sickbay. None are listed as critical."

"Well done, Commander." Picard was obviously pleased.

"Thank you, sir."

The captain stood up, walking closer to the viewscreen. He seemed to be examining the *Prospector*. The warp nacelle was still slightly tilted to one side. The blackened hole with its rough edges of twisted tritanium framework was clearly visible on the underside.

"Malfunction or attack?" Picard said speculatively to Data.

"There are no ships in the immediate area, and there was no further attempt while the shields were lowered."

Picard thoughtfully rubbed his chin, supporting his elbow with his other hand. "Perhaps it was a fault in the ship's structure or in the integrity field itself. Whatever it was, I'd like to know how this happened. There's something not quite right about the situation." He straightened up and addressed Data directly. "Find out if the damage is as bad as Walch reported. And see if you and Lieutenant La Forge can repair the synthetic gravity field. Perhaps we can call a tug from Starbase 87—"

"Captain Picard, this is Dr. Crusher."

The captain broke off, tapping his communicator. "Picard here."

Her voice was cautious. "You'd better come down here, Captain. We might have a problem with the Sli."

Chapter Six

Dr. Crusher let her hand fall from her comm badge, still staring at the transport container holding the Sli.

The light was shining through the faintly orange, luminous gas, tinting the air of the cargo bay around her. There were four Sli inside, each a little more than two meters tall. Their bodies were elongated and tubular, with the top pointed and the bottom flared into twelve long, slender tentacles. They were composed of a semi-transparent gelatinous tissue that was difficult to distinguish from the surrounding gas.

Yet as Crusher watched, each of the gauzy orange creatures began to change color, with the ruddy tone gradually shifting toward yellow, and becoming deeper and brighter in tone. The change happened so slowly, so subtly, that she couldn't take her eyes off them. She kept expecting it to stop, for the transition to become complete and the Sli to be a dazzling, brilliant yellow. But just when it seemed they could go no further, faint swirls of smoky gray started to twine down from the very top, working their way around the bodies of the Sli. The transformation never stopped.

In spite of the mesmerizing sight, Crusher's professional eye noted that the Sli had no cranial or internal skeletal structure. Movement was achieved by muscles flexing in the tentacles, and their direction was primarily vertical. Two transparent dorsal fins in the upper part of the body apparently served as equilibrium stabilizers.

Most important—whereas four of the Sli were moving around and changing color, a fifth lay in a gray gelatinous mass on the bottom of the tank.

"It's dead, I tell you!" a Ferengi was shouting right next to her, pointing a skinny arm toward the transport container. "It was the explosion. I was lucky to get these four out alive!"

"I understand," Crusher tried to say soothingly. "I've notified the captain and he'll be here in a moment. If you'll let me get to the tank—"

"No!" The short Ferengi glared up at her, belligerently dismissive as Ferengi usually were with humanoid females. "I want everything left as it is. I want my just compensation!"

"Sir, whoever you are—"

"I'm Mon Hartog, wo-man." He pulled himself up as tall as he could. "I'm the Sli's manager, and I'm responsible for making sure they get justice. Murdered! One of them has been outright murdered!"

"I can see that." She held up her tricorder. "But I need to examine the Sli who are still alive to make sure they're in no danger."

One side of his upper lip twisted in an ugly sneer. "How do I know you won't try to hurt them?"

She stared at him. "What are you saying? I'm a doctor! I'm trying to help them."

"Someone tried to kill them. Someone managed to kill one already."

She couldn't believe what she was hearing. "I'm a doctor, Mon Hartog. Do you know what that means? I save lives, I don't take them."

Hartog shoved himself in front of her as she tried to step around. "You're Starfleet, and Starfleet hates the Sli."

Crusher stepped back rather than physically touch the Ferengi. But before she could deny his outrageous accusations, the cargo bay door opened, letting in Lieutenant Worf and Medical Technician Tarses. Tarses was ushering along an octagonal unit, but he hesitated when he saw the tension between Crusher and the Ferengi.

"Good," Crusher said at the sight of them. "Bring the stasis unit over here, Tarses. And, Worf," she added sweetly, "I'm glad you're here. Please ask Mon Hartog to wait outside until we're done."

She pretended to ignore them both, examining the Sli with her tricorder as Tarses moved the stasis module closer to the transport unit. She noticed Tarses trying not to stare at the Sli, but a couple of times he had to shake his head to tear himself away from the sight of the swirling hues.

"You can't do this to me!" Hartog shouted from behind them, as he tried to circumvent Worf. The security chief seized the Ferengi by his upper arm, and easily withstood his attempts to wrest away. "I have the right to be here!"

"You are interfering with my examination," Dr. Crusher informed Hartog in an even voice. "I would allow you to stay if you provide medical background and information regarding biological functions of the Sli."

"I won't allow it!" The olive skin of Hartog's face darkened as he screamed. "You have no right—"

Crusher simply returned to her examination of the Sli as Worf spoke for the first time. His voice was low and menacingly restrained. "Will you make it necessary for me to forcibly eject you from this room?"

The Ferengi still struggled, but he was looking up at Worf, easily twice his size. Without another word, Worf guided Hartog to the door and ushered him out. As it slid closed, the Klingon silently took up a stance directly in front.

Picard acknowledged Dr. Crusher's call and gestured toward the turbolift, ordering, "With me, Commander Data."

Data was already swinging back his control panel. "Aye, Captain."

When the turbolift took longer than usual to get to the lower decks, Picard realized Data must have rerouted the tube movement to allow for uninterrupted distribution of the evacuees. That's what made Data so good at Ops—it was his nature to consider every final detail of a problem.

"Data, tell me about the Sli."

Data cocked his head slightly, signs of accessing. "Little is known, sir. The Sli were discovered in the Qizan Qal'at system thirty-two years ago by the Starfleet scout ship *Crockett NC-600*. Qizan is the primary, and Qal'at is a gas giant—apparently a 'failed' star of what almost became a binary system. Life signs of the Sli were discovered in the hydrogen/nitrogen atmosphere of the gas giant, but the crew was unable to make contact before their ship was destroyed."

Picard glanced at him sharply. "I thought the *Crockett* was destroyed during a battle with a Klingon vessel. Are you implying the Sli had something to do with it?"

"The details are unknown, sir. The *Crockett* was in the Qizan Qal'at system when they relayed a message to Starbase 1 that a Klingon warship had arrived. When the *Crockett* didn't respond to subsequent messages, Starfleet sent the *Bridger* to investigate." Data paused, as if imitating human reluctance to impart bad news. "When the *Bridger* arrived, they found only debris in the area."

Picard did not like the sound of this. "What is your supposition?"

"The Sli are incapable of leaving Qal'at unassisted. However, insufficient testing has been done regarding their emotive capabilities and the effects on humanoid life-forms. In addition, the Klingon Empire claims the Sli were responsible."

They both shifted as the balance changed slightly in the turbolift. Picard was still frowning. "Why wasn't there an investigation?"

"Two Starfleet diplomatic envoys were sent to the system, one right after the incident and the other two years ago, establishing the sentience of the Sli. However, neither envoy was successful in their investigation due to translation difficulties. The Sli resisted efforts at formal relations with the Federation and are now officially allied with the Ferengi Consortia."

"Apparently the Ferengi have had better luck in communicating with them. What are the Sli doing on board a starliner?"

Data raised his brows slightly. "The Sli are performance artists, sir. A Ferengi known as Mon Hartog is their manager."

"Artists?" Picard demanded.

"Yes, sir," Data told him. The lights slowed, then stopped, and the turbolift door hissed open. There was more activity in the corridor than usual. They started toward the cargo bay as Data continued, "The Sli are currently engaged on a tour that includes twelve star systems. They perform 'emotive concerts' wherein the emotions of the audience are directly stimulated during a three-hour, intricately choreographed production." Data's tone became more eager, revealing his curiosity about anything that could be considered creative. "As an artistic endeavor, the Sli are receiving mixed reviews. Yet they have managed to generate an unusual amount of public response."

"Thank you, Mr. Data." Picard raised his head, stepping forward a little more quickly. "It doesn't sound too serious, does it? Perhaps Dr. Crusher is simply having trouble dealing with temperamental artists."

"Perhaps, sir." Data turned his head slightly, one brow raised. "However, the location of the explosion was adjacent to the cargo hold which had been equipped with class-K environmental conditions for the Sli."

Picard stopped, narrowing his eyes at Data. "Mr. Data, are you telling me these Sli might be responsible for the explosion?"

"Not at all, sir. Other than their proximity, there is no evidence to that effect."

"It was Walch, that's who did it!" a whining voice suddenly called out from the alcove they were passing by. A small, wiry Ferengi scurried out to them, his arms crooked and his elbows held in close. He blocked their way, yet was half cringing in the typical Ferengi fashion that tried to deceive by its subservience. "I know it! That man Walch is responsible for this!" He tilted his head, squinting up at Picard, letting the light play across the beaded pattern of his headpiece. "That ship is a pile of junk! I should have guessed when that speculator was so eager to cut his price."

Picard drew back slightly. He didn't much like dealing with Ferengi in the best of circumstances, and in this case he wasn't going to unless it was absolutely necessary.

The captain started to edge around him. "Mon Hartog, I'm sure the proper authorities—"

"You! You're the authorities here." The Ferengi rubbed his hands together, unable to keep the sly yearning from his voice. "I want my just compensation."

"Data, could you please determine who this . . . gentleman should see about his claim," Picard said.

"No!" Hartog exclaimed, suddenly turning belligerent as he stepped right up, peering moistly into Picard's face.

His crooked brown fangs were streaked with yellow. Picard tried not to breathe. "My Sli were booked as a quintet. When the promoters find out—"

Picard stepped back, firmly moving the Ferengi to arm's length. "You're detaining me from an urgent call from the ship's doctor."

"It's already too late," Hartog sneered, his lips pulled back. "One of my Sli is dead. Murdered by malfunctioning equipment! I want my just compensation."

The captain grew very still. So much for hoping it was something minor. "Come with me, Mon Hartog."

Dr. Crusher struggled to stand up. She'd been crouched so long beside the Sli's transport container that her legs were cramped. Technician Tarses reached out a hand to help her up.

She tried to smile to thank Tarses, but she just couldn't manage it. Of all the duties she had to perform as chief medical officer, postmortems were the most difficult. It was worse in this case, because the Sli had died before she could reach it. Luckily, the other Sli didn't appear to be in any danger, but the medical data on Sli was extremely limited.

"Is the stasis field ready yet?" she asked the tech, brushing back a loose strand of hair.

Tarses carefully checked the dials on one side of the octagonal module. "Yes, Doctor. All systems on-line." Tarses made one final adjustment on the position of the module.

Beverly stood back a moment, preparing for the next step of extracting the dead Sli from the transport container. She'd never dealt with a helium/hydrogen lifeform before, and it was an intricate and demanding experience.

An impatient movement from Worf by the door finally prompted her back into action. "All right, Simon, set the reduction on the lowest level. Let's be gentle with—"

Beverly broke off as the door of the cargo bay slid to the side, revealing Captain Picard and Commander Data. The Ferengi manager was sneaking in behind them.

"Sir!" Worf protested when he saw the Ferengi sidling in next to the captain.

Picard held up a restraining hand. "Return to your post," he told Worf. "Status, Doctor?"

Beverly tightened her lips for a moment, but she could ignore the Ferengi. The captain always had his reasons for doing things. "One Sli is dead, Captain. Cause unknown, but readings indicate a severe decompression occurred at the time of the explosion." She nodded toward the Ferengi. "Mon Hartog says their large environment module was completely destroyed. That much force is bound to cause damage to an organism."

Hartog rasped out from behind Picard, "I barely got them out alive!"

Tarses cleared his throat softly behind her. She turned. "Yes, Tarses?"

"I'm ready to begin the catchment reduction, Doctor."

The Ferengi unit had been difficult to decipher, but now things seemed to be moving along smoothly. As far as she could tell from the readouts, the dead Sli was being drawn into the catchment. When she looked back up, Captain Picard seemed entranced by the sight of the Sli. His faint smile was one of growing wonder, and the creases in his forehead began to smooth. Even Data was gazing up at the Sli with his amber eyes.

Though she'd had more time to get used to the sight of the Sli, it didn't mean much. It wasn't the shape of the Sli as much as the amazing kaleidoscope of colors that continually bloomed and faded and shifted into a myriad of other tones deep within that slick-looking flesh.

She stepped around to the captain, closing her medical tricorder. "They're beautiful, aren't they, Jean-Luc?"

"Exquisite," he murmured, watching as one drifted

slowly to the top of the ten-meter tank, then flitted back down to the bottom, performing a pirouette just before them. All four Sli were still coordinating their colors. At the moment, dark pink streaks curled around their bodies, with a pale peach undertone. Then green spots appeared like tiny whirlpools of violent water before fading away. One Sli reached out with a dark orange tentacle, placing the tip with its row of tiny knobs against the containment barrier. The bottoms of the knobs were black. Beverly gently touched her finger to the same spot on the outside.

Picard drew in his breath. "Can they see?"

"There are no centers of visual nerve clusters. We're going to have to reconfigure a bioscanner to cope with their physical structure." She looked back at Tarses, giving him an encouraging nod as he monitored the reduction. "They *are* a DNA-based life-form, surprisingly enough, so that should make it easier."

"Enough of this!" Hartog spit out, stepping right between Dr. Crusher and Captain Picard. "You accomplish nothing."

Jolted from his contemplation of the Sli, Picard shot Beverly a grave look over Hartog's head. "Doctor, what about these other Sli? Were they injured?"

"I'm not even sure what makes them alive yet." As the Sli drifted away, she removed her finger from the barrier and put some distance between herself and the Ferengi. "Their life support unit is extremely complex. I'm recording different mixtures of gases that feed in periodically while the noble gases are drawn off. I'll have to hook the medical computer directly to the unit to find out more."

The Sli were shifting toward blue now, with vivid purple smears and tangled golden threads shooting through the mottled surface.

"What causes the change in color?" Picard asked.

"It has to do with the gas," Hartog thrust in aggressively.

Beverly thought about it a moment. "It could be. As the Sli absorb the different atoms, the chemical reaction could cause different visual wavelengths to be absorbed. The shifts do appear to happen as frequently as the gases are added to the environment tank."

Picard nodded, turning back to Mon Hartog. "How do you communicate with them?"

The Ferengi drew away slightly, settling his short jacket more easily on his shoulders. "They won't talk to you now. They're too upset. My Sli are very sensitive."

Picard continued looking down at Hartog. "I'd like to hear that from them, if you don't mind."

"Excuse me, sir," Data put in. "I believe the panel directly beneath the transport module is a translator. It does not appear to be in operating mode."

Picard gestured to the transport unit. "Please activate the translator, Mon Hartog."

"I tell you they won't talk right now."

The captain turned to Data. "Commander, would you please establish contact."

Data immediately started for the console, but Hartog pushed in front of him with an irritated whine. "Okay, okay. Have it your way. But they won't talk."

"Very possessive," Beverly murmured to the captain as Hartog keyed in an elaborate sequence. Picard gave a brief nod of acknowledgment.

"There!" Hartog said with an exaggerated flourish at the panel. "For all the good it will do you."

Picard stepped up to the console. A narrow screen across the top carried a moving line of type. Beverly craned her head to see, but it looked like gibberish to her.

Picard read aloud, tracing his finger along the screen, "Relief of hearts . . . feel more . . . feel more time . . . worry to take care . . . time for life . . ." He broke off, narrowing his eyes at Hartog. "What is this?"

53

"It's them." Hartog shrugged, standing near a corner of the tank with his arms crossed.

"How do I speak to them?"

Data leaned over, pressing two of the contact nodes simultaneously. "You should be able to converse with the Sli now, sir."

"Thank you, Data."

Hartog grimaced, but he didn't say anything. He also didn't notice that Beverly was watching him.

Picard faced the Sli. "I am Captain Jean-Luc Picard of the *Starship Enterprise.* I am concerned about your current condition."

The words scrolled out on the screen, apparently being translated into Sli—whatever that was. However, more randomly grouped words were the response.

Picard turned to Data in frustration. "Is the translator malfunctioning?"

"No!" Hartog denied. "Not my translator. They just won't talk, I tell you."

The doctor pursed her lips thoughtfully, wondering how life-forms without sensory organs would communicate with one another. "Perhaps you should get Deanna down here," she suggested. "The Sli are an emotive species."

"Excellent idea, Doctor." He tapped his communicator. "Picard to Counselor Troi. Please report to Cargo Bay 38."

"I'm dealing with some of the tourists, sir," came her quick response. "I'll be down as soon as I can."

"Acknowledged," Picard said, turning to Mon Hartog. "Now, you keep referring to 'my translator' and 'my Sli.' You seem to have a rather personal stake in these beings."

Hartog drew himself up as if he was offended. "I'm their manager! I take care of them while they're on tour."

Picard exchanged a dubious look with Beverly. "What exactly do the Sli get from this relationship?"

The Ferengi smiled, a ghastly sight, as he spread his skinny arms wide. "Fame. Fortune. The opportunity for others to appreciate their art form."

"Fortune?" Beverly couldn't help saying. "Look at them! Just what do they do with their fortune? Give it to you to spend?"

"The Ferengi made an agreement with the Sli!" Hartog insisted. "We're giving them life support units and helping them colonize in exchange for processed fuel. It's a profitable deal for both parties."

"I'm sure it is," Beverly said under her breath.

"Doctor!" Tarses called out as he bobbed back into view. "I have the Sli in the catchment."

"Good," she said, giving Hartog one last look before moving to Tarses' side.

Together, they bent and pulled out the catchment, swinging it onto the stasis module. Tarses activated the stasis and transferred the deceased Sli onto the module. Its body was slightly more puffed up than the living Sli, and its tentacles were shriveled into tight curls. Unlike the others, this Sli had no color and appeared to be made of thin layers of cloudy glass. Startled, Beverly glanced back at the living Sli, confirming that this was indeed the same creature. But what looked dense and wet when moving through the heavy gas now seemed insubstantial, almost gossamer.

Beverly felt the captain by her side. He was gazing down at the Sli. "What a shame."

"Yes." She swallowed tightly.

Tarses bumped into Beverly, and when she glanced over, he was bouncing nervously on the balls of his feet, obviously torn between keeping a stand by his equipment and retreating.

Beverly questioned him with her eyes. "What's the matter, Tech?"

"Maybe we should put a forcefield around it until we're sure it's dead.

Beverly swept a professional gaze over the Sli. "I'd say this Sli is dead."

Tarses couldn't meet her eyes. "But aren't they dangerous, Doctor?"

"How?" Beverly gestured to the transport tank. "They're completely isolated."

"Sli aren't dangerous!" Hartog protested, thrusting his chin in the air. "They're as defenseless as croc'rog underwater."

Data added, "According to Starfleet regulations, it is illegal to transport dangerous life-forms within Federation Territory. However, the Sli are considered sentient and therefore are to be judged on an individual basis."

"Ha!" Hartog sneered. "Starfleet doesn't like the Sli, and the Sli know it. No wonder they won't talk to you. The first time you found them, you had a full battle right next to their home world. Sli don't trust Starfleet—or Klingons for that matter." He snuck a look over his shoulder back at Worf, who had remained near the door.

"Starfleet holds no animosity toward any life-form." Picard was quite serious. "We would like to make our intentions of peace and cooperation clear to the Sli."

"You've tried!" Hartog twitched his shoulders back. "It just bothers them more when you push at them."

There was a strained silence. Tarses shifted his worried eyes from Beverly to the security guards on the other side of the cargo bay. "B-But the security chief said we were to take all precautions."

"We have," she said flatly. Just because she thought Worf was basically paranoid, it wouldn't do for her to criticize another senior officer to her technician.

"Hey! Watch out!" Hartog called out, rushing toward the Sli on the stasis module.

The dead Sli was expanding right in front of their eyes. A sudden wisp of smoke ran along the outer edge, spiraling upward until it was caught by the artificial ceiling of the stasis field.

Tarses leaped for the controls as Beverly asked, "Was the integrity field broken?"

"Negative! I don't understand . . ." he trailed off, consulting the readings. "Oh, no . . ."

Data joined Tarses, making queries of his own on the control panel. Pale blue smoke was filling the stasis chamber, seemingly more dense than the Sli itself.

"Data, what's happening?" Picard demanded. Worf had advanced to stand behind the captain, his phaser drawn.

"The pressure level is too low for this life-form," Data informed them. "The organic remains are rupturing. I am attempting to reconfigure the stasis field."

Beverly turned on Mon Hartog, who'd been silent after his first outburst, watching the Sli vaporize right in front of their eyes. "You never said anything about pressure levels!"

"I told you it wouldn't work, hu-man!" He sneered right into her face. "We've tried."

Data's fingers slowed, but he didn't take his eyes off the readings as he reported, "Hydrogen atoms are spontaneously igniting. Stasis has been compromised."

The stasis shimmered as the field broke, releasing the smoky gas. Everyone flinched back as it started to curl up into the room, but it almost immediately disintegrated. A rim of deep blue flame ran around the edge of what was left of the transparent Sli.

A warning alarm rang out and a containment forcefield was instantly erected by the overhead sensor cluster. The computer usually suffocated a fire in seconds, but the hydrogen/helium compounds of the Sli continued to burn within the field. Beverly could only watch as her specimen fizzled to nothing.

Finally the computer gave another warning beep before deactivating the forcefield. All that was left was a small smear of organic goo.

Beverly started laughing. She couldn't help it. "Did you see that?"

Picard's forehead was wrinkled. "Dr. Crusher, please."

She grinned full into his face, seeing his perfectly even, white teeth and that dent in the center of his chin. It was really quite arresting. Not to mention those clear, hazel eyes of his, and the proud lift of his head. Jean-Luc was a distinguished man, but she'd heard enough about his past to know he had been considered quite dashing when he was younger. When had it happened? When did that joyous Gascon acquire the dignity she'd known ever since she met him as Jack's captain?

Then she noticed that none of the others were laughing. "I can't believe . . ." She tried to smother the last traces of her giggles. "That was . . ."

"Captain," Data put in. "I believe that prolonged exposure to the Sli affects emotional responses. That result is consistent with reports regarding their performances."

Tarses blurted out, "I knew they were dangerous! I knew it."

"Captain," Worf put in, still holding his phaser. "I must agree."

Picard glanced from them to Beverly, who was trying to control herself. Then he confronted Mon Hartog. "Please tell the Sli to desist from affecting my crew."

The Ferengi raised his upper lip, perhaps a weak attempt at a smile. "Sli choose who they focus on. Usually it's someone they're angry or upset with. I'd say they don't like this wo-man. They probably think she did that to the Sli."

Picard fixed his gaze on him. "You will inform the Sli that the incineration was an accident."

Hartog shrugged, holding both skinny hands palm up. "They won't listen to me. I told you. They're upset."

Picard glanced back at Dr. Crusher, and by this time

Beverly had managed to stop laughing. She was able to meet his worried eyes with something like composure. "I'm all right now. I don't know what came over me."

She flipped open her medical tricorder as she stepped closer to the remains of the dead Sli. Her fit of helpless laughter had been so strange. An odd part of her truly found it funny the way the Sli had gone up in smoke—the episode hadn't been a delusion or something that felt completely foreign to her. But normally she wouldn't have paid any attention to such an irreverent feeling, as was in keeping with her medical decorum.

She glanced up from her tricorder to check on the surviving Sli. They had turned tawny yellow with swirls of lighter cream streaking their bodies. Lavender blotches emerged and began to swallow the yellow, emitting fine wavy lines of pitch black. Their tentacles had become dark purple.

Picard was scanning the readout of the translator unit. "They're attempting to communicate, aren't they?"

Beverly joined him in time to see his words appear on the blue field of the backlit screen, apparently being translated to the Sli.

It was quickly followed by: "Aren't you impressed? It's not fair, is it? Why can't we . . . why can't we . . . Now what?"

"Do you understand what they mean by this?" Picard asked Mon Hartog.

"Seems they're upset," Hartog said with a shrug.

"Do they usually combust upon death?"

"Only in our kind of atmosphere." The Ferengi twisted his fingers together, sounding a little petulant. "It doesn't matter."

"On the contrary, it matters a great deal to me. I would like to be able to communicate with the Sli. Particularly if they are capable of affecting the reactions of my crew."

The Sli began to shift from the lavender and yellow quickly through green into blue, running the gamut from powder blue to indigo in a vast mottled pattern that covered them from top to tentacle. They pulled together into a diamond formation, with one slightly higher than the others.

The screen read: "Isn't it wonderful. . . . Why does it have to be this way? Dreadful too bad."

Picard addressed the Sli again. "We are attempting to assist you."

He waited as the words disappeared into the translator. As they did, a delicate pink wash began to stain the tips of the Sli's horns, seeping down to gradually cover the blue. Specks of magenta rose to the surface, then disappeared, as if a bloody snowstorm were whirling beneath their skin.

On the screen: "Oh, how awful! Does it hurt? Serves you right. It's a shame, isn't it?"

Picard straightened up, looking at Data. "Would a connection to the Universal Translator be of any help?"

"That would require a computer interface with the Ferengi hardware," Data said.

"What's wrong with my translator?" Hartog demanded. "Works fine! See the words there? That's what they want to say."

"A translation by its very definition means that communication is taking place. This," Picard said, pointing to the screen, "makes no sense."

The Ferengi sputtered wordlessly for a moment, waving his hands. "That's just the way they are. Who ever said Sli were easy to figure out?" He reached out and patted the casing of the translator console. His lips were shiny wet. "Ferengi are traders. We know translators—better than your Starfleet."

"Mon Hartog is correct, sir," Data said. "Ferengi translators incorporate technology superior to that of the Federation."

"See there?" Hartog taunted.

Beverly could tell the captain was trying very hard not

to let his distaste for Hartog show. Not that Ferengi ever cared what you thought of them. The only sign thus far had been his narrowed eyes. "Data, I'd like you to make an attempt to interface this translator with the Universal Translator."

"Aye, sir." Data began keying in commands.

"Hey, that's my machinery!" Hartog hovered near Data. "You can't do that!"

Picard raised one hand. "As you yourself stated, Mon Hartog, you'd like to be justly compensated. Simply consider this part of Starfleet's formal investigation." He nodded to Beverly as he turned to leave. "I'd like a full report as soon as you're done, Doctor."

"Yes, sir." She lifted the tricorder with a rueful smile. "I seem to be back to my old self."

"The Sli did express some concern. Perhaps they understood my statements."

Beverly nodded. "Well, I feel fine now."

"Hey!" Hartog interrupted, having reluctantly yielded his translator to Data. "You can't leave my Sli here. They'll die if they stay in the transport container too long. They need more space."

Dr. Crusher just shrugged when Picard glanced at her. "Mon Hartog is the current expert on the Sli."

"Very well. Shuttlebay 3 can be converted to a K environment. Will that be large enough?"

"Oh, more than we need, I assure you." The Ferengi bowed several times, suddenly nauseatingly obeisant.

"Yes, fine," Picard said. "Mr. Worf, please see to the transfer of the Sli."

"Aye, sir!" Worf replied. He called his two security guards over and began giving them instructions.

The captain was looking much more cheerful when he left the cargo bay, but Beverly noticed that Tarses was still eyeing the Sli with distrust. She almost expected that sort of behavior from Worf by now, but not from her medical technician.

But when she went to his side to reassure him once again, she suddenly realized that Tarses wasn't looking at the Sli at all. He was staring past them to Worf.

"Simon, are you all right?"

He couldn't keep from glancing over at Worf again. "I don't want to make another mistake."

It *was* Worf. "Everything will be fine, Tarses. I'll have the computer run redundant bioscans during the transfer. We should have no more problems."

She waited until Tarses nodded and then she sent him on to Shuttlebay 3 to program the K environment. She sighed when she saw the tech hurry past Worf. She knew it was no use talking to Worf about his behavior. Sometimes Worf felt it was necessary to intimidate people to get the job done, and nothing she could say about that would change his mind.

Chapter Seven

Lieutenant Worf was in the flight control booth of Shuttlebay 3, waiting for Dr. Crusher to give the go-ahead for transportation of the Sli, when he was paged by the bridge. "Lieutenant Worf, incoming subspace message!"

Worf frowned slightly. They were going to transport at any moment. "Send it to this terminal, Ensign."

"Aye, sir."

The blue field on the small screen faded to reveal the smiling but, as always, faintly worried face of his foster mother. She was wearing a dark green dress with a rounded neckline trimmed with white cord.

Her Russian accent was pronounced. "Worf, my darling. I just spoke with Miriah Walch. She got a message from Jake telling her that the *Prospector* has been destroyed and that the *Enterprise* rescued him and his crew. Worf, what is happening? Is he with you now?"

His foster father poked his head into the screen. His beard had white streaks from the corners of his mouth down to his chin. His mustache and the patch directly under his mouth were still the same ginger color that Worf remembered when he was younger.

"Son, what's going on? You're taking care of my old friend, yes? It's very bad, I hear."

"Yes, Father." The call was like a shock—it was completely unexpected. They were still on yellow alert. Worf had to quickly find his balance. "The *Enterprise* will be investigating the situation."

"It's terrible. Terrible. Everything gone."

"The *Prospector* was not completely destroyed," Worf tried to assure them.

"He had to evacuate his passengers," his mother insisted. "People were hurt."

Sergy couldn't seem to sit still. "Is Jake all right, Worf? Tell us the truth."

"Father, Mother," Worf said as reasonably as he could. "Jake is fine. No one was seriously injured."

"Thank heavens," Helena said, absently smoothing her dark hair back into the large bun, with its dangling loops of slender braids. "Jake does tend to exaggerate sometimes. From the message Miriah got, we thought it was hopeless."

"Tell us what happened, Worf."

"Father, I cannot discuss the situation at this time. There will be a formal investigation."

"But we're family," Helena said with a small smile.

Sergy added, "And Jake is like family."

"I am sorry," Worf told them, trying to keep the irritation out of his voice. "Captain Walch is fine. We hope to transport the evacuees back to their ship shortly. But I cannot discuss this with you—it is a matter of ship's security."

They were both silent for a moment, with Helena blinking just a little faster.

"We understand, Worf," she said. "As long as you say Jake is doing all right. . . . I know you'll tell us later."

Then she brightened up. "Where's Alexander? I want to see my big grandson."

"Yes, call him, Worf." Sergy leaned forward, nodding. "Alexander liked Jake. I bet he's glad to see an old friend."

"I am on duty," Worf informed his parents. "Alexander will see Captain Walch tonight."

"Oh, I wish I could talk to him." Helena made a sad face. "How is he, Worf? He told us in his last communiqué that he's been having nightmares. How long has this been going on?"

Worf's eyes widened. He didn't know Alexander had informed his grandparents about his bad dreams. "It is a temporary situation."

Helena glanced at Sergy, raising one hand. "Ah, that's good. All children have bad dreams every once in a while."

"No sweets before bedtime," Sergy put in. "That will fix the dreams. It always makes me sleep uneasy when I have—"

"But you can't be too careful with these things," Helena interrupted. "Sometimes it starts out small like this, then it can haunt you for a long, long time. Vina, my friend from Unett, the nightmares she tells me about. . . . Talk to him, Worf. Find out if anything is bothering him."

"Warm milk," Sergy was saying. "Give him warm milk before he goes to bed. That will take care of the dreams."

Worf clenched his hands together. "I can deal with Alexander."

"Of course you can, my darling. Of course." Helena glanced to one side, checking something. "Our five minutes are almost up, Father." The fond look she gave Worf was concerned. She knew something was bothering him. Worf had to glance away.

"Don't worry, darling," she said. "Just remember

what we've said. It's probably nothing. But talk to the boy."

"And warm milk," Sergy added.

Helena quickly shushed him. "We love you. Tell Alexander we're sorry we missed him. Good-bye."

Smiling and nodding, their images disappeared as the message was terminated.

Worf stared blankly through the window of the flight control booth, into the orange gas. His foster parents meant no harm—they only wanted to help. Yet it irritated him.

"Lieutenant Worf!" Dr. Crusher paged him. "We're beaming the Sli into Shuttlebay 3."

Commander Riker strode toward Shuttlebay 2, his expression grim. He was trying to ignore the fact that his away team was leaving two hours later than scheduled departure time.

The door hissed open to reveal shuttles packed tightly together inside Shuttlebay 2. The pilots had had to scramble their shuttles and supplies out of the Main Shuttlebay to allow room for the deposit of the emergency pods during the evacuation of the *Prospector*. The shuttles that had been sent to Shuttlebay 3 had received priority departure and were already on their way down to their drop-off coordinates on Lessenar, leaving the shuttlebay empty for the Sli.

"What a mess," Riker muttered as he looked around. His carefully calculated flight plan had been blown to pieces along with the *Prospector*.

Pilots and technicians were shouting final instructions to one another, trying to get things reorganized. Shuttles were stacked so close together that it was difficult to move between them. As Riker watched, a shuttle surged up a little shakily, clearing another shuttle with only inches to spare.

The flight control technician, Ensign Korn, was standing behind the deck control console, coordinating with the flight control booth in the wall high above them. Her blond hair was gathered into a knot at the top of her head, with the loose strands forming a short plume. She hardly glanced up from her panel, and her small fingers were dancing over the controls. Another cargo shuttle lifted slowly up from the pack and turned to aim toward the pressurized door of the shuttlebay.

"Sir!" she exclaimed, when she caught sight of Commander Riker. Her voice was breathless, worried. "I'm sorry! Your shuttle is still trapped behind three others. I'm working on it, but it'll be a few minutes before it's free."

Riker quickly swallowed his own impatience, and gave Korn a slow, easy smile. "Relax, Ensign. This is only a minor delay. We're getting the job done."

"Aye, sir," she acknowledged with relief. She returned to her panel with renewed determination, her movements less harried than before.

Riker took up a position nearby, silently watching the shuttle dispatch. Each shuttle had different coordinates to deliver its supplies to. Several shuttles, including his own, were programmed to test the atmosphere, and carried scientific equipment for the atmospheric specialists. Lieutenant Chryso's assistant, Ensign Puckee, was already setting up a ground-based testing module near the equator that would automatically perform a battery of tests at various altitudes. Lieutenant Chryso was going down in Riker's shuttle, to set up a dual relay to the nearby location. Without the relay, the condition of the atmosphere would distort the data during transmission.

"Where is Lieutenant Chryso?" he asked Korn.

Korn straightened up. "She's in shuttlecraft *Voltaire,* sir. I have only one more shuttle to go before yours."

"Thank you. I'll wait for dispatch in the *Voltaire.*"

"Aye, sir."

When Riker got into the shuttle and sealed the door, he

noticed Chryso was poised on her chair. She obviously couldn't wait to get into the atmosphere to start the interactive testing.

He ran through the preliminary launch sequence and was ready to lift when he got the go-ahead from Ensign Korn. He effortlessly maneuvered the *Voltaire* past the last few shuttlecraft. As they broke through the blue annular forcefield, moving outside the *Enterprise,* Riker felt a familiar surge of energy. Sometimes it felt as if piloting a shuttle was the most natural thing he ever did.

He hardly noticed when Chryso got up to stand beside the computer access panel behind the seats. As the shuttle brushed through the first tendrils of green in the atmosphere, the small craft reacted to the change in field density. He compensated with the thrusters and continued their slow spiral down.

In a few minutes, all he could see was murky light. The rings were indistinguishable from within. The ionization was draining the shields, but at the current rate of dissipation, they would have several hours before shield integrity was compromised.

The atmosphere remained dense and impenetrable to sight almost all the way down. When they finally broke through the hanging, opaque layer, they were entering a vast valley, flying less than a hundred meters above the surface of the planet.

As he went into landing sequence, Riker caught a glimpse of a vast gray bowl of land. They flashed past several buildings with a large crowd of people gathered neatly to one side. As he set the shuttle down on the coordinates some distance from the structures, he realized he couldn't see the people on the other side. Then the impact sent up a cloud of dust that completely covered the front window.

Lieutenant Chryso was still working with the computer. Riker handed her a biofilter and gestured for her to put it over her nose and mouth. She grimaced, but copied his movements, tightening the small cup against her face.

With his own filter in place, Riker made his way through the webbed containers holding the relief supplies and opened up the shuttlecraft. Two figures were making their way through the hanging dust.

"Ho-ya!" one called out, both hands raised in greeting. His fingers were drawn tightly together, as if atrophied into claws. He cleared his throat before speaking into the old-model Universal Translator he was wearing around his neck. "It is good you are here."

"I'm Commander Riker." The words were muffled by the filter. He gestured back into the shuttle. "Lieutenant Chryso is inside. We've brought the relief supplies you requested."

"Water?" the other man asked breathlessly. The skin of his neck was wrinkled and loose, hanging from his chinless face.

"Three hundred liters," Riker confirmed. The expressions of gratitude on their thin, angular faces was almost painful.

Lieutenant Chryso appeared in the doorway. "We also need a place to set up the relay terminal."

"Come this way," the first man rasped out. "We'll show you where."

The two men started toward the buildings, bending their heads and waving their hands against the still-hanging dust. They moved slowly, as if their joints were dry and lacking lubricating nutrients. Riker fell in behind them. Lieutenant Chryso was a slender woman, but walking next to these two men, she looked almost plump.

"I'm Reeves," the first man wheezed. He had to take a deep breath before he could get out, "And this is Sebast."

"Nice to meet you," Riker said automatically. He was watching his footing. Every few steps either his heel or his toe would sink several centimeters into the ash-colored soil. As he waded through it, the dense substance floated up knee-high before settling heavily back down. Overhead, the sky was soupy gray, nothing like the spectacular view from space.

"You don't know how glad we are to see you," Reeves told him. "We ran out of water yesterday."

"Ran out?" Chryso asked, holding her filter more firmly against her face.

"The well is dry," Reeves said. "We've been moving everyone here to the capital—it's just over that mountain range. But it's slow work."

Sebast added, "The people in the capital aren't much better off."

Riker noted the information. The capital hadn't requested relief, and Council Head Wiccy had proposed it as the location of the reception he had insisted they schedule for the following day.

As they neared the buildings, the ground was dotted here and there by small, flat plants of tangled threads, laid out like burgundy snowflakes. They served to somewhat anchor the ashy soil. Rosy-gray boulders were also scattered across the ground, with smaller rocks embedded in the dirt. Many of the larger boulders were cracked, seemingly ready to fall apart at the slightest touch. Riker leaned against one to see if it was as fragile as it appeared, but the lower regions were planted firmly in the ground. Lieutenant Chryso moved her tricorder over the rock.

"Severe temperature fluctuations created those fissures," she informed Riker.

"Do you need temperature control?" Riker asked Reeves. "Heaters, blankets, clothing?"

"No," Reeves replied. "We don't have that problem anymore. But about eighty cycles ago, the whole planet suffered through radical weather swings. Now it stays close to *demond.*"

"Thirty-one degrees Celsius," Chryso murmured to Riker.

Six more people emerged from around the sides of the buildings. Sebast gestured toward the shuttle. "Can they begin unloading the supplies?"

Riker noticed a battered antigrav sledge parked near one of the prefabricated structures. "Of course. The containers are loaded on antigravity pallets. They shouldn't have a problem with the controls."

Sebast called out something to his people in the Lessenarian dialect, motioning for them to proceed. Riker noticed that the natives compensated for the soft ground by walking in a loose-kneed gait. Chryso didn't seem to be having as much difficulty as he was.

"This used to be farmland," Reeves told them. He swept his arm toward a row of bracken visible some distance to one side of the structures. Most of it was collapsed in on itself, blackened skeletons with gray-tipped branches splayed toward the sky. "An enormous river valley. This was the last location water could be found. People made their way here." He paused to catch his breath. "There're mountain ranges out there, but you can't see them for the haze."

"This is the way I've always known it," Sebast told them.

The two Lessenarians were so open about their situation that Riker didn't feel uncomfortable asking, "Couldn't your people stop this from happening?" He kicked at the lifeless soil.

"The system worked for the ones in power," Reeves said simply.

Taken aback, Riker glanced at Chryso. She was frowning, obviously expecting a biological or natural explanation.

"Who's in charge here?" Riker asked him.

Reeves exchanged a long look with Sebast. "I suppose we are. Trinid died two phases ago."

They rounded the sheds, which, upon closer look, appeared ready to fall apart in a good wind. Riker squinted up at the unmoving air. A good wind wasn't likely to come along. He glanced back at the half dozen Lessenarians unloading the shuttle, then forward again, and stopped.

Hundreds, no thousands, of people spread out before them, hunched on the ground that sloped down to the dry riverbed. Riker had thought Reeves and Sebast were thin; these people were transparent. Their skin was the same ashy color as the ground, partially covered by dark rags. Their sparse hair lay in wispy patches across their heads. Eerily, there was little sound, and a few raised their heads to look at his bright uniform. Their eyes were huge and protruding as they stared up at him.

Riker drew in his breath, and next to him, Chryso raised her hand to her mouth, shaking her head slightly. Riker thought he heard her murmur something under her breath.

"We'll prepare the food," Reeves was saying next to him, "and begin distribution." He walked into the crowd as if drawn forward. As he moved among the people, he reached out, absently touching hands that were held up or gently brushing a bowed head. His breathing was labored, as was that of the others.

Chryso swayed as she looked up from her tricorder, sweeping her eyes across the crowd. "Eight thousand four hundred and thirty-two."

The silence was frightening. Thousands of people, and except for the thin, weak cries of children, there was nothing. Hardly any movement. No talking.

Then Riker heard the low, swelling roar of a shuttlecraft high in the atmosphere. The sound seemed to echo on forever, before finally fading away.

"A relief shuttle," Chryso murmured next to him.

Chapter Eight

DEANNA SHOOK HERSELF from a daze, and found herself staring through the window of the flight operations control booth of Shuttlebay 3. That was the fourth time it had happened since she'd started her observation of the Sli.

She glanced over her shoulder, but Worf hadn't noticed. He was watching the four Sli with narrowed eyes as they drifted near the middle of the huge, empty chamber. The space doors were closed and the glowing blue forcefield had been deactivated. The gently swirling orange gas had completely transformed the vast space into a sea of sunny layered mists.

Deanna drew in her breath as the Sli shifted into a patchwork pattern of darker tones—navy, purple, and crimson, with their tentacles shading toward brilliant fuchsia. The shimmering colors reminded her of the gorgeous stained-glass artwork she'd seen in the ancient cathedrals on Earth. She felt as if she could dive right into the color, it was so deep and rich . . .

She caught herself just before slipping into a mesmerized state again. She shook her head sharply. The security guard closest to her, Ensign Hassett, was also completely engrossed, gazing unblinking into the bay. She considered snapping him out of it, but he was doing his job. Keep an eye on the Sli, Worf had said. He'd posted two guards in the control booth, as well as alarm seals on the main-floor access doors. Ensign Potter was at the other end of the booth, but he didn't seem to have the same problem as Hassett. Potter was jittery, if anything. Deanna noted his behavior on her padd. So little was known about the Sli that any bit of empirical data was valuable.

Troi counted herself lucky that she'd been able to figure out a way to dampen the emotional prods the Sli were sending out. When they'd first come on the *Enterprise,* she'd had a hard time coping. But now she had it back to the way it had been when the Sli were still on the *Prospector*—a continuous background mosaic of feelings. It was beautiful, really, the way their emanations performed an intricate dance through her highly trained empathic responses—that is, it was beautiful when it was properly dampened by her shields.

After accessing everything she could find on the Sli— mostly concert reviews and inquiries by psychologists and health officials—she was certain of one thing. The Sli affected humanoid emotional responses. Their range had been tested by concertgoers, and the limit of their reach was approximately seven hundred meters in diameter. She wondered if the Sli were less powerful now that one of them had died.

She also wondered if the effects were stronger the closer one was to the Sli. Hassett's gaze was still unfocused.

"Worf, is it absolutely necessary to post guards?"

She had surprised him.

"Yes! It is." He briefly met her eyes before returning to his scrutiny of the Sli.

Deanna raised her brows. "Why?"

He didn't look at her. "These . . . creatures are dangerous."

"You call them creatures, as if they weren't sentient."

This time he looked at her. "Sentience requires judgment and reason."

"Worf, sentience is also determined by the degree to which a life-form receives and reacts to sensory stimuli. It's sensation as well as perception." She gestured to the slowly revolving quartet. "Apparently the Sli sense humanoid emotions and react by directly stimulating reactions in us."

"Their response is irrational."

"The Starfleet diplomatic corps seems to believe it's a translation problem," she said. The computer was working with the Universal Translator, but Deanna had a feeling it wouldn't be as easy as that. Emotions were usually indecipherable to machine analysis. Just look at Data. Despite all of his efforts, emotions were still an enigma to the android.

Worf lifted his lip slightly. "That will tell us nothing. Sli are insane, and they provoke insanity."

Deanna frowned. He was serious. "I agree the effects can be disturbing, but I don't think the Sli are powerful enough to be truly dangerous."

Worf didn't bother to answer. He just stared with cold determination at the slowly pinkening Sli.

"Worf, how do you know so much about the Sli?"

He stiffened slightly, his head up and eyes slightly hooded in perfect Klingon posture. He didn't want to say, she could tell.

Then she said, "Oh, that's right," as she remembered. "One of the vessels that was destroyed when the Sli were first discovered was Klingon, wasn't it?"

"Yes." He glanced at the two security guards, but as usual, they appeared not to be listening.

Susan Wright

Deanna lifted her padd slightly, making it an official request. "What do the Klingons think of that first encounter with the Sli?"

Worf clenched his teeth for a moment, then reluctantly told her, "The Sli caused the dishonor and destruction of the warship *Blr Hud.* The captain surrendered to a Starfleet scout ship without engaging in defensive maneuvers. He then notified the Klingon home planet. When additional warships arrived, both ships had been destroyed."

"And you blame the Sli?"

"A Klingon warship would never surrender to a weaker vessel, then allow itself to be destroyed. The crew of the *Blr Hud* were judged insane, and their deaths were dishonorable." He gestured with his chin to the Sli. "I do not trust those creatures."

Deanna sighed, wishing she were better at sensing Worf's emotions. It would help her through spots like this, when she hit the impenetrable wall of culture.

"Well," she finally said. "The Sli aren't going anywhere, and I'm more concerned about the guards being in such close contact with them. Maybe they can be posted out in the corridor."

"We cannot afford to appear weak."

"Worf," she said, trying to keep her tone calm. "I think the guards are making it worse. It just gives the Sli more people to focus their attention on."

Worf bared his teeth. "The Sli have adversely affected members of the crew. According to regulations, guards must be posted until the danger can be contained." His eyes flicked to the side. "Besides, I do not trust the Ferengi."

She flung up one hand. "What could Mon Hartog do?"

"Ferengi are capable of anything they can get away with."

Deanna shook her head. "We're going in circles." She

76

straightened up, her tone firm. "Fine, leave the guards then, but their shifts may only be three hours long. I recommend that you call for reliefs for these two men." Worf was nodding agreement when she added, "And I think that you should leave, too. You've been here even longer than they have."

"Me?" Worf broke his stance. "Definitely not—"

"Yes, you," Deanna insisted. "If the Sli are dangerous, as you say, then the most danger lies in prolonged exposure. As counselor, that will be my recommendation to the captain."

She kept her eyes on him until, reluctantly, he gave the orders for a shift change. He finally left when the new guards arrived. Hassett seemed woozy when he started out, and Deanna told him to report to sickbay. She wanted all the information she could get about the Sli and their effects.

Worf returned to his quarters. His shift on the bridge would begin shortly, but meanwhile he couldn't shake the feeling that Counselor Troi had managed to chastise him like a child. It bothered him.

Alexander was home from school. Worf paused at the open door to his bedroom, checking to see that it was clean, then nodded silently to his son before turning away.

He seated himself on his tall leather chair, leaning back against the hard, round cushions. Absently he gazed into the round, bevel-edged mirror, seeing his foster mother's concerned face instead of his own reflection.

Counselor Troi didn't trust his opinion about the Sli. It was typical for him to disagree with her, but Troi usually had little influence when it came to matters of security. It wasn't that he didn't trust the counselor—quite the contrary. He and Alexander had engaged in counseling with her for some time. But he would not allow her to sway his personal decisions, and he had to admit he was glad he no longer had to endure those weekly chatter sessions.

"Lieutenant Worf!"

Worf tapped his comm badge. "Worf here."

Ensign de Groodt told him, "Incoming subspace message from the Klingon home world, sir."

Another message? Worf pushed himself out of the chair. "Relay it to my quarters, Ensign."

"Aye, sir."

Worf thoughtfully went to his desk and keyed the screen. The Klingon seal faded to a recording of his brother's face. Worf sat down slowly, as Kurn bared his teeth in that mock-sinister smile of his.

"*QaleghneS*, Older Brother. I trust this finds you prosperous."

By the honorable address and Kurn's seat in front of his ritual *taj*, Worf immediately knew this had to do with clan business.

"I formally wish to make a request of the future head of the clan—your son," Kurn continued. "Alexander must come to the Klingon home world to be introduced to our ways if he is to one day properly rule the clan." Kurn's smile widened. "When I have a son, he will give allegiance to your son. I would not give my trust, or have my sons misplace theirs, in one who is not of us." His smile disappeared. "My *juH* is ready to receive you. I await your response."

Worf was growling low in his throat. He didn't like the glint in Kurn's eye. Who was Kurn to say how Alexander should be raised?

He cleared the screen and immediately logged his return message.

"*LoDnI'*. I refuse your request. It is not yet time for Alexander and me to return to the *juHqo'*. Worf out."

He hesitated, his finger poised over the button, before he finally pressed it. Part of him wanted to be even more curt. After all, he knew that Alexander would be eaten alive among other Klingon boys. Alexander was so much more tender than Worf had been at his age. Yet he wondered if he shouldn't take more time to think about it. Alexander would have to see the home world someday.

"I'm glad," came his son's voice from beside him. "I don't want to go."

Alexander was wearing a green jumper. Worf noticed that he'd grown a lot in the past year. "You have never been there, son. Would you not like to see the Klingon home world?"

Alexander quickly shook his head.

"You would eat real *rokeg* blood pie. Perhaps you could even have a *targ* of your own for a short time." Worf almost smiled at the faint memories of his family's town house in the capital city. He remembered much more about their home on Khitomer, but Kurn had lived in that same sector on the home planet almost his entire life.

"No, I don't want to." Alexander's lower lip stuck out. "I never want to go there."

"Alexander. Do not speak that way to your father."

"You can't make me," he called out, retreating toward his room. "I'll tell Counselor Troi and she'll let me stay!"

Worf's hands clenched and he let out a strained sound. "Counselor Troi has nothing to do with this! You will return to the home world when I wish it."

Alexander slipped into his room without a backward look.

Frustrated, Worf ground his teeth together. "It's time for your music lesson, Alexander! Must I come in there and—"

Alexander appeared in his door again, his padd under his arm. "I'm going."

With difficulty, Worf got himself under control. "Do not leave the room when—"

The page interrupted, "Lieutenant Worf, this is Commander Riker."

Worf took a deep breath, steadying his voice. "Aye, sir?"

"Report to Transporter Room 1 for away team duty."

"On my way, Commander!"

When Worf turned, his son was gone.

Chapter Nine

GEORDI STARTED the preliminary engage sequence on his low-pressure suit. He wished he didn't have to wear one—like Data. The suit wasn't the most comfortable thing he ever wore, but it sure did the trick. With the suits, the away team would be able to work on the *Prospector* in spite of the malfunctioning gravity field. The atmospheric conditions on board the starliner continued to meet class-M standards, but they would have to keep their suits sealed to compensate for the gravity fluctuations.

Data was standing to one side, waiting for them to finish suiting up. Except for the hood and gloves, the low-pressure suits were similar to the regular uniforms— red shoulder panels and black bodies—but the material was much thicker. Riker and Worf looked like someone had pumped air into them.

Geordi suppressed a laugh behind his faceplate. Data would have been curious, and this wasn't the time for a long explanation about a stray thought as strange as a blowup Worf doll.

Worf stepped up into the transport chamber. He

looked even more massive than usual in his padded red and black suit. So did Riker. Geordi joined them, holding a portable diagnostic unit that had already been programmed with data downloaded from the *Prospector*'s computers. The captain had instructed them to repair the graviton field and determine whether the ship was capable of movement.

"Ready?" Riker asked. His voice was only slightly distorted from the tiny speaker in the throat of his suit.

They all acknowledged. As the commander nodded and gave his go-ahead to the transporter chief, Geordi took a deep, calming breath. He noticed that Worf tensed as he always did just before transport, but Geordi found it was less disorienting if he arrived relaxed.

The *Enterprise* faded and the *Prospector*'s main transporter room shimmered into sight around them.

They were standing under a small, round temple with a domed ceiling supported by columns. Geordi absently noted the synthetic plasticide that concealed the transporter chamber. His VISOR could perceive a greater range of the electromagnetic spectrum than human eyesight, and he easily detected the coil structures and pattern buffers underneath.

Data held out his tricorder. "The fluctuations in the gravity field vary from 1.23g to 0.74g. The microgyros in your suits will compensate, but there could be a delay of up to two milliseconds."

"Understood. We walk softly." Riker was glancing around sharply. "And what about this? Is it an optical illusion?"

A rectangular fountain stretched away in front of them, with the water reflecting an opalescent glow. Behind them was a flowering bush that concealed the transporter operator console.

"All I see is a large room," Geordi said. "About ten meters square."

"Ten point four meters," Data corrected.

Riker glanced at Worf. "Do you see the stars?"

"We appear to be standing in an open structure within a circle of light." Worf was standing stiffly. "Beyond that is a starfield. I do not recognize the sector."

"I also see a night sky." Riker's voice got a little sharper. "But what is it? A holograph?"

"No, I'd see a holograph." Geordi touched a hand to the faceplate of his suit, pushing it closer to his VISOR as he examined the room. "There's a thin layer of keiyurium and silicon animide applied to the walls— similar to the material we use in our holo diodes. There aren't any energy emissions, so it must be a passive visual distortion."

"Trumpery," Worf growled. "To impress empty minds."

"Right. It's for the tourists." Riker dismissed it. "Come on. Let's get this done so we can get the evacuees back where they belong."

Geordi took a closer look at the commander as he fell in beside him, walking along the fountain. He knew this was Riker's second away team mission of the day, but he sounded unusually tense.

"You say that like you want to get rid of them," Geordi commented.

"They've done nothing but complain since they arrived. It wouldn't be bad except they're interfering with our primary mission." Riker's lips pressed together. "If you'd seen those people down there, Geordi. They're the ones who need our help, not a bunch of—"

Worf made an indistinguishable noise deep in his throat.

Riker glanced back at him. "Something on your mind, Worf?"

"The Sli should be removed from the *Enterprise*. They are a security risk."

"I just want this resolved. Then we could get on—"

Riker lurched a little from a localized gravity fluctuation as they went through the door.

"Are you all right, Commander?" Geordi followed more carefully.

Riker nodded, turning right as Captain Walch had instructed and continuing down the corridor. The floor was covered with a bold-patterned carpet of interlocking swirls in red, blue, and purple. The wall lamps were large and rounded, giving off a warm amber glow. It was very different from the cool efficiency of most Starfleet vessels.

They entered the turbolift—all gleaming white angles with filigreed gold trim. Geordi half smiled when he saw the old-style turbolift handles. When he was twelve, he and his mother had lived on an ancient science ship with the same sort of turbolifts. He'd known by the specs that the starliner was sixty-five years old, but turning a handle to operate the lift was something he'd forgotten about.

"Bridge," Riker ordered, grasping his handle.

The lift started, but it was jolted back and forth as the lights flashed past.

"The gravitational field is affecting the inertial damping field of the turbolift," Data evenly announced.

Geordi was hanging on, his feet braced far apart, as they were all thrown back and forth. One second he was light-headed, and the next he felt as if he were twice as heavy as he should have been. He knew the distortion couldn't have been that severe, but it sure felt that way. His stomach was queasy by the time they arrived at the bridge.

Commander Riker was also looking a little green through his faceplate. Geordi couldn't tell if Worf was affected, but he knew Data could have walked to the bridge on the ceiling and not blinked an eye. Sometimes he envied his friend's unflappable calm.

"The environmental station is this way," Data announced.

Geordi followed slowly, holding the diagnostic unit slightly out to his side so he didn't bump it against his leg. The bridge had low ceilings, and was long and narrow. It was also rather dim, with light knobs glowing different colors on all the panels.

Worf immediately went to the communications/sensors station, the closest the *Prospector* had to a tactical display.

There was no central captain's chair, so Riker sat down at one of the seats nearest the lift, letting his breath out. "Well, this looks efficient enough. If a little outdated."

"Aye, sir." Data was carefully manipulating the control panel with his gloved fingers.

Geordi set the diagnostic unit on the floor and carefully bent down to unlock the access panel. Any sudden movement or change in the gravity field sent a rush of blood to his head. It took almost ten minutes for him to create an interface link between the sophisticated diagnostic unit and the hardware of the *Prospector*'s subprocessors, but he finally managed it.

"Ready, Data?"

"Structural integrity field generators off-line. Beginning information retrieval for Level Two diagnostic."

Geordi watched the readout of the portable unit for a few seconds. "Retrieval running. That's it, Commander. It'll be almost an hour before the automated routines are finished."

"Then let's examine the site of the explosion." Riker pushed himself out of his chair. "I don't suppose there's any way we could get there without using the turbolift?"

"Access to Deck A cargo hold is at the rear of the ship, fourteen decks below our current position. It is accessible through Jeffries Tube 03-18." The tilt of Data's head was exaggerated by his suit. "However, I do not understand why you wish to avoid the turbolifts."

Riker raised one corner of his mouth. "The gravity fluctuation is irritating."

"Irritating?" Data repeated, puzzled.

"Data, it tosses around the fluid in our inner ear, messing up our balance," Geordi gently explained. "Does it do that to you, too, Worf?"

Worf glanced over, his face unreadable. "It can be endured."

Geordi grimaced, but he let it pass. He'd learned not to take Worf's occasional surliness personally. That was part of being a Klingon, he supposed.

Riker was already heading out of the bridge. "We'll walk back along this deck to the rear, then we'll take the turbolift. It's better than climbing a ladder down fourteen decks."

Getting to the rear lift was an adventure in itself. For all his years in space, Geordi had never been on a starliner. The furniture that lined the halls and lounges was overstuffed, with worn plushy fabric and rows of tassels. There were plenty of tiny throw pillows everywhere in contrasting colors. They passed recreation rooms, gymnasiums, and a huge flora-filled promenade with a fake waterfall at one end, splashing madly from the gravity fluctuations. There were also massage tables, steam rooms, saunas, ice plunges, and two swimming pools.

Geordi read all the signs and wished they had time to look around. One open door in particular, marked Vibration Room, caught his eye. But the gravity shifted violently as they were passing by, and Geordi stumbled into Data before dropping to his knees. The gray padded walls of the room next to them thrummed gently in response, and a soft scent wafted into the corridor.

"Um . . ." Geordi said, a delighted smile on his face as Data helped him to his feet. "Smell that."

Puzzled, Data took a sniff. Then he breathed deeply in and out through his nose as if trying to determine exactly what was in the air that was so appealing.

Geordi knew what he was doing. That thoughtful

expression could only mean the android was analyzing something.

Data frowned slightly. "Sage and Holbri musk. Wine of a sweet grain. The scent of burned seed oil. Human flesh . . ." He glanced at Geordi. "I can detect several components of the scent that I am unable to define without further analysis."

Geordi sighed as Commander Riker called back, "Stay together!"

Geordi gently slapped his hand against Data's shoulder. "Come on."

As they continued down the corridor, Data said, "If you wish, Geordi, I can replicate the scent when we return to the *Enterprise*. Perhaps you would like to program it into a holodeck simulation?"

Geordi's smile deepened; he was touched by his friend's thoughtfulness. Data always tried so hard.

"That would be great, Data. I think a lot of people would enjoy that."

Their second turbolift ride was just as bad as the first one. Data was the only one able to maintain some sort of balance. It lasted less than a minute, but sweat broke out on Geordi's face and neck, and he could feel a trickle run down his back. The suit's humidity control hummed slightly, valiantly trying to compensate.

The turbolift stopped on Deck 2, indicating there was a forcefield seal between their current position and Deck 1. The cargo holds were in Decks A, B, and C, with C the outermost hold. Parts of all three lower decks had been destroyed by the explosion, and apparently Deck 1 had also sustained damage or the seal wouldn't have been in place.

Geordi watched as Data accessed the *Prospector*'s computer and tripped the double seal in the corridor where the Jeffries Tube led down to Deck 1. That created a temporary airlock in their section, and sent their pressure suits into full life support mode. Geordi checked his readouts one last time, as the atmosphere was slowly bled off.

Once vacuum was reached, Data deactivated the seal on the Jeffries Tube. Riker gestured for Worf to go first, and the security chief quickly climbed down out of sight.

Geordi was the last to go down. The others had climbed past Deck 1 and were waiting for him by the access door to Deck A cargo hold. According to the computer logs, this was where the Sli had been quartered in their huge environment module.

Riker gestured for Geordi to attach his umbilical to the magnetic strip beside the ladder. "All right, Data. You can open it up."

The thick compression doors slid apart. Geordi was pushed forward by the slight difference in pressure, though he was careful to keep hold with at least one foot on the deck at all times.

The rest of the away team moved into the huge, open space, but their gestures and steps were slower, as if they were walking underwater. Geordi loved working in vacuum, and he watched the others for a moment before going in after them.

To his right, most of the cargo hold had been sealed off with emergency bulkheads when the Sli had withdrawn from the explosion, apparently the only thing that had saved them. The rest of the equipment had been forcibly stripped from the cargo hold by the explosion. Through the torn-out floor, Geordi could see the enormous gaping hole in the next cargo hold. A portion of the sweeping curve of the planet's huge diameter was visible through the jagged edges.

Suddenly Geordi couldn't move. Bursts of spangled light permeated Lessenar's atmosphere, blanketing it with tiny bars of moving, flashing color. His VISOR sent a concentrated stream of data directly into his optical nerve, threatening to overload his brain.

Geordi winced and quickly bent down, concentrating

on not keeling over in the airless chamber. When he finally got himself under control, Data was already on the other side of the hold, examining the torn metal. Worf was standing near him, his magnetic boots planted firmly against the deck, holding his tricorder out.

Halfway there, Riker turned back, his faceplate catching the light. "Something wrong, La Forge?"

He had to swallow. "I've only seen the planet on a viewscreen, Commander. It's overpowering on direct sight." He felt a stab of warning pain in his temples as he tried to look at the others. He swayed and quickly fastened his eyes back on his boots.

"Go back up, Geordi." Riker glanced at the hole and the planet below. "This won't take long."

"Commander!" Worf called out.

Geordi was already turning away, but he hesitated at Worf's tone.

Riker also heard it. "What is it, Lieutenant?"

Worf snapped his tricorder shut, every muscle in his body on the defensive. "This was not caused by a failure of the skeletal structure or the structural integrity field. An explosive was planted on the outside of the hull."

Chapter Ten

WHEN THE AWAY TEAM finally arrived back at the *Enterprise*, Captain Walch was standing in front of the console, impatiently shifting from one booted foot to the other. His white beard looked as if he'd been raking his fingers through it, separating the mass into long, straggling strands. He was still wearing his leather chapped pants with buckles at the knees and ankles, and a brown polynylon jacket.

Worf could tell that Jake must have been waiting for some time, because Ensign Standish was looking a little glazed. Worf stripped back his hood and took a deep breath of *Enterprise* air. He hated being closed inside the low-pressure suit.

Jake was watching him closely. "Well . . . how is she, son?"

Worf hesitated, then became angry at himself. His first instinct had been to soften the blow for the older man. He ground his teeth together, fighting his compassion.

"It's not good, is it?" Jake realized.

Worf glanced at Riker, but the commander was busy

removing his own hood and gloves. Apparently Commander Riker had decided to leave this to him.

"No, sir," Worf told him, tensely trying not to let his voice betray him. "The structural integrity has been compromised beyond repair capacities."

As Jake started shaking his head, Geordi added kindly, "I'm sorry, Captain Walch. That was a pretty big chunk torn out of both the primary and secondary frameworks. The forcefield network will collapse under impulse or warp flight."

Jake was looking with question at Geordi, and Worf quickly informed him, "Captain, this is the chief engineer of the *Enterprise*, Geordi La Forge."

"You would know," Jake told Geordi, giving him a firm shake of his hand. He nodded to Riker and Data, whom he'd met during the evacuation of the *Prospector*. "Are you saying you boys can't fix it—or it can't be fixed at all?"

"It would need a complete refit," Geordi said slowly. "And I don't know of any yard that would refit such an old ship."

"You sure? Maybe there's something . . ." The old man's voice trailed off as he looked from one certain face to another.

Worf didn't know what to say.

Riker stepped closer, almost coming to attention. "My sympathies, Captain Walch." Geordi nodded, as did Data.

"Well, I guess that's it, then." Walch stared blankly past them. "She was my pa's ship, you know. Me and him ran her on purt near this same tour. Started when I was nine years old. He . . . Well, I'm glad he's not here to see her like this—"

"Picard to Commander Riker."

The commander glanced up, a habit all senior officers picked up from signaling communications on the bridge. "Riker here."

"Please report to the bridge with your away team."

"Aye, sir," Riker acknowledged. He nodded once more to Walch. "You'll receive a full report on our findings, Captain. We'll also let you know where you'll be dropped off, so you can make arrangements for your passengers and crew."

Jake grimaced at that.

The others started out, but Worf stayed back for a moment, reluctant to be too hard on the man. Jake had been like an uncle to him, and Worf had played and fought and grown up with his large brood of kids. To all the children, including his own, Jake had been larger than life. He would sweep in a couple of times a year when the *Prospector* put in at the Earth Station Facility with dozens of new stories and descriptions of aliens and places that were beyond imagination. He was a favorite of everyone, both those who believed him and those who didn't.

Worf finally said in low voice, "We will speak at a later time, Captain."

"Sure, Worf." Jake made a good stab at a smile, but his blue eyes were tired. He waved Worf off. "Get on with you, now."

Deanna hurried into the lounge just as the debriefing was getting underway. Dr. Crusher was already there, as were the four members of the away team.

"So the ship's a derelict," Picard was saying as she rounded the table to her seat.

"Aye, sir." Riker paused as Deanna sat down. "The hull was breached from the outside, rupturing the helium/hydrogen environment of the Sli. The resulting explosion did most of the structural damage."

"What caused the initial hull breach?"

Riker glanced at Data, who smoothly answered, "An explosive charge of some kind, sir."

"It wouldn't have done much damage to the ship," Riker pointed out, "if the Sli's environment module hadn't exploded."

Picard looked at Data. "Could it have been aimed at the Sli's environment to create just such an effect?"

"Unknown at this time, sir."

They were silent for a moment. Then Beverly asked, "Why would anyone want to destroy a starliner?"

"Terrorism," Worf immediately replied. "Sabotage. Assassination."

Deanna let out a controlled breath. Worf's tension was so strong that it was drowning out everyone else in the room. It wasn't just aggression—that would blunt her empathy. If she didn't know better, she'd say that anxiety was driving him.

Beverly shook her head at him. "That's pretty extreme, don't you think, Worf? Killing off almost four hundred people to get one target."

"However," Data said thoughtfully, "there is a precedent for such behavior from the Picanou Protectorate, the Gatherers of Acamaria, the Intaran—"

"Thank you, Data," Picard interrupted with a nod.

"Maybe we should check out the passengers," Riker suggested. "Find out if there was anyone on board targeted by groups like the Picanou Protectorate. Or even the Cardassians. They'd blow up an entire ship if they thought they had good reason to."

Geordi leaned back, but there was a frown creasing his forehead. "Maybe someone was after Captain Walch. He's the one who's suffered the most from this, losing his ship."

Worf was staring at the top of the table. His voice was low. "Captain Walch has no enemies that I know of."

"It seems to me that the Sli were the most likely targets," Deanna felt compelled to say. "One was killed, and the others were lucky to get out alive."

93

Worf growled something under his breath.

Picard glanced sharply at Worf. "Do you have something to say, Mr. Worf?"

"Yes, sir. It's about the Sli." Worf straightened up in his chair. "Their presence on board is a security risk."

"Well, they can't go back to the *Prospector*," Geordi told him. "Without the structural integrity field, the gravity overlap has nowhere to bleed off. That causes the sharp fluctuations."

Riker gave a short laugh. "It's just bad enough to be hazardous. Or we'd send the whole lot of them back where they belong."

"Something must be done," Worf insisted.

Deanna raised her brows, noting how his eyes seemed to burn.

But Beverly was already nodding. "Worf may be right. Sickbay has received complaints from Decks 9 through 17 regarding unusual behavior patterns."

"According to the logs of the *Prospector*," Data informed them, "the first two passenger decks above the cargo holds remained vacant throughout the current tour."

"Perhaps we should clear the decks around the shuttlebay." Riker glanced at the captain with a grim expression. "The evacuees are on Decks 9 and 11. They won't appreciate being moved again so soon . . ."

"They'll like it a lot better than violent mood swings," Dr. Crusher told him. "The Sli are upset about what's happened, and according to the Ferengi, they can aim their emanations at those they are particularly angry with. They could see the people who were on board the *Prospector* as a threat because that's where the explosion happened."

"I agree," Picard said. "Worf, make the arrangements for evacuation of these decks. Make sure that contact with the Sli is limited until we know how to lessen their impact." He turned to Deanna. "Have you found out anything about the Sli that can help us, Counselor?"

"There isn't much information on them, sir." She swung her chair to face him directly. "The Sli just started touring this past year, and only a limited number of people have been exposed. I do have reports from various health organizations who compared the effects of the Sli to a mood-altering drug. We know that the Sli tap buried desires and feelings—making it a powerful release for most humanoids. It's not just entertainment, it's an emotional stimulant."

Worf muttered, "They are dangerous."

Deanna tried to keep her voice calm. "The effects can be very therapeutic for some, Worf. We're having trouble because the Sli are upset. It intensifies their projections and gives them reason to enhance the more negative emotions they sense around them."

"Be glad there aren't more of them," Dr. Crusher threw in.

"Perhaps," Picard said. "But I'd like to be sure we can control the Sli that are here."

"What about a forcefield around the shuttlebay?" Geordi asked.

Deanna shook her head. "They're communicating on a very low frequency. It falls in the range of humanoid brain waves, which are larger than the diameter of Lessenar. There's no way to contain wavelengths that long. Not even full ship's shields and vacuum could keep them out—it's the same reason my empathic sense works over great distances."

Riker narrowed his eyes. "What about neutralizing the effects in our minds? Can we block the neural transmitters that carry these emotions?"

The doctor was already shaking her head, her mouth compressed. "That's a highly specialized procedure. Any attempt would block all emotion-carrying transmitters, and I can't do that unless the emanations are completely stopped first."

"Very well." Picard sat back a moment. "If we can't stop them, is there any way we can calm the Sli?"

"Perhaps Mon Hartog knows something he isn't telling us," Riker put in.

"I'm not sure he has any control over them," Deanna disagreed. "He says the reason he isn't being affected, and the security guards are, is because the Sli see the guards as a threat."

Worf was absolute. "We cannot leave the Sli unguarded."

"Worf, they've been on board the *Prospector* for most of the past year, and Captain Walch hasn't had any complaints. In fact, he credits the Sli with reviving his business." She shifted a little. "Many have hailed their performance as one of the most pleasurable interludes they've ever experienced."

Riker nodded in agreement. "I bet the Sli are a big draw despite Walch's ship. It's pretty old, and creaky opulence doesn't go far in this day and age."

Worf frowned. "Captain Walch relies on clients who prefer 'old world' elegance."

"And new world drugs in the form of the Sli," Crusher added.

Deanna focused on the doctor. Beverly was being unusually flippant. "According to the evacuees I've interviewed, they view exposure to the Sli as an emotional symphony—very exhilarating. Both passengers and crew were allowed to rent the empty cabins when they wanted a private session. As they toured the planets, Hartog beamed up the inhabitants for concerts held in the Deck B cargo hold."

"But that's not what's happening here," Dr. Crusher protested. "I'm getting reports of people experiencing mild forms of paranoia, depression, and hysteria. Also

96

confusion, irritability, and manic fits." She glanced down at the last.

"You're being affected, aren't you?" Deanna quickly asked. "Beverly, don't spend so much time with them. They're upset and see anyone who comes in contact with them as a threat."

"I have to run my tests," the doctor insisted. "The medical library is being programmed for the analysis, but I've already gathered some interesting data. Do you know that the helium in their bodies has remained isolated atoms? I can't understand how it's interacting with the hydrogen and carbon atoms to form living creatures. According to Hartog, they take in radiant energy like plants. Don't ask me about that either—it's nothing like photosynthesis."

"Let your technicians take over some of the work," Deanna insisted. "I've recommended that no one stay near the Sli for more than a few hours at a time." She looked harder at Worf. "Including security personnel. Unfortunately, you don't have to be in their presence for them to affect you."

"How serious is it?" the captain asked.

"The emanations are fairly weak. With a little effort, it's easy to resist," Deanna assured him. "I've been instructing everyone who comes in contact with them to do so. I'm also hoping the Sli will calm down now that we have them settled in the shuttlebay."

"Very well," Picard said briskly. "We'll discuss this with Mon Hartog, Counselor, and see if we can reach some sort of accord. In the meantime, you and the doctor continue your examinations." He nodded to his security chief. "Worf, I also want you and Counselor Troi to proceed with a security investigation of the passengers and crew of the *Prospector*. There must be a connection somewhere between the people on board and the explosion."

"Yes, Captain." Worf nodded sharply.

Deanna also acknowledged. She was glad she'd have an opportunity to work with Worf. It might provide the opening she was looking for to discuss his more personal problems.

"As for the operational status of the *Prospector,*" Picard continued, "I'll inform Captain Walch that it may be wiser to request a tow ship rather than wait for us to finish our mission here. His tourists could become impatient with the delay."

Riker shifted irritably. "About those tourists, sir. We're getting complaints every few minutes as it is."

"I suppose we should make arrangements for salvage of their belongings," Picard said thoughtfully. "That seems to be the biggest cause for complaint so far. Commander Data, I want you to work with Captain Walch and his crew to speed the process along."

"Aye, sir."

Before they could continue, the door of the observation lounge opened, admitting Lieutenant Chryso. Her dark skin was flushed and she was trying to hide the fact that she was out of breath. She hesitated when she realized everyone was seated and looking at her.

"I'm sorry for the delay, sir," she told Riker in her low voice.

"We were just getting to your report, Lieutenant," Riker said. "Have a seat."

Chryso acknowledged, "Sir," to the captain before sitting in the chair next to Riker. She also nodded greetings to Deanna, Dr. Crusher, and Commander Data. Her glance slid past La Forge and Worf, and Deanna realized Chryso had never worked directly with them before.

"I have a preliminary assessment," Riker started, toying with a disk case sitting in front of him. "Overall, the situation is worse than Starfleet was led to believe. It could be the Lessenarians are in so deep that they don't realize what's facing them. Or they might have been afraid we wouldn't help if we knew the full extent of the damage."

"How bad is it, Number One?"

"The inhabitants are desperate. At thirty-four of the drop-off sites, the environment was almost incapable of supporting life. Every report from the relief shuttles was the same—dead and dying crowds of people, barely holding on with the help of the strongest survivors. Three of the drop-off sites were to fair-sized cities on the western continent. Government organization tends to be restricted to these more populous areas, and the people there are in better shape. Apparently all of the information we were given pertains to the inhabitants of the cities."

"It's as if the government has given up on the outlying regions," Chryso agreed.

Dr. Crusher shrugged one shoulder, shaking her head. "The population base is pretty small—less than a million people. But according to the records I received, related diseases and deaths from the quality of their atmosphere, water, and food supply are at least ten times what I would normally expect." She looked directly at the captain. "If the commander is correct, the real statistics must be appalling."

Riker's voice was harsh. "Fires are burning constantly —incinerating the dead. On low-level flights the most prominent sights are the black smoke smudges. There's hardly any vegetation, and most of the rivers and lakes have dried up." He nodded to Chryso. "Proceed with your report, Lieutenant."

Chryso took a deep breath as she inserted a disk and gestured to the monitor. "This is a planetary map of Lessenar. Approximately fifty percent is land mass, and the other half is covered by oceans high in saline content."

Deanna leaned forward to see better. Lessenar had six

large continents, equally distributed. Distinct bands of brightness ringed the planet in four spots—narrow bands on either side of the equator and even smaller ones closer to the poles.

"The drop-off sites were located in the darker bands, the areas that receive precipitation." A series of indicator lights appeared, marking each coordinate. "As you can see, most of the surface of the planet is uninhabitable. In addition, our preliminary analysis indicates that the atmosphere is no longer within the parameters of class-M."

Dr. Crusher sat forward, disturbed. "Every one of those people down there should be wearing a biofilter."

"I agree," Chryso said. She met the captain's eyes.

"Is the situation irreversible?" Picard asked her.

Chryso briefly shook her head. "Our analysis isn't complete yet, sir. It's a very complex problem. Every aspect of the ecosystem, from the atmosphere to landmasses to the oceans, must be surveyed and correlated." She keyed the monitor, bringing up a sensor graph. "For example, the high degree of ozone in the stratosphere and mesosphere sets in motion a series of chemical processes. The excited oxygen electrons destroy molecules such as water vapor, methane, molecular hydrogen, and nitrous oxide. The resulting molecular oxygen molecules absorb solar ultraviolet radiation from three thousand to eighteen hundred angstroms, damaging the reproductive tissue of living organisms." She clicked off the monitor. "There isn't one solution that will solve their problems. A very delicate balance has been violated, deliberately violated, by the Lessenarians."

"You're saying this situation is not due to natural causes?" Picard asked.

"No, sir. The biosphere once created a viable ecosystem. The Lessenarians altered their environment."

"What're they doing about it?" La Forge asked.

Riker glanced at Chryso, then answered for her. "They called us."

"That's it?" Worf demanded, surprised out of his silence.

"That's it. There've been no planetwide efforts to halt the pollution or attempt at cleanup other than contacting the Federation. It even took them years to reach that decision."

Deanna laced her hands in her lap. "Even with people sickening and dying, they haven't done anything?"

Data met her gaze, unruffled by the implications. "According to my studies, the pollution is a by-product of Lessenar's economy. Change would entail a complete revamping of their food and power sources. In recent history, isolated factions within the society have attempted to warn the inhabitants about the danger, or have actively attempted to prevent the worst of the abuses. Their efforts have proved ineffective thus far."

Beverly looked like she was caught between shock and outrage. "I can hardly believe this. How could they let this happen?"

Riker met the doctor's eyes. "I didn't understand at first, either. But it's their way of life. They seem to have accepted it. They're definitely used to it."

"They know no other way," Chryso agreed. "Apparently the situation worsened gradually enough for them to adjust to the restrictions. Yet it's driven them almost to extinction in just eight generations."

"I'd like your report as soon as possible, Lieutenant," Picard told her. She acknowledged as he turned to Riker. "I understand your presence has been requested in the capital city tomorrow morning."

"Yes, sir." His tone was barely polite. "Council Head Wiccy informed me there would be a 'celebration' of our arrival. What that really means, from what I can gather from their media reports, is that the upper castes will be celebrating while the rest continue to starve to death."

"Perhaps they're in need of a tangible sign of hope," Deanna suggested.

"They're much more in need of something else," Riker returned. "Like an education on excess and abuse of power."

Riker's sharp words created a slightly strained silence.

"I understand, Number One," Picard told him. "And I share your sentiments. However, it is not our place to make the Lessenarians change the way in which they live. Our recommendations can be given, but ultimately it is up to them to choose for themselves."

"Sir," Riker insisted, "the source of their problems must be addressed for anything substantial to be done."

"Again, I agree. However, let us not shove our philosophy down their throats. That's a direct violation of the Prime Directive."

In spite of the serious topic, Deanna noted Picard's use of metaphor. He so rarely allowed that of himself.

"Continue the relief efforts," Picard ordered, "and begin distribution of biofilters to the inhabitants. Coordinate with the council, Number One." The captain held up a hand to stave off Riker's interruption. "By all means, include filters with the relief supplies to the outlying areas. But if we begin working with the council now, perhaps they'll be accustomed to cooperating with us by the time we reach the more difficult issues." He met glances around the table. "Very well, let's get to work. Dismissed."

Chapter Eleven

CAPTAIN PICARD WAS STEPPING into his ready room when behind him he heard Commander Riker say to Counselor Troi, "This is one time I think the Prime Directive does more harm than good. We should be allowed to teach those people the lesson they need."

"Will, it's not that easy—"

The door slid shut behind Picard, keeping him from having to say anything. He stood there for a moment. It was difficult for him, too. He, too, wished he could go down there and rally the populace into helping themselves; to encourage them with hope and brave words into being a healthier, more productive people. How could he explain how dangerous it was to think that Starfleet would sweep down and solve the problems of a world? Superior technology didn't make the Federation supermen, and it was far too easy to slip into that role when a less developed species called for help. Such a thing could play insidious tricks on the mind.

"Captain Picard, incoming message on long-range subspace relay from Starbase 17."

"In here," he said, swiveling the monitor to him.

The brilliant Starfleet logo was replaced by the image of Admiral Rosso. She was impeccable as usual—every short gray hair in place, and the fit of her uniform revealing her superb condition. But Picard knew Maria Rosso, and he could tell she was disturbed.

"Admiral Rosso, it's good to see you again."

"And I, you, Jean-Luc."

Taking a cue from her informal tone, he asked, "How is Jono doing? Have you heard from him lately?"

Her smile was wistful, almost pained. "He's doing wonderfully well. I received a message from him a few months ago. He's in the Talarian space fleet now, on board the *Minat Rii*. His rank is equivalent to one of our ensigns."

"You must be proud of your grandson." He remembered how the blond teenager would lie in that hammock he jury-rigged in the captain's cabin and would stare at the stars for hours. Picard had been just as space-mad when he was young.

"I am. I wish I could see him, but the Diplomacy Corps is desperately understaffed right now. I can't seem to get away." She smiled as Picard leaned back. "Yes, I'm leading up to something, Jean-Luc. You're the man I'd pick for this job even if you weren't on the spot."

"Oh, no." He shook his head, raising his hands. "No, you can't do that to me, Maria. I know it's a delicate situation with the Lessenarians, but I'm not going to replace Commander Riker as the Federation's liaison."

"We don't want you to." She raised her brows slightly. "I have every confidence in Commander Riker. No, it's the Sli we're concerned about."

"The Sli?" He narrowed his eyes. "Why the Sli?"

"We've been keeping a close watch on the Ferengi-Sli alliance. The Ferengi are currently getting more than half of their processed fuel from the Sli colonies they've established on class-K planets. Until recently, as far as we could see, the Sli didn't get much from the deal. But now there are two groups of Sli touring with Ferengi 'managers,' and we've had several reports of Sli on board Ferengi merchant vessels. The Ferengi do nothing without receiving something. So why are they suddenly transporting the Sli everywhere?"

"You're worried that the Ferengi are using the Sli somehow? It's not hard to believe. They're certainly having an effect on my crew."

"We don't know enough about the Sli to know what might be happening." She leaned forward. "The data your people have gathered is invaluable, Jean-Luc. But I want more. With the Sli on board the *Enterprise*, you have a unique opportunity. We tried to make contact with that very group when they were on the *Prospector*, but they became so agitated that our diplomat was asked to depart by the captain of the ship."

"Captain Walch didn't mention that."

"It wasn't an unexpected reaction. When the last diplomatic team was sent to Qal'at, to the main fuel depository, they were forced to retreat when the Sli began to negatively affect their reactions."

"Yes, I accessed that report," Picard told her. "The emotional swings leading to the dissolution of the team are similar to what my crew is experiencing. Making contact with them may be difficult," he warned. "It appears the Sli are the most likely target of the explosion that damaged the *Prospector*."

"Very interesting." The admiral slowly tapped her fingers on her desk. "Who would want to kill the Sli?"

"We were asking ourselves that. Yet it appears to lend credence to the theory that the Ferengi are using the Sli to manipulate them into better bargaining positions. Perhaps a dissatisfied customer is attempting to even an old score."

"If you could just get the Sli to trust you . . ." the admiral murmured, with a gleam in her eye. Her tone changed slightly. "I don't believe there is a tow ship

Susan Wright

currently available in your sector. The *Enterprise* will
have to tow the *Prospector* back to Starbase 81 upon the
completion of your current mission."

He was surprised at her candor. "You diplomats will
do anything to establish communication, won't you?"

"It's our only indulgence, Jean-Luc. You know that.
Misunderstanding can be more dangerous to us than
anything—it breeds war."

Picard drew in his breath. It was true. "Very well, my
crew will simply have to put up with the inconvenience.
Commander Data is reconfiguring the Ferengi translation unit, and Counselor Troi has begun empathic attempts at contact."

"Good. Use every method available. Emotional ma-
nipulation would be a powerful tool in the hands of the
Ferengi, one that can easily be abused."

Picard agreed as he signed off with Admiral Rosso.
Then he immediately hit his communicator.

"Counselor Troi, please meet me at Shuttlebay 3. It's
time we had a talk with Mon Hartog."

Mon Hartog was leaning against the flight operations
console, sneering down at the young Klingon boy beside
him as he said, "Your father knows nothing about my Sli.
His narrow mind can't understand these beautiful creatures."

The Sli were floating just on the other side of the
window. They were very dark, mottled purple and plum
with charcoal gray tentacles. Burnt orange smears
streaked through the darkness, like light shining through
rents in the fabric of their skin.

"Alexander!" Deanna exclaimed when she saw the
boy. "What are you doing here?"

He instantly turned, his anger at the Ferengi shocked
into guilt, then just as quickly transformed into defiance.
"I was looking for Father."

"Is something wrong? Why didn't you use the computer to call him?"

"Nothing's exactly wrong," Alexander hedged, twisting his fingers together.

"Enough of that, Alexander. If you were curious about the Sli, why didn't you say so?"

He was wide-eyed. "I didn't think Father would let me see them."

Deanna deliberately kept herself from answering back sharply. Childish honesty was too precious to suppress with anger. "You're right, Alexander. Your father wouldn't like you to be here. The Sli can make people feel things they don't want to. He'll be worried when he finds out you were here."

Hartog leaned closer, the wet sounds of his words loud in the narrow room. "It can be our secret." He tried to grin at Alexander, but the boy drew away. "The father won't understand."

Alexander's eyes were pleading up at her.

She turned her head slightly. "Alexander, I have to tell Worf about this. He's your father."

From behind her, Picard asked, "What's going on? What's this child doing near the Sli?"

"Alexander was just leaving," Deanna said, ushering the boy out. "Go back to your quarters. I'll speak to you later."

Picard looked at the senior security guard on duty. "There's an evacuation order in effect for this deck, Ensign. Perhaps you weren't aware of that?"

The woman had a fine fuzz of dark hair on her head, and round black eyes that looked perpetually startled. "No, sir. I mean, I knew there was. But nobody told us to keep people out."

Picard went very still, his eyes narrowing somewhat. The other guard shifted uneasily when Deanna glanced at him.

"What are your orders, Ensign Saart?"

Saart shot a quick look at Mon Hartog, who'd silently withdrawn into the far corner. The Ferengi was smiling.

"Sir, we are to monitor the actions of the Sli and Mon Hartog when he is in the flight operations booth. No contact is allowed between them. Any suspicious moves are to be immediately reported."

"Well, that's clear enough anyway." Picard nodded. "Add to that—no unauthorized personnel are to be allowed admittance. Particularly children."

"Aye, Captain."

Picard was turning to Deanna when Saart mumbled, "I can just see it now. Another reprimand."

"What—" Picard stopped himself, staring back at the guard. "Explain yourself."

Saart ran a hand across her shorn head. "It wasn't our fault! We weren't told."

"Shut up, Saart!" her buddy hissed.

"You're both temporarily relieved of duty," Picard told them.

They broke from their positions from the force of his command, but they were obviously confused.

"Return to your quarters," Picard ordered. "Lieutenant Worf will inform you when you may return to duty." The captain waited until they slowly started out, then turned back to Deanna.

She felt compelled to say on their behalf, "It's the effects of the Sli, sir."

"I'm aware of that, Counselor. Please see to it that crew members don't stay in close contact with the Sli for more than an hour. That includes yourself."

"Captain, I've been trained to block emotional projections." She tried to keep her tone calm, despite his peremptory order. "I shouldn't have any problem with the Sli."

He gave her a considering look. "Perhaps not."

She lowered her voice, gesturing to the presence of Hartog. "I need to work with the Sli to learn how they communicate, sir."

Picard finally nodded, also turning his attention to Mon Hartog. The captain seemed to don his diplomat's hat right in front of her eyes.

"Mon Hartog, if I could have a moment with you?" Picard's tone was reasonable, and he even summoned up a pleasant expression for the Ferengi. "Surely there must be something we can do to calm the Sli."

Hartog was as polite as Deanna had ever seen him, but his answer was abrupt. "I know of nothing."

It was stated just bluntly enough to stop the captain for a moment. "Yes, well," he started again. "You were able to maintain some sort of control over them while you were on board the *Prospector*, correct?"

Hartog shrugged. "They never got this upset. Oh, except for that once. Starfleet personnel were involved then, too."

"Well," Picard said patiently, "what can we do to make their current situation more agreeable?"

"They're not like us," Hartog was quick to point out. "They don't feel how we feel. Not for the same reasons."

"They're upset because one of their number has died. That seems reasonable enough to me."

"That's not why!" Hartog gestured to the translator board mounted on the console. "Ask them and see."

Deanna nodded. "Data and I have adjusted the translator unit, Captain. We've eliminated the lesser reactions and are getting a more accurate picture of what they're trying to express."

The captain stepped up to the unit and cleared his throat. He greeted the Sli, then asked, "Is there anything we can do for you?" He waited, but when they didn't respond, he added, "Your emotional projections are disturbing my crew. If there is anything we can do to make you feel more comfortable, I would be glad to arrange it."

The words scrolled across the screen: "Resent/hate being told what to do. No one understands/cares."

Picard drew in his breath. "I'm attempting to understand your situation. Please tell me what you need."

The Sli went from predominantly purple to a brownish olive green mixed with black. "Hopeless/trapped we are."

"You're not trapped on board my ship," Picard quickly contradicted. "You will be returned home when it can be arranged."

"Frustration/anger."

Picard shook his head. "This isn't getting us anywhere."

"But it's clear they want something," Deanna insisted, looking up from the screen. "Hartog, what do you give them for their 'performances'?"

"They haven't asked for anything."

"What?" Deanna's mouth opened, then closed. "You're telling me you make a profit from the Sli, and they don't receive anything? How do you know they want to do this?"

"They haven't complained until now."

Exasperated, Deanna met Picard's eyes. "I don't believe this. He's treating them like circus animals."

"I take care of them!" Hartog insisted, ducking his head repeatedly. "What else do you want? When they ask for something I give it to them. They don't like the transport container, so I make sure they get this big room. They want to see people, so I arrange concerts. Other than that, I leave them alone." His voice grew more snide. "It's better than some do—someone just tried to kill them!"

Picard raised his hands. "We haven't established the origin of the explosion yet."

"I say we have!" Hartog scuttled over to the glass, peering out at the Sli as their dark colors slowly revolved. "Sli don't brood on anything. They're quick on to the next thing. But look at this," he said, pointing to the Sli. "They're still excited because they know someone's after them."

"How would they know that?"

Deanna told the captain, "It's likely the Sli are as good at sensing our emotions as they are at projecting theirs. Mon Hartog could be right that they sense someone who has murderous intentions toward them."

"Who would want to kill Sli?" Picard asked, his eyes shifting nonchalantly toward the Ferengi.

Mon Hartog shrugged, his voice taking on an irritating whine. "Perhaps someone wanted the group to leave my employ. Perhaps there's someone out there interested in my profits."

Deanna knew Picard wasn't convinced. "Perhaps someone is angry at the Sli," he said. "This could be an attempt at revenge." He was watching Hartog closely.

"That's it! Someone wants them dead. So smart, you are, Captain," Hartog sniveled ingratiatingly, tilting his head to look up at him.

Deanna frowned. "You don't believe that at all," she told him.

"Yes, this must be it," Hartog insisted. "There're many people that don't appreciate their talent. They're scared of my Sli."

"We don't even know what caused the explosion," Deanna told him. She knew the captain was studying Hartog's reaction. "Worf's still running a computer check on the passengers and crew of the *Prospector*. He's also checking the trade vessels that have entered this system in the past quarter. We'll know soon enough if there are any connections."

"Don't bother," Hartog said dismissively. "The killer

is here, on board this ship, or the Sli wouldn't be so upset." His voice grew sly. "Why don't you start investigating the *Enterprise* crew?"

"My crew!" Picard stared harder at the Ferengi. "What are you suggesting, Mon Hartog?"

"I'm not saying for sure—but it could be that Starfleet wants my Sli dead. Those diplomats of yours sure upset my group when they came on the *Prospector*. And everyone knows there've been bad feelings ever since your *Crockett* was destroyed, now hasn't there?"

"You're jumping to conclusions, Mon Hartog."

Hartog quickly licked his lips. "You said it yourself, my dear captain. It just seems to me as if someone finally decided to take revenge on the Sli."

Chapter Twelve

LIEUTENANT CHRYSO STRAIGHTENED UP from the science station on the bridge. The end of Alpha shift was nearing, but that didn't matter to her. She expected to be working through the night on the planetary analysis. She would have preferred to be working in her lab in Atmospheric Sciences, but she had to coordinate the volumes of data for the research teams, and that was done better directly on the bridge.

Chryso glanced back at Riker, seated in the command chair. He had requested hourly updates on her analysis, which she'd been providing. She wasn't sure if he was pleased with their progress or not.

They had already received the first of the test results from the ground-based module. The situation on the planet was complicated by natural factors, making the problem much more complex than she'd first anticipated. The electron influx from the primary was reacting with the pollutants in the air, creating an array of lethal secondary pollutants. Additional particulates were produced by Lessenar's hot core and unstable crust, with the resulting incidence of volcanic eruption unusually high for a class-M planet. In addition, the destruction of the natural ecosystem had allowed bacteria to multiply and flourish, both in the water and airborne growth.

Chryso was turning back to her computer when her assistant, Ensign Puckee, burst through the turbolift. Puckee's pale skin was flushed, and small curls of copper-colored hair had sprung from the waist-length braid she wore down her back, to gently frame her round face.

"Lieutenant!" she said breathlessly, quickly crossing the upper tier to her side. "Why don't we integrate the spectroscopy lab analysis with the reconfigured sensors in the ground-based module? It would speed things up and—"

"The object of our analysis," Chryso corrected, pitching her voice deliberately low to remind Puckee that they were on the bridge, "isn't to be fast, but to be thorough. Error rate would rise to plus or minus six percent with integration, and that is unacceptable."

Chastened, Puckee cast a quick look at the bridge officers before she nodded and swallowed. "I knew Commander Riker was waiting for our results," she said apologetically.

Chryso smiled. "He is. Keep coming up with ideas, Ensign. Your solution for stabilizing the ground module was innovative."

Puckee brightened. "Thank you, Lieutenant."

"Anyway, you've had a long day," Chryso told her, remembering that Puckee had gone down to the surface in one of the first shuttles to leave the *Enterprise*. Then she'd had to set up the ground module, which was a slow, intricate process. "Why don't you go relax for a few hours until the second test sequences come in?"

"But . . ." the redhead started hesitantly, "you're still working. I really shouldn't—"

"I'll want you to be in the lab at oh nine hundred hours

to coordinate the analysis. Until then," Chryso ordered with a grin, "go rest. And get something to eat."

Puckee nodded acknowledgment, turning smartly toward the turbolift, her long braid swinging out behind her.

Chryso's smile faded. Puckee had a brilliant mind, and tended to become impatient with routine cross-checks. Chryso knew she was excited about their current mission, but she hoped by sending Puckee away from the labs, her assistant would cool off a little. A biosphere as delicately poised on the brink of annihilation as Lessenar required careful, thoughtful investigation. If they made just one mistake, misjudged one outcome, the planet could be lost forever.

Chryso took a deep breath, and brought up the spectroscopy analysis once more to verify the preliminary analysis.

"You're off shift early," was the first thing Guinan said to Simon Tarses when he sat down at the bar.

Simon chewed on the inside of his lip. "It's only an hour. Dr. Crusher said I'd been running tests with the Sli too long."

Guinan dipped her head silently in understanding, setting his usual burgundy fizz in front of him. Her pale green hat was almost round, but the brim flared just over her forehead. Her tunic was thin green cloth that shimmered when she moved.

Simon slowly made himself relax—he knew he could trust Guinan. If it had been anyone else who'd asked, he wouldn't have been so quick to tell the truth. Not that it was such a bad thing to be sent off shift early, but some people might think he wasn't capable of doing his job if they heard about it.

A crowd of off-duty personnel had gathered by the view window. The *Enterprise* was at full stop, so

Lessenar was farther away than was usual in standard orbit. They could see the entire planet through the window, green fuzzy rings and all. Simon looked at it for a moment, then away. Everyone seemed so pleased with the sight—they should get a look at the Sli. He'd never seen anything as strange in his life.

"It's quite amazing. Don't you want to look?" Guinan asked.

"No. It's not so great." He heard his voice go up at the end, hating how uncertain it made him sound.

"Well, I'm glad. It was getting lonely over here," the hostess said, really seeming to mean it. "Everyone seems to be drawn to the view. The captain had to make Ten-Forward off limits to the tourists."

"They're everywhere else."

Guinan's eyes were smiling. "I think the tourists are thrilled to be on board the *Enterprise.* Most people like things that are unusual."

"Sometimes." Simon bent his head, then forced himself to meet her eyes. "Sometimes people are scared of things that are different."

"Perhaps." Guinan shrugged lightly. "But you won't find many of those people in Starfleet."

"I guess not. It's just that I . . ." he stumbled, closing his eyes. He gestured to his slightly pointed ears. "I have to watch out for it."

"Because of your grandfather?"

He rubbed his hands together, nodding quickly.

Guinan's voice was soft. "I see. You think people are judging you because of your Romulan blood."

He quickly looked to see if anyone else had heard. One of the atmospheric scientists, Ensign Puckee, was sitting nearby, but she seemed more interested in her soup than what Guinan was saying. Just in case, he lowered his voice, so only Guinan could possibly hear. "Nobody trusts Romulans."

"Simon." Guinan leaned forward, with her hands on

the gleaming silver counter. "As long as the Federation has an uneasy peace with the Romulan Empire, people will be curious about you. Don't mistake that as a personal judgment."

"Th-That's what . . . Counselor Troi says everyone knows I'm part Romulan."

Guinan smiled. "I consider you one of my more exotic friends, Simon. Your kind is rare—just like mine."

"S-So you also think of me as Romulan?"

"Simon, I think of you as my friend," Guinan corrected, not taking her eyes off him. "Something is bothering you."

"Why do you say that?" he asked, drawing back. Could everyone tell?

"The Sli could have something to do with it," Guinan suggested.

Suddenly Ensign Ro appeared next to Tarses, almost breathless in her hurry. She leaned over the counter. "Guinan, have you heard? They think it might be someone from the *Enterprise* who sabotaged the *Prospector.*"

Simon gripped his thighs with his hands. It couldn't be true. Not again.

"Really? It hasn't been announced," Guinan was saying.

"Well, it's true. The captain is fighting to keep them from investigating the crew."

"Who exactly is 'they'?"

Ro flipped her hand in the air. "You know—Starfleet. The Ferengi . . ."

From behind them, security officer Potter was suddenly yelling, "That's an ignorant lie!" He got up from his table, ignoring his friends who grabbed at his arms, trying to keep him there. "It was the Sli who did it. That's why there's a guard posted—"

"Not here, Potter." Hassett got up and tried to stand in front of him. "You're talking about our orders."

117

Potter pushed him away, advancing on Ro. "I don't think you should be spreading rumors like that."

"Hey, mister, this is a private conversation." Ro glared right into his eyes. "Turn around and I'll forget it happened."

Potter raised his chin, his straw-colored hair catching the light. *"You* have no right to talk. You've been court-martialed . . ."

"Why, you—" Ro flared up, her hands clenching into fists.

Ensign Puckee stepped up to Ro, putting her hand on her arm. But she spoke to Potter. "You're out of line, Ensign."

"No!" he blurted out. "She is!"

"That's enough." Guinan moved from behind the counter to insert herself between them. Her tunic swirled around her, but she didn't move a muscle.

"Give it a rest," Ensign Puckee added firmly.

Ro and Potter glared at each other. But just when Tarses thought they would start fighting again, they both backed away slightly.

"That's better," the hostess said, lowering her hands. "I'm surprised at both of you. You'll never lack for enemies fighting over gossip."

Guinan knew Ensign Potter would subside quickly, so it was Ro she kept her eyes on.

"You're right," Ro finally admitted. She who used to hold a grudge for days backed down quickly enough under Guinan's penetrating gaze. Ro nodded to Potter, who sheepishly shrugged and returned to his friends.

"What's going on around here?" Puckee asked, as Ro left the lounge in a huff.

"I believe Potter was posted guard duty on the Sli." Guinan turned back to the bar. "Well, Simon—"

Tarses' chair was empty, his burgundy fizz only half finished. Clasping her hands thoughtfully in front of her waist, Guinan glanced around the room. He was gone.

"Would you like anything else?" she asked Puckee as she made her way to the replicator. Meanwhile, she dialed up a synthehol for Potter, certain he would ask for another any moment now.

"You cannot be serious."

Deanna drew back. Worf was staring at her so hard, she had to remind herself that he was in complete control of himself. "It's Captain's orders, Worf."

"I cannot believe the captain suspects one of the crew."

"Maybe not, but he's attempting to get Mon Hartog to cooperate with us. If a perfunctory investigation of our crew helps calm the Sli, then what can it hurt?"

Worf looked offended. "It is bad for morale!"

"It's a closed investigation, Worf. The crew won't know about it."

Worf clenched his teeth, and turned away toward the view windows. The *Prospector* was drifting just behind and above them, its hull plates worn and old compared to the shiny warp nacelle of the *Enterprise.*

Deanna had brought Worf into the lounge to give him the captain's updated orders, and now she was glad she'd had the foresight. This was not the type of conversation she wanted to have in front of everyone on the bridge.

"That Ferengi is responsible for this," Worf muttered.

"I don't trust him either, Worf." Deanna sighed. "But we don't have any choice. I empathically interviewed the people from the *Prospector* that the computer search came up with—six passengers and one crewman. None of them was hiding anything about this. We've sent messages to all the planets on the tour, looking for anyone who filed a complaint against the Sli, but that will take time. What would you suggest?"

"Investigate the Ferengi!"

"Fine. Do that. But when I gave the captain my report, he instructed us to run a routine check on the people on board the *Enterprise* as well. It will placate Mon Hartog, and perhaps—" She broke off when Worf growled low in his throat. "Worf—"

"I will follow the captain's orders, Counselor." His face was impassive once more.

Deanna took a deep breath. It had been a long day—starting far too early with the explosion on board the *Prospector*. But she'd avoided this discussion longer than a ship's counselor should have. Not only were Worf's emotions difficult to decipher, but her common bond with the Klingon was through Alexander, and he'd been resisting her input in that area for months.

"Worf, you seem to be on edge lately," she started in a diplomatic tone. "Perhaps it would help if we talked about it."

"That would not help."

"Let's just say it would help me—and everyone else— to know what's been bothering you."

"Nothing, Counselor," Worf insisted in a flat voice.

"Nothing?" Deanna shook her head. "Worf, we aren't blind. You've issued more reprimands in this quarter than you have in the past year. Talk about problems with morale! And now you've put the Sli under a triple ring of guards, and mobilized the ship as if we're under attack."

Worf seemed to snap to attention. "As security chief, I am entrusted with the safety of the *Enterprise*. Security must not be compromised."

"Compromised?" Deanna paused, calming herself as she tried to defuse the tension between them. *"Enterprise* security has never been better. If you feel you have to be strict to maintain that standard—well, it's not for me to dispute that. But you never see your son—"

"I must not become soft."

"Soft?" Deanna was frustrated in the face of his

implacability. "No one would ever consider you soft, Worf. You have an excellent record." She stopped herself when she remembered that the only blemish on his record was his murder of K'Ehleyr's assassin.

Apparently Worf remembered, too. He shifted irritably. "My responsibilities as security chief require my attention."

Deanna sighed, hesitating to say more. It was easy to overdo it with Worf. "Well then, tell me, are you being bothered by the emanations from the Sli?"

"No!" Worf quickly denied. He realized she was waiting for more, and he reluctantly admitted, "However, I can feel their attempts to control my mind."

"Worf, our findings are conclusive at this point. The Sli aren't mind controllers—they manipulate emotions."

"The result is the same."

The door slid aside before she could try to explain further. At first she couldn't see who it was because of the strong light from the bridge shining behind him.

Then she sensed an oddly elusive anxiety, like a sneaking fear that the man was trying to conceal.

"Simon!" she exclaimed, when she recognized the medical technician.

"You do not have access to the bridge," Worf informed Tarses. "You must leave immediately."

"Wait," Tarses protested. "I—I have to talk . . . to tell you. I didn't mean to do it."

"What did you do?" Worf asked suspiciously.

"It wasn't my fault." He swallowed. "It just . . . went up in smoke before I could do anything. I tried to stop it, really I did."

Deanna shook her head. "Simon, what are you talking about?"

"The Sli," he said, as if she should know. "I didn't mean to make it burn up."

"Oh," Deanna said, finally understanding. She turned

to Worf. "Dr. Crusher told me that the dead Sli disintegrated when they removed it from the transport tank. The other Sli apparently weren't happy about it."

"They're mad at me," Tarses told them. "But I didn't sabotage the *P-Prospector.*"

"This is of no importance," Worf said dismissively. "And you do not have clearance for the bridge." He moved forward as if to usher Tarses out, but Deanna stopped him.

"Can't you see, Worf? It's the Sli doing this to him." She went to Tarses' side, placing her hand gently on his arm. "You're overreacting, Simon."

"But I—I heard." He glanced uneasily at Worf. "You think someone on the *Enterprise* did it. I thought since it was my fault about that Sli . . ."

Worf's head suddenly went up, his eyes hooded in typical Klingon defense posture. "Counselor, you said this would be a closed investigation!"

"It is." Startled, she faced Tarses. "How did you find out about our investigation?"

Tarses nervously looked from her to Worf. He backed up a step, rubbing his palms against his trousers. "Uh . . ."

"Simon," Deanna said firmly. "Who told you?"

"I . . . everyone's talking about it."

"Who?" she insisted.

Worf hadn't taken his eyes off Tarses. "He knows more than he should."

"I don't!" Simon insisted, his forehead wrinkled up. "N-Nobody trusts me."

Worf didn't even bother to reply. He continued to stare at Tarses like a predatory creature, waiting for the technician to answer.

"Please, Worf," Deanna said, taken aback by his intensity. The whole situation had become almost frightening.

"He will talk," Worf insisted. "Or I will summon security."

"Simon," Deanna said, trying to sound as reasonable as she could. "Just tell us how you found out about our investigation."

Tarses was opening and closing his mouth, obviously stunned by Worf's threat. "Ensign Ro!" he finally managed to blurt out. "It was her. In Ten-Forward."

"Ensign Ro?" Worf confirmed.

"You have to b-believe me," Tarses pleaded. "Don't call security."

"Don't worry, we won't," Deanna tried to assure him. But Worf had an odd gleam in his eye.

"No need," Worf muttered, as if to himself. Moving quickly, he put one hand around Tarses' arm. Tarses cried out, struggling a little until Worf gave him a hard shake, almost jolting him off his feet. He forcibly began dragging Tarses toward the door.

"Worf!" Deanna exclaimed. "Calm down!" She ran after them. "He's leaving. You don't have to do that—"

Deanna broke off as the door opened onto the bridge. Worf was not going to let Tarses go, and that was bad enough without her screaming after them.

Riker stood up when they entered. Most of the other bridge officers were watching as well, as if they had been waiting for Tarses to reappear.

Tarses let himself be pulled past the aft science stations. Lieutenant Chryso drew back out of Worf's way. Deanna hurried after them, not liking the way Tarses stumbled along as if he were in shock.

The turbolift opened in front of Worf, and he thrust Tarses inside. "You will be on report. Return to your quarters immediately."

Tarses was hunched over, leaning against one wall. Deanna didn't trust herself to look at Worf as he turned and brushed past her. Instead, she stepped into the

123

doorway of the lift, her voice low. "This isn't your fault, Simon. The Sli must be focusing on you because you've had close contact with them." Tarses looked up, as if grasping a lifeline with desperate hope. "Go back to your quarters and relax. And don't give in to these feelings. You're being influenced."

She gave him a reassuring nod, then stepped back out on the bridge. The door shut between them. Tarses didn't look as haunted as he had a moment ago, but it wasn't a good situation. She would probably have to send Beverly to give him a light sedative. With any luck, the Sli would calm down and Tarses would be better by morning.

She turned around and found that everyone was staring at her. Crew members just didn't violate the sanctity of the bridge.

She lifted her chin slightly, bracing her defenses. First she nodded to Riker, acknowledging to the commanding officer that the situation had ended. Then with a determined stride, she went straight to Worf and said in a tone audible to everyone, "We aren't finished, Lieutenant Worf."

Worf looked like he wanted to spit. His anger slapped into her, then sharply recoiled as he struggled to get hold of himself. With a brief, stilted acknowledgment, he turned and went toward the lounge. It reminded her of the way Alexander had stalked away from the Sli earlier in the day. And that reminded her that she still had to tell Worf about Alexander's visit to the Sli.

The way things were going, it was definitely going to be a chocolate evening.

Worf left the bridge in a black mood. Talk, talk, talk—that's all Counselor Troi ever wanted to do. Their course of action seemed clear enough to him. Make a show of investigating the *Enterprise* crew while focusing their attention on the Sli and their Ferengi keeper. He had wanted his next stop to be Ensign Ro. Security leaks were always revealing. But Troi wanted to approach the ensign on her own since she could empathically sense any nuances in regard to their investigation. He had reluctantly agreed.

Then Counselor Troi had insisted on keeping him in the lounge to discuss his handling of Tarses. She requested that Tarses not be held responsible for his infraction. When she blamed the Sli, Worf had pointed out that this proved the creatures were a threat to the crew. But Troi had refused to argue that point and instead pursued the source of Worf's own reaction to the medical technician, claiming that the Sli were affecting him as well.

Worf had been hard-pressed to avoid her probes. It wasn't that he thought the technician was capable of sabotage—the idea was absurd. It may have seemed a bold move to intrude on the bridge, but Worf recognized a weak and unstable character in Tarses. It reminded him of the way Alexander sometimes behaved—erratic bursts of rebellion, followed by defensive wordplay. After all, Tarses was of mixed heritage just like Alexander, and the tech was obviously uneasy about his Romulan ancestry. It made Worf think down lines he didn't want to explore, and how could he explain that to Troi?

However, he finally did inform her that he disliked being reminded of his participation in Admiral Satie's treason hearings. It had not been an honorable thing for anyone involved, except perhaps Captain Picard. Worf had managed to avoid Tarses since then, believing it was none of his concern that Tarses had lied on his Starfleet application and been put on probation.

Worf reached his quarters on Deck 5, having not said a word to anyone en route. Apparently the crew recognized when their security chief was in a sour mood, and stayed out of his way. Worf didn't mind.

Alexander wasn't home from organized play yet. Worf

went to his desk and busied himself with checking routine reports filed by his duty officers, but he knew his mind wasn't on his work. That irritated him. He also didn't like it that Alexander had been to see the Sli. He would be forced to censure his son for that disobedient visit.

Finally he hit the button to close the operations file. Sitting there steaming for a few moments did nothing to relieve the pressure building inside of him.

He found himself opening the slide drawer before he was aware of what he was doing. It was an indulgence he rarely allowed himself. But today, after that disturbing encounter with the Romulan technician . . .

Worf pulled out a small holographic projection base and set it on the polished black surface of his desk. He hesitated, almost reluctant to touch it. His eyes were fierce, even hateful, but he finally reached out and activated the holograph.

A miniature image of K'Ehleyr appeared, with a much younger Alexander holding on to one of her legs. She moved, placing a hand on her son's head as she gave Worf one of her classic, wry smiles directly into his eyes. It was as if she'd planned it that way, knowing he would set the holograph on a table to view it.

It went like a knife through his heart. K'Ehleyr was so supremely sure of herself, so glowing and confident.

Worf clenched his hands into fists, throwing his head back and straining the muscles in his neck. The barest hint of a low cry escaped his throat.

Panting harshly, he lowered his head, staring at the projection. K'Ehleyr had taken the holograph and given it to him shortly before she was killed. He remembered how she'd slid it across this very desk, her mocking words so sweetly provocative in his ears. "Here you are, Worf. A little something you can growl at when I'm not around."

He searched the image of her face again, those knowing eyes, then looked down at the boy. Alexander was wearing a blue romper, and seemed so small and defenseless next to his mother. But even the transparency of the holograph couldn't hide his son's steady gaze and his small, serious mouth. If K'Ehleyr were here, he knew he would not be having these problems. K'Ehleyr would have known exactly what to do and say to help Alexander accept both his Klingon and human blood, just as she had done so brilliantly for herself, garnering the best from both worlds.

He groped out to disengage the image. As it flickered and vanished, his shoulders sagged forward. He was fighting a far different fight than he had ever faced before. He knew how to battle the flesh. He knew the steps to take to be master over his desires. He could bring his emotions under control, and response was always dictated by tradition. But none of that mattered now. He didn't have K'Ehleyr—

Worf sat very still. Control was what he sought. A trickle of sweat ran down the side of his face. Control and calm.

He slowly reached out and picked up the disk with the security reports. He jammed it toward the slot, but it went in crooked, sticking. He pulled it out and was reinserting it when he remembered how his brother had said in his last message, "I would not place my trust in one who is not of us."

Worf slammed the disk down. He began to beat it into the plasteel surface of the desk, striking it down again and again as chips and splinters of the disk flashed and darted off all around him.

When he finally stopped he was panting and his teeth were clenched. Only then did his blind fury begin to recede. He dropped the destroyed disk, turning his fist to look at a pair of meaty slashes in the side of his palm. Blood welled up, running darkly down to his wrist. Thick droplets of violet splattered heavily on the desktop.

The computer signaled a message coming through. Worf quickly looked up, gratefully seizing on something outside himself.

"Worf, this is La Forge. I need you down in Engineering right away."

"On my way." His voice was hoarse, but Worf was heading through the door before he'd finished his reply. His hand would have to wait.

Chapter Thirteen

GEORDI WAS NOT HAPPY. In fact, everything seemed to be going wrong.

He hadn't had much luck establishing a forcefield around the Sli. Just as Counselor Troi had predicted, the wave frequency was too low to be able to block the resonances. He tried atomic rays with tiny, staticlike wavelengths, then he tried synchronizing the Sli emanations with larger waves and redirecting them. Since sensors were unreliable with regard to telepathy and empathy, Counselor Troi was the only one who could tell him if he was accomplishing anything, but she was busy investigating the *Prospector* crew and passengers. Every time he had been ready to test his fields, he had to call her back to the shuttlebay.

He would have still been up there working on the Sli, except his duty engineers seemed to be doing everything they could to botch up the routine change-out of the impulse reaction chamber. He had finally come down to Engineering to oversee the final stages of replacing the inner lining. It had seemed like the perfect opportunity to do the change-out while the *Enterprise* was at full stop near the disabled *Prospector,* but apparently his engineers had other ideas. They were making mistakes in the most rudimentary procedures.

Sitting in his chief engineer's office, Geordi pulled off his VISOR, letting out a sigh as he rubbed the skin around the contact nodes at his temples. An irritable headache seemed to pulse within his forehead. He wondered if the pain was caused by that glimpse he'd caught of the planet's atmosphere. He knew he should go down to sickbay and get a hypospray, but he had been so busy, he hadn't had time to get to it.

Geordi stood up, clicking his VISOR back into place. He took a couple of steps closer to the duty engineer's console. "I'm going to sickbay. Just monitor the change-out rate and we'll be done with this in no time."

"Aye, sir," the ensign said.

Geordi hadn't made it past the master systems display when Data appeared in the doorway, followed by Jacob Walch. Captain Walch was looking a little more cheerful than the last time Geordi had seen him.

Geordi smiled and nodded at Data and the burly man, but he stopped when he saw more than two dozen people filing in behind them. Most of them were wearing odd, baggy clothing in bright colors and carried miniature optical recording sensors.

"What's going on, Data?" Geordi asked.

"This is the tour I informed you about," stated Data. "These are some of the former passengers of the *Prospector.*"

Captain Walch was ushering everyone forward, waving to the pulsing core and calling out loudly, "Everyone, this here's the warp reactor core! The living heart of the *Enterprise.* That light you see there is the reaction patterns inside the core."

Data gently corrected, "The reinforced optical window allows visual access to the matter-antimatter reaction assembly."

The tourists edged forward, murmuring among themselves.

"Data," Geordi warned, feeling the stabbing at his temples. He had completely forgotten that Data had told him he was going to bring some of Captain Walch's tourists down.

"Yes, Geordi?"

Geordi didn't want to bluntly throw them all out, but he didn't want them in Engineering right now, either. Things had been going wrong all day—it would only make matters worse if something else developed a glitch while there were a bunch of tourists in his way.

Data was still looking at him, politely waiting for him to say what was on his mind.

Before he could, Walch called out, "Your captain was mighty helpful! Gave me a whole list of nonrestricted areas I could show my folks around." He jerked a thumb their way. "This here gentleman has already showed us the arboretum and science labs." Then Walch gathered the attention of the tourists with one sweeping look as if he were letting them in on a secret. "Well, folks, what Starfleet won't tell you about this here ship is, she's an experiment. Pure and simple. They didn't quite know what they was doing when they built her, and had to run on guesswork many a time."

Data was standing next to Geordi at the outer edge of the group. As Walch paused for a breath, Data informed him, "That is not quite correct, Captain Walch. The primary design and fabrication specifications were verified in the production of the *U.S.S. Galaxy* and the *U.S.S. Yamato* at the Utopia Planitia Fleet Yards."

"You see? It's one of the first." Walch was nodding, drawing their eyes back to him. "And it was the warp engine—what you see here—that caused the most problems. They couldn't even get the materials to hold up—kept sorta collapsing in on itself."

Data added, "The materials failures were common to all three Galaxy starships in production."

"See there?" Walch asked again, checking for nods from the crowd. "And they were having to do warp tests without the coils in place. I can't show you them—we'd have to suit up like real spacemen to do that."

"The warp nacelles—"

"That's enough, Data!" Geordi pressed his lips together, not trusting himself to say more. They were driving him crazy. He didn't want to undermine the last vestiges of Captain Walch's authority, and he felt bad for the man losing his ship and all, but enough was enough.

The tourists were listening to Walch again, and Data turned to Geordi, keeping his voice low. "Captain Walch is not always correct; however, I find his style of delivery quite intriguing."

Geordi closed his eyes, wishing he could take off his VISOR again. "Listen, Data, I think tomorrow would be a better time for your tour."

"I have already scheduled a tour with Captain Walch for this hour tomorrow."

"No, you haven't," Geordi suddenly said, grimly moving forward. The tourists weren't paying any attention, following Captain Walch around the core. "Hey, people, nice to have you here, but the tour's ov—"

"Commander!" Walch called out. "Come tell us about this thingy here."

Data obediently went to his side, telling him, "That is the housing for the dilithium crystal articulation frame."

Geordi flung his hands out in frustration. Why should he have to deal with this? He turned his back on them, tapping his communicator. "Worf, this is La Forge. I need you down in Engineering right away."

Data was explaining the matter-antimatter reaction assembly to the tourists when Worf interrupted him midsentence.

"Engineering is off limits to tourists until further notice," Worf announced to the group. "Please leave the area."

Walch appeared to be so pleased by Worf's appearance that he instantly cut off his tour. He waved his hands at his passengers, telling them, "Get along, folks, get along. We've taken up too much of these boys' time. We'll see other parts of the ship tomorrow."

"When will a schedule be posted?" one pink-skinned man asked.

"Tomorrow, main lounge," Walch assured them. "Go on, now." He grabbed hold of Worf's arm, smiling and nodding at the tourists as they slowly filed away. When the last one rounded the corner, he started after them, drawing Worf along. "Glad you happened along, son! Let's grab a bite to eat and talk about the home folks. Say, where's that son of yours? Let's get him—" Worf and Captain Walch disappeared into the corridor, with the captain obviously leading Worf.

When Data turned, Geordi was gone.

The situation was very odd. Data was unable to come to a conclusion when he attempted to analyze the situation. Geordi had agreed to allow tourists access to Engineering at this hour. Why had he changed his mind?

Data decided to log the incident in his daily report. He also intended to inform Dr. Crusher about the injury he had noticed on Worf's hand. From his angle, it had appeared there were two cuts on the side of his right palm, with signs of smeared and drying blood. There were dozens of possible causes for Worf's wounds, but upon further analysis of the position and depth of the cuts, Data narrowed it down to two probabilities. Either the injury had been caused while Worf was in a defensive posture or the damage was self-inflicted.

Jake had urged that they all go to Ten-Forward, but Worf refused, citing the Sli's presence on the ship as reason to be cautious. Worf took him back to his own quarters.

Alexander was there waiting for his father. His face lit up when he saw Jake, and he enthusiastically gave the big man a hug when the captain asked for one. During dinner, Jake managed to center the talk around Alexander, finding out about places the *Enterprise* had been and what the boy had seen and learned. Jake also told Alexander what was happening with his old friends back on Earth. One of Jake's grandchildren had broken his leg with a new antigravity game, and another had won the decathlon in the local school meet. Alexander liked hearing about people he knew, but when Jake started talking about old times with Worf—barbecues he and Miriah used to have, trips the two families had taken— Alexander started to get restless.

Then the door chimed.

Alexander jumped up, throwing down his napkin. "That's Timnia. You said she could come over tonight, Father."

"We have another guest tonight, son."

Alexander was stopped halfway to the door. "But I already told her. You said I could day before yesterday."

"You may see her tomorrow evening," Worf said firmly.

"But she can't come tomorrow!"

Jake shifted comfortably in his seat. "Let the boy play with his friend, Worf. Young folk don't want to sit here listening to us gabbing on."

Worf drew in a slow breath, ready to insist, when the door chimed again more impatiently.

Alexander ran the rest of the way, opening the door. "Hi, Timnia. Did you bring your shield?"

"Yeth." It was a slender human with brown hair hanging in bangs over her large eyes. Her mouth and chin were tiny. She was holding a round, embossed shield.

Alexander turned to his father with pleading eyes.

"We're going to play samurai soldiers. See," he said, pulling a folded piece of cloth out of his pocket. "This is the ceremonial headgear. My teacher helped me make it for our history lesson today."

Worf was pleased that Alexander liked his samurai *miskazi* enough to find out more about it. "Very well, Alexander. Despite the fact that you went to the shuttlebay today." His voice became firmer as Alexander's face fell. "However, we will discuss that at a later time. Now you may play with your friend for one hour."

"Thank you, Father." Alexander grabbed Timnia's hand and pulled her into his room. "Come on."

Walch got up from the table with a grunt of satisfaction. He stretched, then made his way to the couch, relaxing back.

"Just like his father," he said of Alexander.

"Um," Worf said, noncommittally. He joined Jake. "I received a call from my parents this morning. They are worried about you."

"No need to worry anymore," Jake said with a smile.

"Indeed?" Worf asked, thinking it was typical of Jake Walch to recover so quickly. The man was irrepressible.

"Oh, I'll miss the old girl, don't get me wrong," Jake assured him. "But she was 'bout ready to put to pasture anyways. Insurance—Miriah always insisted on that, you know. That'll get me another ship. I'll be back out on the tour before you know it."

"My parents will be pleased to hear that," Worf said.

"Even my passengers." He gave Worf a wink. "Half of them are ready to sue, but insurance will take care of that, too."

"Does the Ferengi have any claim on you?"

"Hartog? Nah," Walch drawled. "We had a consignment deal—he worked for me. And with their contracts, none of my crew can say boo. I'll get them back to Earth, and then if my new ship comes through quick enough, I'll just rehire the lot of them. Excepting the Sli."

Worf seized on that. "You no longer trust the Sli?"

"I tell you, I was mighty eager to take them on." Walch nodded to himself, staring at the floor. "Miriah made sure we tested and found out they had a limited range, being only five in all. Now four." He shrugged, pursing his lips. "But your counselor says they're causing problems for you people. I don't like the sound of that. It reminded me of the time I gave those diplomats a ride to Starbase 81. The passengers started getting edgy. The Ferengi said then the Sli were upset 'cause of the Starfleet people, but I didn't take him too serious. Now, well, looks like he may be right, eh?"

"Is that the only time you had a problem with the Sli?" Worf asked insistently.

"Only that once." He stabbed a thick finger down. "Mostly I didn't know they was down there. The tourii would use them all the time. They went nuts over 'em."

"The Federation believes the Sli are sentient." Worf couldn't manage to make his tone more neutral, indicating how much he disbelieved that theory.

"Wulp," he exclaimed thoughtfully, "they always seem more like animals than people, you ask me. I got nothing against them, but the whole lot of 'em could have got wiped—it's better than one of the paying customers getting it." Walch suddenly grinned, running his hand through his long beard. "That's why I'm showing the tourii round the *Enterprise*. Can't complain if they get more than the brochure said, now can they?"

Worf cautioned, "Engineering is now off limits to your tourists."

Walch's mouth twisted wryly. "See what you can do about that, Worf, will you? Engineering's one of the best parts."

"The chief engineer would not restrict access without good reason."

Suddenly a shrill scream echoed out from Alexander's

room. Worf and Captain Walch were instantly on their feet as the young girl ran through the door. Alexander was right on her heels, brandishing the samurai sword over his head and yelling at the top of his lungs. In the boy's hands, the short sword looked enormous.

"Alexander!" Worf bellowed, cutting through the din.

Timnia continued to scream, darting into Worf's room. The shield she was holding caught the light with a brief blinding glare.

But Alexander skidded to a halt in front of his father, realizing that he'd done something wrong.

"Alexander," Worf repeated, quietly incensed. "What are you doing with that sword?"

"We're . . ." Alexander started, then he looked at it in his hand. "We're just playing samurai warriors."

Worf reached down and took the sword from Alexander. He had to restrain himself from being too rough. The small human girl was peeking around the corner, afraid to come out.

Worf stepped forward, addressing her. "Are you injured?"

She drew back, her mouth puckered into a silent O.

Worf quickly scanned the child. She appeared to be unharmed and was exhibiting no signs of pain.

He returned his attention to his son with redoubled anger. "You could have hurt your friend, Alexander—or yourself!"

Alexander rubbed his arm where his father had gripped it pulling away the sword. "It's how I do it on the holodeck."

"This is *not* the holodeck." Worf held up the knife. "This is a deadly weapon, Alexander, not a toy. From now on, you will only use it in holograph training simulations."

Alexander looked at his sword in his father's hands. "But you gave it to me."

"Go get the scabbard, Alexander." Worf waited as his son reluctantly went into his room and returned with the scabbard. He slid the short sword into it and placed it on top of the high table next to his Klingon *bast.* "Say good night to your friend."

"But we still have half an—"

"Say good night, Alexander."

His son tightened his lips, glaring at him. For a moment, Worf thought he would openly defy him. "Alexander," he said in warning. "Now."

Alexander let out a frustrated sound, then stomped over to Worf's room to get his friend. "Come on, Timnia. My father says you have to go." He grabbed her hand and pulled her toward the door. She dragged her feet, staring wide-eyed at Worf the entire time. "I'll see you tomorrow."

"Bye, Alekthander," she called out as the door slid shut behind her.

"Go to your room," Worf told his son. He didn't trust himself to administer the proper punishment at this time. "I will discuss this with you tomorrow."

Alexander broke and ran to his room. Worf thought his son was more angry than upset.

Suddenly the communicator alerted him to a page. "Lieutenant Worf, this is Dr. Crusher."

Worf snapped, "What is it, Doctor?"

There was a slight pause, then Dr. Crusher said, "I understand you need medical treatment."

"I do not." Worf clenched his teeth together, then made an effort to sound calm. "I am currently occupied, Doctor. Worf out."

Worf held his breath until it was clear the doctor wasn't going to call right back. He stared for a moment longer at his son's sword lying next to his *bast,* his ceremonial dagger, and the other Klingon battle accoutrements.

"Just like his father," Walch said from behind him. It

sounded like he was chuckling softly. "Don't be too hard on the boy, Worf."

The Klingon gripped his hands into fists. "I can deal with Alexander."

Walch got up and walked over. Worf tensed as the man put a hand on his shoulder.

"Now, son," Jake said kindly. "Don't get all prickly with me. Wasn't I always the one to stick up for you? I remember your parents fit to be tied at some of the high jinks you pulled. But what did I tell them?" Worf turned to face him, shrugging off his hand. Jake just threw out both arms. "It's the Klingon way, I told 'em—and you should see real Klingons. Our Worf ain't half aggressive compared to them, I says. Barroom brawlers, most of 'em are."

Worf heard Jake through a distant roaring, as if he were far away, yet the older man's words had an strangely depleting effect on him. He swayed and put out a hand to the table.

"Your son's fine," Walch was saying. "You'll see. He'll get what he needs before he manages to cut his own throat. You did. We all do. Just give him his head every now and again, or you'll break his spirit."

Worf forced himself to speak. "My son will be a strong warrior."

Alexander suddenly appeared in the doorway of his bedroom. He glared at both of them, yelling, "I don't want to be a warrior! I don't want to!"

Worf snapped up straight. "Alexander, go to bed!"

His son started to protest, "You told me to stay in my room—"

Worf stared up at the ceiling, his eyes wide as he tried to control his breathing. Alexander abruptly shut his mouth, taking in his father's silent fury. He must have seen something that told him this was serious, because he quickly disappeared without another word.

"Wulp, time for me to be getting along," Jake said with

a hearty smack on Worf's arm, startling him. "Take her easy, there, Worf. You've got a fine son. Night, Alexander! See you tomorrow."

"G'night," Alexander called softly from the other room.

Worf quickly nodded at Jake, then looked back at the ceiling, almost humiliated at his son's misbehavior and the sneaking suspicion that he had overreacted. Either he was losing control of himself or those alien Sli were controlling his reactions. He didn't know which possibility was worse.

Chapter Fourteen

DEANNA WENT TO CHECK on the Sli again after Worf and
Simon Tarses left the lounge. Captain Picard had told her
the Federation Council considered it important to establish diplomatic ties with the Sli. She was busy with the
Prospector investigation, but she also tried to take time to
communicate with the Sli. But the Sli weren't responding
to empathic probes or the new translator.

She went to Ten-Forward next. Ensign Ro was probably still there, and she could find out about the rumor,
relax for a while, and have that chocolate sundae all at
the same time.

Deanna was already braced to ward off the emanations
of the Sli, but she tightened her defenses before entering
the lounge. Emotions were keyed higher than normal
among the crew, and in addition to Tarses', there had
been dozens of unusual incidents reported. All were
relatively minor, though, and Deanna couldn't fault the
Sli for being frightened and doing what came naturally to
protect themselves. If only she could communicate
Starfleet's peaceful intentions, then the Sli would know
they were safe.

Ten-Forward was full, and the voices and laughter seemed louder than usual. Guinan was silently nodding at a Tricon crew member who was trying to tell her a story. He kept forgetting what he wanted to say, tangling himself into knots by going off on punning tangents.

Deanna listened for a few minutes, amused.

"Can I do something for you, Counselor?" Guinan asked. The Tricon shrugged and turned to Ensign Puckee, who was sitting on the other side of him, starting his story all over again.

"Is Ensign Ro still here?"

"No," Guinan said. "She left not long ago."

Deanna nodded. "Maybe she's in her quarters." She continued to look at the hostess, wondering if she should talk to her about the investigation. Guinan was intuitive, and Deanna had nothing else to try at the moment.

"Anything else I can do for you?" Guinan asked, turning her head slightly.

"Yes, thank you." Deanna liked being around Guinan. She emanated a warm calm that was soothing to her empathic senses. "I'd like a chocolate sundae and an answer to a question."

"The sundae's coming right up. Would you like that answer first?"

Deanna smiled. "Yes. Did you hear any rumors today about our investigation into the explosion on the *Prospector?*"

Guinan nodded, folding her hands in front of her. "Ensign Ro mentioned it. You suspect *Enterprise* crew members might somehow be involved."

"Not really." Deanna slid onto a stool at the counter. "But we have to investigate every possibility. Do you know how she heard about it?"

Guinan blinked. "Apparently there is a loose-lipped Ferengi on board."

Deanna quickly looked up. "Mon Hartog?" She let out her breath, shaking her head. "Worf was right."

"I see. It was supposed to be covert information." Guinan glanced around the room. "Well, you're too late, Counselor. Everyone in this room knows about it."

"I figured that, since Tarses knew."

Guinan turned to the replicator and pressed two places on the panel. She had worked out several chocolate sundae recipes that Deanna particularly liked. Deanna usually let the hostess choose which one she'd get, and she watched eagerly to see what it would be this time.

The particles swirled, seeming to take longer than usual, until a silver dish appeared.

"Umm . . ." Deanna sighed in appreciation. Chocolate ice cream with bittersweet chocolate syrup and white whipped cream.

Guinan picked up the dish with both hands and set it in front of Deanna. She watched as Deanna took the first bite, savoring the combination of flavors. "Wonderful, Guinan."

"I'm glad you like it." Guinan was casually rubbing the edge of the counter with the tips of her fingers. She didn't look up as she asked, "Tell me something, Counselor. Simon Tarses was here this afternoon. How is he doing?"

"The Sli are aggravating him, and this investigation reminds him too much of last time," Deanna told the hostess. She let her hand holding the spoon rest on the counter, as she stared thoughtfully into a corner. "I don't know what to do about him, Guinan. He won't relax. You've been very kind to him, I know. I appreciate that—he needs friends."

Guinan shook her head at her thanks. "I enjoy talking to Simon. He believes he's faced with the impossible task of transcending what he is."

Deanna quickly glanced up at her. "Interesting. He's locked into a label he's put on himself."

"Something like that." Guinan shrugged. "Sometimes I think I see what's right in front of my eyes, but I don't."

"The Sli," she murmured, digging her spoon in again and licking it clean.

"Yes," Guinan agreed. "The Sli. They are an interesting group of beings."

"You know, Guinan, they're the strongest empaths I've ever encountered. They possess emotions we've never even dreamed. If only I could understand them better, somehow talk to them. I can feel them, but their intent isn't clear."

"Others also feel the Sli," Guinan cautioned.

"I know. There's no way to stop the emanations. All I can do is warn everyone. The problem is, half the time those being affected don't even realize what's happening until it's over. That's because what we're feeling is familiar and real, yet it's reactions we normally wouldn't express."

"Are the Sli stronger than you thought they would be?"

Deanna took another bite of her sundae. It tasted better than usual. Slowly she said, "The Sli aren't stronger than I thought. But they are . . . elusive. Somehow they can creep into your mind and manipulate you without your being aware of it—"

Deanna stopped, feeling something tickling at the back of her mind. Wary, she lowered her shields to take a quick probe.

Her spoon hit the counter with a splatter of syrup. She was staring straight ahead.

"Deanna, what is it?"

"More Sli." Deanna blinked rapidly, re-forming her shields and bracing them as fast as she could. Without thinking, she turned to the bay windows across Ten-Forward to gaze into the blackness of space. "I feel them out there. They're coming."

Picard told Counselor Troi to meet him in his ready room when she called. Commander Riker was confirming that a Ferengi vessel was entering sensor range as she arrived.

"You can feel the Sli from this distance?" Picard asked her as soon as she entered the room. There was a tiny line between her eyes, as if she was under some sort of strain.

"The emanations are very powerful," Troi said. "There must be hundreds of Sli on board that ship."

"Then the effect will be that much stronger for the rest of the crew."

"I'm afraid so, Captain."

Picard nodded, considering the situation. "Have you had any luck determining what the Sli want?"

The counselor tightened her lips. "No, sir."

Riker's voice paged though, interrupting them. "Captain, we are being hailed by the Ferengi marauder, the *Tampanium.*"

Picard took a deep breath as he stood up, pulling his uniform into place. "Well, then, perhaps Mon Hartog should be present when we greet the new arrivals."

"Captain, there's something you should know," Troi said, stopping him before the door to the bridge opened. "Mon Hartog has told crew members that we suspect someone on board sabotaged the *Prospector.*"

Picard glanced sharply at her. "How does that benefit Hartog?"

"I'm not sure. But you know it must or he wouldn't bother to do it."

Picard knew that was true, yet it wasn't important enough to pursue right now. "Perhaps Hartog is simply one of those Ferengi who plays every card that comes to hand, hoping that one will pay off."

The counselor seemed satisfied with that, and she followed him without another word onto the bridge. Picard could feel the Sli emanations now, a tangible force pushing into him, opening him up and urging him to action, any action at all in order to correct the situation. Picard suddenly swayed, catching the back of Data's chair.

"Something wrong, sir?" Riker immediately asked.

"Light-headed for a moment, Number One," Picard said, sternly marshaling his thoughts. He wondered what kind of effect this was having on his crew.

The Marauder was on the screen, crossing in front of the *Enterprise*. The rust-colored, horseshoe-shaped vessel was distinctively Ferengi, with its two slender bow points and heavy, curving stern where the warp grid glowed white-hot.

"Status?" Picard asked.

"The Ferengi are still hailing us, sir," Riker replied, standing up. "Daimon Brund is in command."

"Please ask Mon Hartog to come to the bridge," Picard ordered. He faced the viewscreen, hesitating just long enough to quickly review his options. Communication with the Sli was what he most desired. "Give me Daimon Brund."

Almost immediately a Ferengi appeared on the large screen. His face was very wide and his body quite bulky for a Ferengi. He didn't have the ferretlike quickness and bright eyes of Mon Hartog, but there was a certain shrewdness about him.

"Captain!" he said, his face lifted petulantly. "I protest the treatment of the Sli in your charge!"

"The Sli are not in my charge," Picard told him. "However, they were granted asylum on my ship when the starliner they were on suffered an explosion. What I would like to know, Daimon Brund, is why are you transporting such a large number of Sli?"

"We were taking them to a new colony on Sketti Iota Three."

"You are considerably off your course," said Picard.

Brund ignored him. "Is it true that Sli have died?"

"Did the Sli tell you this?" Picard asked quickly.

"Then it's true." The daimon's upper lip pulled back

146

over the teeth on one side of his mouth. "That explains why they're so violent."

"Since you apparently have some sort of communication with the Sli, perhaps you could suggest what we can do to calm them."

"I know what my lot want." Brund grinned into the screen. "They want your Sli dead."

"What?" Deanna cried out.

Daimon Brund seemed to enjoy what he had to say. "Kill the ones on your ship and then we can be on our way."

Mon Hartog had just stepped out of the turbolift. He scurried down the ramp, shouting, "Don't let him do it!" He was hunched over and gesturing with both arms. "He can't kill my Sli!"

"Hartog!" the daimon sneered. "I should have known this was your doing."

"Only one Sli died, Daimon Brund. And you can't have the others! I don't care who you know in the consortia!"

"Gentlemen, please! No one will be killed on board the *Enterprise,*" Picard informed them. "I can hardly believe you're serious, Daimon Brund."

"Got any better ideas?" Daimon Brund shrugged negligently. "As soon as yours are gone, then I can take these on to their colony."

"You're trying to make murder sound reasonable," Picard pointed out.

"The colony won't leave as long as those four are upset. They knew about it from almost ten sectors away. They're sensitive to death—"

"Enough!" Hartog interrupted, becoming even more agitated. "Just take the colony away from here! I'll find the murderer and my Sli will be fine again."

"I'd like nothing better." The daimon had a wounded expression. "I would appreciate immediate action on this matter, Captain Picard."

"Again, Daimon Brund," Picard insisted, "I request that you aid me in communicating with the Sli."

"That won't solve my problem," Brund bluntly told Picard. "But I'll make you a deal—kill the ones on your ship, and I'll let you talk with my bunch. How's that for a bargain? We both get what we want."

Picard stepped forward. "Your proposal is unacceptable, Daimon Brund. Picard out," he added, turning to Ensign de Groodt at Tactical and making a sharp motion with his hand to cut the Ferengi off. Then he looked at Deanna. "Is Brund truly communicating with the Sli?"

"I'm not sure, Captain. I know he's being deceitful, but it's difficult to tell what exactly he's lying about."

Picard turned to the Ferengi. "Mon Hartog, you dispute his assessment of what his Sli want. Why is that?"

"I know what my Sli want," Hartog said in a surly voice, staring down at the floor. "Let me help in the investigation, Picard. It will make the Sli feel better to know that I'm doing something to protect them. Then they'll be happy."

Commander Riker stiffened at the suggestion, obviously not liking it one bit. The counselor shifted uneasily, but she didn't protest out loud.

Hartog saw Picard's hesitation, and tried something altogether new. "Please, Captain. If they think I'm doing something to protect them, then they might redirect their attention to the Sli on the *Tampanium*. It would give your crew a little relief."

Picard fought off another wave of dizziness. He noticed Lieutenant Chryso was leaning against her comm panel, shaking her head as if she was trying to clear it. The situation was unacceptable.

"Very well," Picard agreed, sitting down in his chair. "The information will be made available, but you must immediately notify the Sli that you are taking care of the situation."

148

Hartog made his thanks, bowing and smiling his way off the bridge. Commander Riker watched him go with a frown. "Shouldn't we get some distance between us and that Ferengi ship?"

"You'd have to leave this solar system to get far enough away," Deanna told him.

"What about going to yellow alert, Captain?" Riker asked.

Picard rubbed a finger across his lips. "Not immediately, Number One. Let's see what the situation brings. Alert Security, however, and announce to the crew that I would prefer all nonessential personnel to remain in their quarters tonight."

Chapter Fifteen

DEANNA STAYED IN HER QUARTERS that night as the captain had ordered, but she was restless and couldn't settle down to anything productive. She tried reviewing her notes on the Sli, but she felt as if she'd read them so many times, she could say them in her sleep. So instead, she rearranged the next day's schedule, knowing that if the extra Sli continued to affect the crew, people were going to be wanting to see her.

With that done, she changed from her uniform into a soft spider-silk robe. She watered her plants and thought about having more chocolate, but decided that would be too indulgent. For a while she just sat down at her dressing table, studying her unsmiling face in the mirror. She thought her expression was too serious in repose. When had that happened? It bothered her, though she wasn't sure why. Then she tried to forget about it, feeling the tickling of the Sli against her mind. They kept sneaking up on her, and every time she sensed them, she quickly tightened her defenses to keep their emotional pull from affecting her. But it was like floating in an ocean, bobbing up and down on the waves, moving without realizing it. Every now and again she found herself staring blankly off into space, sighing. When she glanced back in the mirror, there was a secret little smile on her lips.

The door chimed, startling her.

"Come in," she called. As she stood up, she realized what she was wearing. The robe was made of layers of sheer violet. She hoped it wasn't the captain. He'd be very uncomfortable finding her this way.

But it was Will Riker. His eyes quickly took in the robe, and Deanna drew in her breath with a slight trembling of her hands. It reminded her of so much—

"Purple," Riker said, but his voice was oddly flat. He paced into the room, frowning as he looked around. "You like that color, don't you?"

Deanna actually felt her face flush. The last time her mother had looked through Deanna's closet, she had teased her that most of her sensual outfits were violet. Lwaxana had been amused, but Deanna had been embarrassed.

She crossed her arms, trying to ignore what she was wearing. "Did you want something, Will?"

"I was coming off bridge duty, and I . . ." He trailed off, squinting his eyes out her view window. He seemed uncertain of himself.

"Is something bothering you?"

Will met her eyes briefly. "It's crazy."

"What is?" Deanna took a few steps closer.

He took a deep breath, his chest expanding. Then he let it out, trying to smile. "It's nothing really. I think I'll just go."

Deanna stopped him with a hand on his arm. "Will, I'm here to listen. If it's something the Sli are bringing out, it might be better if you tell me."

"I don't think it's the Sli. That's what makes it so

strange." He shook his head at himself, but he didn't go. "It's about our mission."

"You mean Lessenar?" Deanna asked, unable to keep the surprise out of her voice.

"Nothing's getting done, and I don't know what to do about it," he said in a rush.

"What are you talking about?"

"I can't stop thinking about those people down there." He managed to control his voice, but Deanna could feel his distress.

"You've started distributing the biofilters, haven't you?" She waited until he nodded. "And the relief supplies continue to be delivered. We've already accomplished a great deal for them."

Riker grimaced, rubbing his hand through his beard. "Superficially, I'd say yes. But I don't even know the full extent of the damage yet. Lieutenant Chryso still hasn't turned in her report."

"Is there a problem? As I understood it at the meeting, it's an extremely complex situation."

"She seems to be dragging her steps, being overly meticulous. We already know it's much worse than we first thought. Something has to be done for their ecology right away, or the entire planet will be a wasteland."

Deanna listened, but it didn't make much sense. "Will, it's only been one day."

"Don't you think I know that?" He jerked his head, brushing off her words. "But now there's the Ferengi Marauder out there. With a load of Sli on board. Worf's security teams have broken up two fights since ten hundred hours, and the bridge is getting reports from every deck. Even the science teams are complaining about their distraction, and that's slowing things down even more. No one can keep their mind on their work with all those Sli out there!" He flung his hand at the window, toward the orbiting *Tampanium*. "The captain even suggested I postpone the reception plans tomorrow. He wants me to stay on board."

"A reception won't give the inhabitants the help they need."

"I should be down there," he said, frustrated. "But then I think—what could I do if I was there? All I can do is watch them suffer. Chryso saw it, too, but at least she has something tangible to work on." He stared right into her eyes. "Can you feel it, Deanna? Their pain."

She swallowed, stiffly nodding her head. "My barriers are in place because of the Sli, but they're enhancing my sensitivity. I know what you saw down there, Will."

He broke away, his brow furrowed. "If I could just pilot one of the shuttles, move supplies if nothing else. I'm . . . at a loss."

"It will all get done." She waited, but he didn't acknowledge her. "Will, tell me. What do you feel you've lost?"

"It's . . . not so much a feeling," he admitted. "It's something that I keep seeing in my mind. It's me when I'm old—gray hair and all—and I feel this deadness inside of me. A lack of resolve, as if I can't make . . . as if I'm drifting."

"That's the Sli, Will. You have to fight it. Don't let yourself be carried along by them."

He shook his head once, frowning. "I hate feeling this way, but it *is* me. I've . . . felt it before. But I've never come up against a situation so endlessly hopeless. Generations, this has been going on."

Deanna felt a deep sympathy for Will Riker, and wanted nothing more than to explore his feelings of weakness in order to understand them. But she sternly forced herself to acknowledge that Riker wouldn't be reacting this way if the Sli weren't influencing him. Dealing with his feelings wouldn't address the problem.

"Believe me, you wouldn't be reacting this way if the

153

Sli weren't here." Deanna stepped back, straining to make her tone cool and reasonable. "This is what the Sli do. They open us up and bring out emotions that we lock away inside of us. What you feel is not an appropriate reaction. I certainly don't think it's something that must be dealt with right now."

Deanna watched Riker closely, as he reacted to her blunt dismissal of his feelings. His eyes widened a little, and he shook his head as if coming out of a daze. It was as if she had just slapped him in the face.

She tried to be expressionless. "Keep in mind that the Sli are enhancing your sense of . . . inadequacy. Whenever you feel that way, remind yourself that it's a false sensation. You are getting the job done."

Deanna knew exactly when to stop with Riker. Any more, and he'd be humiliated. He was already extremely uncomfortable and self-conscious. She absently tweaked at her robe, arranging the folds. "If you want to help solve the Sli problem, you're more than welcome. We have to stop them from doing this to everyone."

"I wish I could help you." Riker gave an absent shrug, staring fixedly out the view window. "What about Mon Hartog?"

"I don't think Mon Hartog is capable of communicating with the Sli," Deanna told him. "I don't know about Daimon Brund. They both say the Sli are upset, but that's nothing more than we can see ourselves. The question is—does Daimon Brund know what the Sli really want?"

"The daimon is a daimon," Riker reminded her. He turned away from the window, the flush on his face starting to fade. "Among the Ferengi that means something. Maybe Hartog isn't as canny. Or his equipment isn't as good."

Deanna narrowed her eyes. "I don't think so. Somehow, I think Mon Hartog is getting exactly what he wants."

Riker shrugged again, walking away from the window. "Maybe we should lean on him harder."

He was at the door before Deanna realized that he intended to leave.

"Thanks, Deanna. Good night." He apparently didn't notice her confusion. "I'll remember what you said about the Sli."

"Good night, Will," she repeated dutifully.

When he was gone, she went and stood in front of the mirror. Purple, he'd called it.

She stared at her reflection, slowly shaking her head and thinking about their conversation. Who'd have thought that Will Riker would be insecure about his ability to accomplish something? Still, she had the uneasy feeling she'd done something wrong with him. Was that why she was standing in front of the mirror, feeling frustrated? What had she expected from him? That he would have at least noticed the allure of her robe?

Idly she tilted her head to one side. She remembered how her mother had laughed that day, touching her on the cheek. Lwaxana had sent her this very robe the next time a courier ship came through. And now Deanna was wearing it. She almost wanted to rip it off, but it looked so nice—despite Will's lack of appreciation.

Suddenly she looked up, realizing that Guinan was right—often you didn't see what was right in front of your eyes. Deanna knew she wore violet when she was feeling most . . . relaxed. What about the Sli? Their most obvious feature was those swift and vivid color changes.

She slowly nodded. What if those changes weren't a simple chemical reaction but were a biological function that the Sli controlled? What if it was part of their communication?

"Computer," she announced. "Run a continuous scan on the Sli in Shuttlebay 3."

"Working."

She narrowed her eyes thoughtfully. "Compare the sequence of colors and patterns to the readout on the translation unit. I want to know if there's a correlation between the two."

"Specify frequency range," the computer requested.

"Visible light spectrum." Deanna paced a few steps. "Plus infrared and ultraviolet."

"Working." A short pause. "There is insufficient data for analysis at this time."

"Continue program," she ordered. "Let me know if a pattern emerges."

"Acknowledged. Scan in progress."

Picard called a senior staff meeting before their duty shift started the next morning.

Deanna was one of the first to arrive. She'd been woken up eight times during the night by crew members —some she was currently counseling. In each case, she sent a medical technician with a sleeping hypo to them after assuring them that this wasn't a crisis point where something *had* to be resolved immediately.

She sat down in her usual seat and accessed the security report from the third shift. There'd been almost two dozen more incidents that had resulted in calls to Security.

Dr. Crusher came in next. "You're wearing your hair differently," she immediately said.

Deanna nodded, resisting the impulse to touch the coils that twisted around her head and fell across one shoulder. "You look tired, Beverly. Sickbay was busy last night."

"Busy is not the word for it." The doctor gathered her coat around her as she collapsed down in a seat. "It gets like that every once in a while, but last night was different. I'd think everyone on board called in at least once in the past twenty-four hours." She narrowed her eyes. "Except for Worf—and Data reported that he was injured."

"Well, here he is," Deanna said in a low voice.

Lieutenant Worf and Commander Riker came in together. Worf was unreadable, as usual, but Riker seemed to be distracted and worried just as he'd been last night. The doctor waited until Worf was seated, then she went directly to his side, holding out her medical tricorder. Deanna admired the deft way she had trapped the Klingon.

"What is it, Doctor?" Worf demanded.

"You have two abrasions on your right hand, one almost a centimeter deep." She raised her eyes from her tricorder. "Let me see."

Worf reluctantly held out his hand, slightly fisted. He sat expressionless, staring out the window as she examined it.

"You'll have to come to sickbay so I can bond the skin."

"Very well," Worf said, pulling his hand away. He still didn't look at the doctor.

The others had arrived during the brief examination. Data was Data as usual, but Geordi didn't meet Deanna's eyes or say good morning. Lieutenant Chryso gave her a hurried nod. Deanna was glad to see that Captain Picard glanced at them all sharply, alert and in complete control.

"I want to remind you," Picard started right in, "that Starfleet wishes to establish communication leading to diplomatic ties with the Sli. Therefore, leaving this system is not a possibility at this time."

"We can't leave," Riker protested. "We've got a mission to complete."

Picard held up one hand. "Yes, I'll get to that in a moment. Counselor Troi, I understand you have information that may help us with the Sli?"

"Yes, Captain. I believe we can get a better indication of what the Sli are saying by translating the shifts in their coloration."

"It is possible," Data conceded, after a moment's pause. "But I have not had adequate exposure to the Sli to make an analysis at this time."

Beverly was shaking her head. "The color changes correspond to the discharge of gases. I thought it was a biological process."

"Do you know how it happens?" Deanna asked.

"No, not yet."

"Well, I just received the preliminary computer analysis this morning," Deanna said positively, glancing around the table. "There is a correlation between the color changes and the translation of the Sli's emanations. It's extremely complicated, though. The Sli have dozens of emotive frequencies beyond our range. The full analysis will be completed and added to the translation unit within the hour."

"Why didn't the computer pick this up earlier?" Riker asked with a frown.

Data was accessing the program on the small table console. "The association is not arithmetic or geometrical, but based on a fractal equation. A large quantity of empirical data is necessary to complete such an analysis."

"Do you think Mon Hartog was lying?" Beverly put in, raising one brow. "Or was he unaware of this?"

Deanna tightened her hands in her lap. "When Mon Hartog was on the bridge, I felt as if he was hiding something. Particularly when Daimon Brund mentioned the Sli's reaction to death. Hartog immediately silenced him."

"Mon Hartog could have something he's keeping from the daimon," Riker pointed out.

"Ferengi don't trust anyone," Lieutenant Chryso murmured.

"Perhaps. We'll keep the possibility in mind in our dealings with Mon Hartog," Picard agreed. Then he gave Deanna a nod. "Very good, Counselor. This may be the key we've been missing."

"Sir!" Worf leaned forward. "As security chief, I must remind you that the presence of the Sli is endangering the success of our mission as well as the safety of the crew. Their emanations are random and dangerous."

Deanna had to protest. "We just haven't found a way to communicate yet."

Worf ignored her. "Mon Hartog and Daimon Brund are guilty of transporting dangerous life-forms within the Federation. There is a simple solution."

"What is that, Lieutenant?"

"Blow the shuttlebay doors."

"That's what Daimon Brund wants!" Deanna exclaimed, trying to keep the indignation from her voice.

"You can't just kill them," the doctor was just as quick to protest.

"They are seriously disrupting the crew." Worf looked only at Picard. "At least four of the infractions during Delta shift were potentially lethal."

"Not only that," Riker put in, "but every hour we're delayed, dozens more people die on Lessenar. The situation is becoming irreversible."

"With my people being bombarded like this," Chryso added, "I'm afraid errors could be made in the analysis."

Worf leaned forward. "The Sli are dangerous and must be dealt with immediately—before the situation escalates."

Picard shook his head. "What you suggest is impossible. We've been instructed to establish diplomatic relations with the Sli."

"You don't understand, Worf." Deanna watched the frustrated Klingon. "The emotional swings of the Sli only appear erratic to us because we can't interpret them.

Even among humanoids, our emotional response varies intensely from person to person, and culture to culture."

Geordi was leaning back in his chair, gazing at the tabletop in thought. "What I don't understand is how Starfleet decided the Sli were sentient if they haven't been able to communicate with them."

"Exactly!" Worf's eyes burned.

Deanna sighed. "What do you think sentience is? It's a life-form capable of receiving and responding to sensory stimuli. The Sli are certainly capable of stimulating our senses in a very complex and powerful way. Actually, by that standard, the Sli are the most sentient life-forms we've encountered. It's we who are having trouble responding to their level of perception."

"I disagree, Counselor." Worf didn't back down one bit. "The Sli are incapable of following a logical course when it comes to cause and effect. Their response provokes the crew to insubordination."

Data swiveled his chair toward Worf. "Counselor Troi is correct, however. Response is the determining factor of sentience."

"Their sentience is unimportant," Worf shot back. "The Sli are attacking the crew."

"The Sli aren't attacking us," Deanna insisted. "They're stimulating our own emotions—feelings we don't usually allow ourselves to express. That's their way of communicating with us."

"Perhaps their intent is harmless, but I don't like what it's doing to my researchers," Chryso said. "The data must be precisely calculated or one of a million things could go wrong . . ."

Listening to the sound of Chryso's voice rising and falling, without hearing what she said, Deanna suddenly realized that the emanations had increased in strength. She had to fight herself to resist giving in.

"It's happening now!" Deanna forced herself to say out loud. She took a deep breath. "Don't give in to whatever you're feeling. Try to blank your minds. Breathe deeply as if you're entering meditation. It's one of the first techniques of defensive barriers taught at university on Betazed."

They were silenced by her announcement. Deanna bit the inside of her lip, trying to stay objective. "Don't allow yourself to react. I believe it's during these stronger waves of emanations that we are most affected."

"So," Dr. Crusher said, her mouth twitching into a hint of a smile, "all we have to do is grit our teeth and bear it?"

Deanna raised her brows at Beverly, realizing that the doctor was being flippant again. But she was too busy fighting her own languid impulse to reach up into a long, hard stretch, wanting to relax into the emanations. "It's a shame, really," she found herself saying. "If we could allow ourselves to fully experience this sensation, it could be an opportunity for many members of the crew to open new paths of emotional awareness in themselves."

"Too bad we have a ship to run," Beverly put in.

"And a diplomatic mission to accomplish. And a planet to salvage," Picard added. "Am I missing anything?"

Beverly laughed. "You forgot the Ferengi!"

"Never let us forget the Ferengi, Doctor."

Deanna looked back and forth between the two, her mouth falling open. Then she caught Worf's eye. He was glaring at her so hard that she snapped her mouth shut. Then he pulled his lips back, baring his teeth, dismissively glancing in the other direction.

"Is this all we're supposed to do?" Riker asked, worried. "Sit here and take it?"

Data spoke up, sounding just like a computer giving a response. "Possible courses of action include: creating a shield around the Sli, utilizing the magnetic antimatter containment field—"

Susan Wright

"Right!" Geordi cut in. "Blame it on me!"

"Geordi," Data said patiently. "That was not my intention."

"Data, I tried using the antimatter containment."

"Was there an attempt at synchronization?"

"It didn't work!" Geordi practically shouted at his friend. Data was watching him with curious detachment.

"I did what I could!" Geordi insisted, hitting his fist against the table. "There's no way to stop those things."

Picard held out his hand. "Perhaps if you and Data work together, you can come up with a solution."

"Of course," Geordi said bitterly. "Data's always right, isn't he? It doesn't matter what anyone else says or does, just give it to Data and he'll fix it."

"Geordi!" Deanna exclaimed.

Geordi shoved his chair back from the table. "Apparently you don't need me. I'll be down in Engineering."

He got up and stalked out without looking back.

Everyone was very still for a moment. Deanna felt bad for Data, but the android simply glanced around the table. "I believe Geordi is suffering from the influence of the Sli."

"Obviously, Data!" Beverly said, shaking her head.

"That was insubordination," Worf declared, his tone deadly serious. "La Forge should be confined to quarters."

Captain Picard looked to Deanna.

It was becoming easier to think clearly. "This level of intensity doesn't usually last," she told the captain. "Geordi may continue to be irritable, but the worst should be passing already. Can't you feel the difference?"

Picard was nodding. He appeared to be invigorated by the episode. "Issue a statement to the entire crew, Counselor, advising them how to deal with these surges."

"Yes, sir."

Chryso shuddered. "It's terrifying, being manipulated like that."

"We're all a little the worse for wear," Picard said. He looked at Data. "See what you can come up with in the way of a deflector shield for the emanations, Mr. Data. If possible, erect it around the *Enterprise* to protect us from the Sli colony on the *Tampanium.*"

"Aye, Captain," Data said evenly.

Picard broke off to look out the lounge viewports. The Ferengi Marauder was coming toward them in its orbit around Lessenar. For a moment they could see both the *Prospector* and the pointed front of the *Tampanium.* "Have you any new information on the damage to the *Prospector?*" the captain asked Data.

"Reanalysis of readings taken before the explosion reveal there were no objects in the vicinity. Yet the initial impact was on the exterior of the hull."

"Could it have been planted there at the starliner's last stop?" Beverly asked. "Some kind of time bomb?"

"Perhaps," Data conceded. "But there is a 96.4 percent possibility that the sensors of the *Prospector* would have detected such a device attached to the outer hull."

"However, there is a chance that's what it was. Continue along that line of questioning." Picard turned to Worf next. "Has your investigation uncovered anything, Lieutenant Worf?"

"Negative, sir." Worf shifted stiffly. "None of the passengers or crew appears to possess a motive for destroying the *Prospector* or the Sli. *Enterprise* crew members are currently being investigated. In addition, we are receiving reports on the trade ships that have been logged in this area."

"Very well." Picard rubbed a finger across his lips. "I want you to give Mon Hartog access to the information you've gathered so far."

"Sir!" Worf sat forward so quickly, his chair bumped into Deanna's.

"Hartog is the legal representative of the Sli, and as such he is entitled to view our information." Picard narrowed his eyes, almost a smile. "In addition, it could be revealing to see exactly what Mon Hartog is looking for."

"Yes, Captain," Worf said reluctantly. His brow was lowered ominously over his eyes, and he didn't look at anyone.

"Lastly," Picard finished, "Number One, I understand the distribution of the food and medical supplies has almost been completed."

"Yes, sir. Three of our shuttle pilots were pulled from the rotation by sickbay, but we should be finished by this afternoon. Unless we get additional requests."

"Very well," the captain acknowledged. "I know the Advisory Council was upset by the cancellation of their reception and are eager to reschedule. However, I'd prefer you continue to remain on board until our situation is stabilized." The captain waited as if he expected Riker to protest.

"Aye, sir." Riker hardly moved.

Picard raised his brows, but he didn't pursue it.

Beverly turned to Deanna. "What about the inhabitants? Are they being affected by the Sli?"

She shook her head, then had to brush a loose curl from her cheek. "I believe the emanations are being deflected by the world resonance coming from the planet's core."

"Good. That's the last thing we need—the whole planet going crazy while they're already so desperate." Beverly seemed to be making an effort to end things on a positive note, but only the captain gave her a nod in response.

"Proceed with your duties," Picard ordered. "Let me know when your program is completed, Counselor."

Beverly stood up, but she lingered in the lounge as the others started to leave. Deanna absently stayed with her, thinking about the Sli communication program.

"I don't think," Beverly said thoughtfully, "I've ever

164

seen everyone this frustrated after a meeting before. Look at them!"

"This is hard on everyone. We're being forced to deal with emotions we normally ignore."

"The captain seems to be the only one unaffected," Beverly commented.

"He's a little more . . . precipitous."

"You mean rash? I didn't think so."

Deanna didn't want to argue with her friend. She also wondered uneasily if everyone could tell in what way she was being affected. She had to admit it was a little embarrassing that the emotions released inside her were of a more sensual nature. But the Sli emanations coiled into her, drawing her out and making all of her senses tingle with heightened awareness.

She and Beverly were walking onto the bridge when Worf acknowledged a call at his tactical station.

"The Ferengi has signaled Security," he announced. Worf quickly keyed security personnel to proceed to Hartog's quarters, then tied in the ship's computer. He looked up at what he'd found, his voice grim. "Medical Technician Tarses is currently in Mon Hartog's quarters."

Chapter Sixteen

SIMON TARSES TRIED TO HIDE his nervousness as he walked down the corridor of Deck 35.

He had spent much of the morning trying not to look out the viewports at the Ferengi Marauder, circling the planet like a shark ready to attack at the first sign of weakness. He hated the Marauder vessels—they seemed so predatory and mean the way the bow came to two sharp points. And the way the ship just kept going around and around the planet while the *Enterprise* was motionless was both compelling and frightening.

He had reported for duty hours before his shift began, knowing the technicians were in urgent need of help in replicating and packing the medical supplies that were being sent down to the planet. He had felt anxious and useless the entire night while confined to quarters, and he fervently tried to make up for it. The quantity of supplies and the number of sick and injured people they represented were daunting. The urgency of their mission could be clearly read in the piles of stacked containers that were continuously taken from the medical replication lab to the shuttlebays.

Yet he couldn't forget about the Ferengi vessel. Every time it circled the planet, swooping in close as it passed by, it felt as if another band were looped around his body, trapping him. He wondered if the saboteur would be taken away on the *Tampanium* to suffer Ferengi justice for the attempted killing of the Sli. He could imagine Lieutenant Worf turning the culprit over to the Ferengi, maybe even in restraints. Simon knew Worf would be glad to get rid of him. Ever since the investigation that had ruined his life, Simon had known the Klingon didn't trust him. The episode on the bridge just proved his instincts were right. Then the *Tampanium* seemed to leer at him through the viewport as it made another pass, and Tarses knew he had to do something.

He had handed off his replicator duties to another tech and taken the necessary steps that had brought him down to Deck 35. He had made a mistake going so openly to the security chief to find out if he was a suspect, and this time he was going to change his tactics. Subtlety was called for. Dr. Crusher had told Medical Technician Moodet to bring down the medical report to Mon Hartog, but Simon had convinced Moodet to let him do it.

A tourist with orange hair and a transparent jumper passed by, nodding to him. Simon carefully returned his greeting, self-conscious about being on this deck. When he found the right quarters, he had to announce himself a couple of times before he got an answer.

The Ferengi came right to the door and suspiciously blocked his way. "What do you want?"

"I brought you the medical report on the Sli. Dr. Crusher said you wanted a c-copy."

Mon Hartog snatched the disk from his hand, retreating a few steps to bend protectively over it with his back to Simon. He was making eager little noises. Simon hesitated, then followed him in, letting the door shut behind him. He'd seen his fair share of Ferengi, and this

167

one was fairly scrawny even for that species. Not only that, but Hartog's head was shiny and his dark coverall was wrinkled.

"Is this what you wanted?" Simon asked.

Hartog was moving around to sit down at the desk, inserting the disk. "Yes, yes, I suppose so. Are you sure this is all of it?" He shot Simon a quivering glare.

Simon nodded, even though he didn't know what it was the Ferengi had asked for. It didn't matter. His interests lay elsewhere. "D-Do you know what caused it?"

"What?" Hartog didn't look up.

"The explosion." Simon felt a muscle in his neck tighten as he asked outright. He tried to unobtrusively shrug one shoulder to stretch out the tension.

"I've seen nothing but this!" Hartog said irritably. "They haven't given me the report on the damage to the *Prospector*. Or the investigation results."

"They haven't told you yet?" Simon asked, surprised.

Hartog glanced sharply at him, his watery eyes examining every detail until they came to rest rather obviously on his pointed ears. "I know a hu-man didn't do it," the Ferengi said, his tone conspiratorial. "This place is crawling with hu-mans."

"I don't . . ." Simon drew back. "What do you mean?"

Hartog seemed to be taking in every nervous twitch and blink that Simon tried to subdue. He tried to keep his hands still, but it was no use.

"You're not Vulcan," Hartog said with certainty. "Romulan, then."

"How . . ." Simon managed to get out.

"Vulcans are prissy," Hartog sneered. "Vulcans don't pry. But a Romulan would. Romulans are almost worthy of respect. They're downright Ferengi about getting what they want, but they're like the galaxy itself—always shifting and changing. It's hard to see where the stars really lie with them."

Simon had trouble swallowing, almost as if his throat were closing up on him. Hartog had described him perfectly! He had come here to find out if Worf considered him a suspect, and he was doing it on the sly. Not only that, but his trip to the bridge yesterday had been motivated by exactly the same desire—to appear so naively innocent that no one would think him capable of sabatoging anything. Nothing could be more manipulative or treacherous on his part. Except for lying on his Starfleet application.

"I am Romulan," he whispered.

"Of course you're Romulan," Hartog told him. "And you want something—I can see it."

Simon quickly met his eyes, feeling completely exposed.

"Tell me what you want," Hartog told him, returning to his conspiring wheedle. "And I'll tell you what I want. Let's negotiate, Romulan."

Simon managed to barely shake his head. "No."

Hartog wasn't about to give up. His loose black coverall billowed out as he started to circle Simon. "Why are you here? You asked about the investigation . . ." He watched carefully as he drew out his words. Almost deceptively casual, the Ferengi added, "Perhaps you know something about the sabotage?"

"No!" Simon said too loudly. He couldn't let this Ferengi know he wasn't supposed to be here. "I'm . . . I'm curious is all."

"Romulans always have a reason," Hartog said flatly. "You want something. Admit it. What is it you're hiding?"

"Nothing." Simon wiped his hands against his pants. He was losing control of the situation. Maybe if he left, then the Ferengi would forget about him. He glanced at the door and started easing that way. "Call sickbay if you need any additional—"

"Stay right there!" Hartog drew his lips back in an

169

awful smile. "Start talking, Romulan. Or I'll tell the security chief that you've been nosing around. Yes," he said, nodding his head. "You don't want that, do you?"

Simon knew his expression had already betrayed him.

Hartog tilted his head back. "So we are in a position to bargain! Good. You'll find out what I need to know. I'll keep this a secret between the two of us."

"No!" Simon clenched his hands into fists. "I'm not a traitor!"

Hartog crossed the last few steps to the computer control panel. He held his finger poised over the security alarm. "What do they know about the explosive used? Do they know where it came from? Tell me or I'll call," he threatened.

Simon took a step forward. "You can't do this to me!"

Hartog bared his teeth. "Tell me."

"I don't know!" Simon shouted at him. "Honest! I don't have anything to do with the investigation."

Hartog shook his head. "That's not good enough."

"I . . . Y-You don't—"

Hartog hit the security alarm. Simon lunged for him, but he was too late. The light flashed as the message was passed. Hartog was immediately paged by Worf.

Instead of answering, Hartog gazed at Simon, his eyes predatory, as he reached out for a triangular, curved knife lying on the table beside him.

Simon felt light-headed for a moment, staring at the knife. He was drawn forward as if mesmerized by it.

"I could do anything to you." Hartog's voice was hushed. "I have almost two minutes." He held out his hand with the knife. "Listen to me now. You're going to find out what you can about the investigation, and tell me, Romulan—or I'll tell them what you were doing here."

Simon stopped, swaying slightly, an arm's length away from Hartog. The knife was just out of reach, poised and ready.

Simon fixed his eyes on the knife, and Hartog realized too late that he was moving. There was a flurry of arms as Simon slammed the Ferengi back into the wall. They fell apart as Simon screamed out, holding his hand to his head as blood ran through his fingers.

Beverly Crusher strode on Worf's heels as he rushed into Mon Hartog's quarters. Security officers were trying to hold Simon Tarses against the wall, but the man was berserk, screaming out words that made no sense. The cords in his neck were bulging out and his face was streaked with blood, but he continued to thrash in their grip. The Ferengi was rolling on the floor holding his arm and wailing even louder than Tarses.

Beverly immediately went to Tarses, pulling out her hypo. She was carrying more than her usual doses of tranquilizers because of the Sli. She chose benzo-diazepine to put him under quickly. He was hurting himself straining against the men, and she had to stop that bleeding.

"Simon, you're going to be fine," she said in a soothing voice as she pressed the hypo against his neck. She quickly placed a large sealant pack over the left upper quadrant of his face and scalp. The blood was absorbed into the diffusion membrane, leaving the sealant pack transparent. Under it, she could see a gaping horizontal slash, extending from his left ear to just below his eye. The tricorder indicated that there was no deep tissue damage to his skull, yet the cartilage of his ear was almost severed. She'd know more once she got to sickbay.

"What about him?" Worf demanded over the sound of Hartog's cries. Tarses began to fight less, visibly re-laxing.

Beverly waited until she was sure the hypo dosage was adequate, then she went to Hartog. He was moaning and crying out so loudly that she double-checked her readings—but the tricorder indicated only minor damage to his right deltoideus muscle.

"Please, calm down!" she finally ordered, as he writhed into her, knocking her off balance. "You sound like a Magotu ran over you. You're not hurt that badly."

Troi appeared in the doorway, breathless. "The captain sent me. What's the matter with him?"

Beverly grimaced, standing up. "Hartog? A muscle strain. Tarses is worse."

"What's going to happen to me?" Hartog whined.

"We'll take you to sickbay. Just sit right there until we're ready to go."

Troi gently pulled her away from the Ferengi. "What about Tarses?" she asked in a low voice.

"Aside from a nasty knife wound to the head, he's suffering from neurasthenia, as far as I can tell."

"Caused by emotional stress arising from inner conflict," Troi said, almost to herself.

"Usually it doesn't progress this rapidly," Beverly said. "But Tarses makes four that are showing all the symptoms right now." She clicked her tricorder shut.

Medical technicians arrived with an antigrav stretcher and carefully lifted Tarses onto it. Moodet and the other tech worked closely with Tarses, and they were clearly upset by his condition.

As they eased the stretcher from the room, Beverly looked back to find that Troi was standing over Hartog. "What happened here?" the counselor was asking the Ferengi.

"He went crazy! He came after me." Hartog was looking up at her, huddled on the ground. "We were talking. He brought the medical report. Next thing I knew, he attacked me! For no reason."

Worf moved forward as the Ferengi was explaining. "So you used the knife to defend yourself."

"No!" Hartog drew his legs in, sitting up on the floor,

hardly taller than Worf's knees. "He grabbed the knife. Right from that table. He attacked me, I tell you!"

"Then why does Tarses have the injury?" Troi's arms were crossed and her brows were raised in polite disbelief.

"He did it to himself!" Hartog nodded vigorously. "That's what I'm saying. He's crazy!"

Troi looked up at Worf without a word, clearly dismissing what the Ferengi was saying. "He's lying."

Beverly was glad. That meant Tarses probably wasn't entirely at fault, even if he was dangerously unstable emotionally.

"Lying? I'm not! Who are you—"

Worf ignored Hartog. "Is the Ferengi going to sickbay?"

"Yes." Beverly started for Hartog. "Help me, will you, Worf?"

Worf complied, boosting the Ferengi rather firmly to his feet. He gave his orders to the two security officers. "Take this man to sickbay. When he is done, he is to be confined to these quarters under guard."

"What!" Hartog managed to shake Worf off, straightening his coverall. "What did I do? You can't blame me for this! Your captain promised me the investigation report. This is what I get!"

"You will be given the information," Worf growled. "Take him!"

The security officers efficiently removed Hartog from the room.

That left Worf facing Deanna. Troi still had her arms crossed, but the Klingon towered over her. Unlike Hartog, she betrayed no uneasiness about her position. It made a striking impression on Beverly. She'd never seen the two so openly squared off.

"This is the fault of the Sli," Worf told the counselor.

"It's not being done maliciously," Deanna countered.

173

"That does not matter. Something must be done."

Deanna narrowed her eyes. "I am doing something."

"Just a moment, you two," Beverly broke in. "You've already had this argument. Right now we have jobs to do."

Worf said, exasperated, "We accomplish nothing!"

"Beverly's right, though," Deanna agreed. "Our personal feelings don't matter in this. We have to do our duty under these circumstances."

Worf grunted, becoming a silent, intractable wall.

When they reached sickbay, Beverly supervised the sedation and preliminary medical scan of Simon Tarses. Several research and laboratory personnel had been called in to assist the nursing staff in light of the current situation.

When she was finished, Beverly gestured to Troi, and they both went to stand just inside the door of her office.

"An isolation tank might be the best thing for him," Beverly told her.

Deanna was already shaking her head. "For Ensign Cuthbert and that young woman, BeBe, I agree that isolation would be best. Neither were near to having an emotional crisis when the Sli came. But Tarses is different. This nervous breakdown is not a complete surprise to me."

Beverly took a deep breath. "I knew Simon was having difficulty, but I didn't know it had gotten to this point. He's a superior medical technician—his instincts are infallible and he works very hard."

Deanna's eyes were steady. "That's just it. Simon is so meticulous and conscientious that he's been able to suppress his own problems, focusing instead on his probation. That's put him under immense pressure for more than a year now."

"What do you suggest? Psychotherapeutic measures? While the Sli are hammering away at him like this?"

"Well, at least the doubts and suppressed feelings have

risen to the surface. There might be a way to turn his breakdown to good use. I've been saying all along that the Sli would be excellent in a therapeutic environment."

Beverly fidgeted with her tricorder, clicking it open and shut until she realized what she was doing. "Fine. I'll keep him on the benzodiazepine, but I'll lower the dosage. That way he'll be relaxed and you can talk to him." She turned to leave. "As for the others—"

When she pushed open the half-closed door, Worf was revealed on the other side. Her sudden movement startled him, and she realized by his flustered withdrawal that he'd been listening to them.

"Lieutenant Worf! You were eavesdropping on a confidential consultation!" Beverly hardly knew what to think. It was completely unlike Worf to do anything so sneaky.

Deanna also seemed surprised. "Why, Worf? You can't possibly suspect Simon Tarses as a saboteur."

Worf drew himself up stiffly. "It was unintentional."

"But you heard us talking about Tarses?" Beverly asked him.

"Yes."

"What did you hear?"

Worf shifted, obviously wanting to leave. "Enough."

Beverly looked at him with concern. "Worf, there's such a thing as being overzealous. You have to get hold of yourself."

Worf tightened his lips, his eyes burning at the reproof.

"It's the Sli," Troi said. "The emanations feel stronger right now."

"Those creatures are dangerous!" Worf stated, but he subsided when he caught Beverly's steady eyes.

"I don't want to have to relieve you from duty, Worf."

The Klingon barely opened his lips to speak. "That will not be necessary. I know my duty."

Beverly gazed at him for a moment longer. "I hope so."

"My son will not suffer," he added. Then he nodded sharply to her, turning on his heel and striding out of sickbay.

Beverly shook her head after him. She would have to inform the captain that Worf was becoming unstable. Picard would not be pleased by that.

Something else bothered her. "What was he saying there at the end about his son?" she asked Troi.

"I'm not sure. Something's going on with him and Alexander." Troi shook her hair back from her face, catching her lip in her teeth.

"Was he comparing Alexander to Wesley? Wesley isn't even on board anymore."

Troi shrugged. "Perhaps. I'm having difficulty talking to Worf right now." Her voice became more thoughtful. "Not that I don't usually have trouble. Aggression is such a forceful emotion. I can feel it in him, always thrusting forward and overwhelming everything. Worf expects resistance from people, and he relishes the battle. But my empathic response is just the opposite—it's embracing and accepting."

"You don't fight back how he wants," Beverly agreed.

"I think it unsettles us both." Troi glanced down, her fingers lightly laced together in front of her. "He's propelled outward, and I take it in and continually try to direct him back on himself. It's a struggle that feeds on itself, like one of those mythic battles between the gods. Only Worf and I argue over reprimands and Alexander's bedtime."

It was so absurd that Beverly almost wanted to laugh, but it was too terrible. "Worf is spinning out of control while you're waxing poetic about the whole thing."

Troi blushed, suddenly and painfully red. "It's the Sli," she murmured.

Beverly grinned. She couldn't help it. "If you're his nemesis, then according to Worf, I'm his twin. I can't believe he compared Alexander to Wesley!"

Troi nodded, looking a little puzzled.

"As if we're anything alike. Me and Worf." Beverly let out a laugh. "Can't you see the similarities? Worf's got a wonderful beside manner. And I'm great when it comes to firing photon torpedoes."

Troi was watching her with a straight face. "Beverly, it's not funny."

"No?" She laughed harder. "It makes perfect sense to you, doesn't it! Of course Alexander and Wesley will be exactly alike."

"Beverly, get hold of yourself. Fight this feeling."

Troi sounded serious. Beverly remembered her own warning to Worf and suddenly realized that she was overreacting. But it was so funny!

Troi shook her head. "It's all right. You'll be fine in a little while. But why don't you wait in your office until you get hold of yourself?"

Though his duty shift had started, Worf immediately returned to his quarters. He told himself it was to check on Alexander before he went to school.

First, however, he relayed the investigation results to the terminal in Mon Hartog's quarters. He didn't like giving what he considered classified material to the Ferengi, but that was minor compared to the collapse of the medical technician. The counselor had said it was caused by "doubts and suppressed feelings." Those words were vaguely reassuring to Worf, because as any warrior knew, feelings must be properly channeled, and doubt was something to conquer. Yet what if he couldn't bring Alexander to accept his dual heritage? Was that the fate that lay in store for his son?

When he entered his quarters, Alexander was finishing his breakfast. His son was watching the latest issue disk of his comic on the holo-imagery padd. Worf glanced at the tiny, shifting images of humans—apparently this time the group was stranded in an underground cavern, complete with miniature stalagmites and the faint sounds of dripping. It was Alexander's favorite series, with the main thrust being the heroes' attempts to escape from a time-slip that trapped them in different periods on Earth. The counselor had assured him that it was very educational. But when Worf viewed one episode he thought the focus on character interaction made it dull. He'd seen others since that looked much more interesting, with space battles and personal combat between exotic alien rivals, but Alexander didn't like those.

"Eat your cereal," Worf told him.

Alexander dug his spoon in without taking his eyes off the padd. He hesitated, caught by some action, then he slowly raised the spoon to his mouth. He chewed for a few seconds, then stopped. Irritated, Worf watched until Alexander finally started chewing again and swallowed, all the while holding the spoon in midair without realizing it.

Worf restrained himself from correcting Alexander, forcing himself to turn away. His eye was caught by a blinking message light.

He went to his desk. He didn't bother to ask Alexander when the message had come in—sometimes it seemed like the boy didn't pay any attention to the things around him.

The message had the official seal of Qo'noS, the Klingon home world. Worf immediately felt the adrenaline surge through his body.

It was from his brother. Kurn's face was deliberately close to the viewer, cutting off his high, ridged forehead and lending a menacing tone to the entire message.

"Worf." Kurn was angry, Worf could tell, by the negligent sneer and squint of one eye. "Your response is unacceptable."

Worf's eyes widened. Blatant disrespect from a younger brother was not to be tolerated.

"You refuse to properly educate your son, the

cho'DevwI of our clan. According to our laws, I now call you, Worf, and your son to the Dobatlh PuqloD in order to determine legitimacy of succession. Your presence is required on Qo'noS within one *jar*, or *cho'DIb* will be granted to my first son."

Kurn paused as a slow smile spread over his face. "I look forward to seeing you again. Brother."

Worf ground his teeth together. The Dobatlh PuqloD was the test of a son's honor to the clan, requiring both father and son to participate. It was a disgrace simply to be called to such a rite. If they failed, Alexander not only would lose the right of succession, but by Klingon law he could be taken from Worf's custody.

"Father, is something wrong?"

Worf jerked his head toward his son, who was innocently gazing up at him. Worf suddenly realized that Alexander wouldn't be able to pass the Dobatlh PuqloD. The boy could speak Klingon, but even now he had trouble with the formal language patterns required during rituals. More important, Alexander's sense of honor was undeveloped.

Worf clenched the edge of the desk with both hands. By Earth standards his son was doing fine, but this threat of the PuqloD brought back memories of Klingon traditions in all their dark splendor. On Khitomer, he and his young friends had known a boy who had gone through the PuqloD. It had been of vital interest as the only time the adults had descended into their ranks and pulled one of them into public scrutiny. The whispers, the covert looks, the shame that had surrounded the boy . . .

"*Qo'!*" He heaved up the desk, grunting as he flung it away from him. It crashed into the couch and sent the monitor and disks flying.

"Father!" Alexander was standing by the dining table, clutching his padd in front of him with his eyes wide.

Worf felt much better. The blood was rushing through his veins and he was ready to fight.

179

"You *will* have honor!" Worf told his son.

Alexander took a step back, obviously frightened and wondering what he'd done to cause this.

"I was your age when both my parents were killed." Worf drew himself up, his chin high and eyes hooded, though he kept them fixed on his son. "I struggled to bring honor to my existence."

"You always say that!"

"It is true," Worf insisted. "I banished weakness. I proved my worthiness. So will you!"

"Nobody else cares about that," Alexander protested. "Nobody talks about honor like you do."

Worf barely moved his lips. "Klingons do!"

Alexander scowled, refusing to say anything.

"You have human blood, but you *are* Klingon. Just as I am Klingon."

"You lived on Earth."

Worf couldn't have said why that simple, true statement infuriated him. "I am Klingon! When *my* parents were killed by the Romulans, I became strong to avenge their deaths. You do nothing to make yourself strong!"

Visibly stung, Alexander blinked rapidly. "Why should I? Romulans didn't kill my mother! A Klingon killed her!"

Chapter Seventeen

PICARD WAS STANDING at the window of his ready room, gazing at Lessenar as it slowly revolved below. The *Enterprise* was stationed off the north pole, and the borealis was spectacular. Electron emissions were high, making the green rings ripple in tight waves as they spiraled from the pole down toward the equator. The layers were so close that it reminded him of a roll of corrugated tin his father had once brought home, intending to use it to cover an open equipment shed. Picard could remember kneeling in the soft dirt of his family's vineyard and staring mesmerized into the end of the roll of tin. He had liked the way his eyes got lost tracing the tight undulations of the concentric circles. This phenomenon was remarkably similar, except for the fuzzy green color of Lessenar's atmosphere.

Then the *Tampanium* edged into view, approaching from behind the planet and coming toward them. The light from the primary glinted off the sharp curves of the Ferengi Marauder. A grim smile pulled at Picard's mouth, as he felt an answering challenge rise inside of him. Those Ferengi weren't going to get the better of him.

The door chimed, and Picard called out, "Come." He knew who it was.

Guinan walked in. "You too, Picard?"

He glanced over at her. "Excuse me?"

"That planet," she said patiently. "People can't seem to keep their eyes off of it."

The captain stiffly made his way to his desk. "It's an exhilarating sight."

Guinan nodded, taking a seat. "Humans are fascinated by self-destruction."

Picard hesitated as he sat down. "Oh, I don't think so, Guinan. That's not it at all."

"Well," she said with a shrug. "Your eyes may be feasting on the view, but your subconscious is whispering all sorts of subliminal warnings. It's a taboo among your culture to contemplate a self-imposed death. But that's what makes this sight so enticing."

"Aren't you reading more into this than there is? After all, the phenomenon is particularly striking."

"It's pollution, Picard. Those people down there are killing themselves and their planet. Everyone knows it." Her voice was matter-of-fact. "The only crew members facing me at the bar these days are the Tricons, Antarians, Vulcans, and our one half-Romulan. All the humans are queued up to the window, and they usually don't drool this way over a view. It's titillating them on a primal level, provoking them."

"Now you're talking about the Sli."

"No, but that's what you want to talk about."

Picard silently considered her. Her serene expression was in sharp contrast to her startling outfit. He'd never seen this one before. The polished cloth tunic seemed to be made of liquid silver, falling in soft, reflective folds that caught the light in a hundred places, casting off tiny flashing signals as she moved. Her hat was flat on top, creating a mirror image of his ready room when she bent her head.

Picard folded his hands in his lap, leaning back in his chair. "Do you know anything about the Sli, Guinan?"

"Nothing that you want to hear right now."

He raised a brow. "Perhaps you'll let me be the judge of that."

Guinan smiled. "Fine. It's no use trying to reason with the Sli. You may discover what their language is, but that doesn't mean you'll be able to communicate with them."

"Come now, Guinan! Don't tell me you doubt their sentience? You sound like Worf."

"Worf is a warrior. He may have a point in this case. Sometimes life-forms can be so alien that their sentience is no longer the question. Understanding is the key."

"I agree with that." Picard pushed back his chair, standing up and pacing back toward the window. "I've been thinking of a purely human metaphor, but it seems apropos. You know *Cyrano de Bergerac?*"

"The French play? Yes."

"Well, Cyrano didn't know the meaning of moderation—apparently just like the Sli. One physical attribute was of excessive proportion, and he made it a point to make every aspect of his life of equally heroic measure." Picard lifted one hand high in emphasis. "He threw away a year's pay on one grand gesture. He loved a woman for fifteen years, and never breathed a word of his heart. It was all or nothing with Cyrano."

"As I also recall," Guinan put in dryly, "Cyrano challenged an entire theater of people to a duel and sought out a fight with a hundred men at a time, dragging a friend along with him."

Picard stopped his pacing. "I'm not defending the Sli. I have reports here from Data, Dr. Crusher, and Counselor Troi that prove the Sli are a much more subtle danger than we first believed."

"You're right about that. As I said, you're incapable of understanding them."

He frowned down at her. "You must have reason to believe this. Have you encountered the Sli before?"

"Not these creatures specifically." She folded her hands in her lap. "But I feel their emanations and I can recognize the chaos inherent in them."

Picard returned to his desk, thoughtfully examining her expression. "Guinan, is it possible that you're being affected by the Sli as well?"

"I'm not," she said flatly. "But you won't know that until they leave or the crew destroys the ship."

He slowly sat down, resting his chin in his hand. He was in a quandary. He had learned to implicitly trust Guinan, yet this time her opinion might be swayed by the emanations of the Sli. He had no way to be sure.

"I have orders to establish a dialogue with the Sli. We can't just leave—"

The computer chimed, interrupting him, then Worf's voice announced, "Incoming message from Lessenar, sir. Council Head Wiccy."

Picard grimaced at Guinan. "Then there's our mission to aid the planet. Those people are in dire need." He glanced up briefly. "In here, Mr. Worf."

He swiveled the monitor to face him, not at all eager to talk to the council head.

The image was badly broken up, but Worf had managed to improve the audio. "Captain Picard, why aren't you doing anything to help us?" Wiccy demanded without a greeting. He sounded desperate.

Picard blinked. "Medical aid and relief supplies have been delivered to your people. Do you require additional—"

"We need you! We need your people down here now. Something must be done quickly!"

Picard held up one hand. "A full complement of ship's scientists are currently investigating your situation. We require the facilities of the *Enterprise* to analyze possible solutions. To send researchers down to you would slow progress considerably."

"You don't understand. The populace is seriously distressed. At least send Riker down for the reception."

"I'm sure my first officer has informed you of our own problems. As soon as we have this matter under control, we will devote our undivided attention to Lessenar. As of this moment, however, we are unable to do that."

"That is not acceptable! Your arrival has been announced. People are expecting results. Perhaps you should take over for Commander Riker."

Picard took a deep breath. "Commander Riker is more than capable of directing this mission, Council Head. I assure you that his performance has nothing to do with the current delay."

"Maybe I should contact the Federation council . . ." Wiccy trailed off, as if talking to himself.

Picard repeated patiently, "The relief supplies we've delivered will prevent starvation for the present, and medical aid is being dispensed."

"Who cares about that in the cities? I'm talking about showing yourselves. People are doubting you'll be able to do anything."

Picard firmly pushed down a surge of disdain. That was not a diplomatic response. But he had to say, "I'm sure delaying diplomatic exchanges for a few days won't make that much difference."

"A few days! There's talk of recalling the council!" Wiccy exclaimed, as if that explained it all. "We can't wait a few days! We need to give our people a sign that help is coming."

Picard glanced over at Guinan. She was smiling just slightly.

He paused to consider his words. He wanted to make sure he was perfectly clear. "Perhaps in the way you mean it, help is not on the way."

"What?" Wiccy was swaying back and forth, so agitated that he strayed out of the frame of the viewer. "Why do you think we called the Federation?"

"We have gladly provided relief supplies, and once our situation is stabilized, we can repair the damage to your atmosphere." He paused. "But we are not here to be used as political capital."

"Captain Picard! You have to do something!"

"Picard out." He reached over and clicked off the transmission.

Guinan finally broke the silence. "Are you sure you're not being affected by the Sli, Picard?"

"Me? Why do you say that?"

She lifted up a fold of her tunic, sending out a shimmer of light. "Don't you think you were a little high-handed with that poor council head?"

"High-handed!" Picard scoffed. "What, that? You heard the man, Guinan. He's concerned solely about his political future, not taking care of his people."

Innocently she asked, "How far will you go to help them?"

Picard drummed his fingers on his desk. "What are you saying, Guinan?"

She leaned forward. "It's practically a crime the way the Lessenarians have treated their planet. Sort of the same way the Sli have behaved toward us. The Sli are incompatible with logic-based, humanoid life-forms, but they have the upper hand because they can influence our reactions. That makes them more than disruptive—it makes them deadly."

Picard sat back, grim. "Once we have the communication problem solved, it's likely we'll be able to reach some sort of understanding with the Sli."

Guinan stood up to go, smoothing her mirrored tunic. Picard could see a reflection of himself in the cloth.

"Don't count on it, Picard. By sentient standards, the Sli are insane. They have no self-imposed limits. It's deliberate indulgence at the expense of everything and everyone else." She nodded to him silently before she turned and left the ready room.

Picard leaned back in his chair, thinking of emotional provocation, the Lessenarians, and a Frenchman who had thrown away all self-imposed limits in order to prove he was much more than he looked.

Picard tapped his comm badge. "Lieutenant Worf, go to yellow alert."

"Aye, sir!"

Just as the yellow lights began flashing, Picard's communicator signaled a call.

"Captain Picard! This is Counselor Troi."

He quickly glanced up. "Yes, Counselor."

"Please come to Shuttlebay 3, sir. The communication program is complete."

When Captain Picard arrived at Shuttlebay 3, Deanna was silently wringing her hands.

"I'm sorry, sir," she told him before he could ask. "The Sli aren't listening anymore."

"I don't understand." He glanced through the window of the control booth. The two security guards were staring straight ahead. "What about the new translation program?"

"It's working, sir. But the Sli are only in listening mode during the intervals of stronger emanations." Deanna also turned to the window.

The Sli were still in the close diamond formation they'd held for the past two days, drifting slowly through the orange gas. Their colors were a dark, muddled blend of maroon, indigo, and plum, with an opalescent glow that made them more opaque than Deanna had ever seen.

"According to computer tracking of the activity among the crew," Deanna told the captain, "the emanations are strongest when we are being most affected—

Susan Wright

that's when the Sli are open to communicating with us. Their emanations become a running echo, picking up new feelings and enhancing them, then dropping them for something else. To them, it makes sense. Their neural synapses are moving faster than ours, and I know their emotional response is a thousand times more developed than our own."

Picard nodded. "Are we only being affected during these intervals?"

"Unfortunately, no. But it's easier to resist the more random emanations when they aren't trying to communicate."

"I'm sure this caused confusion as far as translation goes. Could it be that the Sli are not as nonsensical as everyone believes?"

"I believe that's possible, sir." She tried to keep her enthusiasm under control, knowing the captain would give less weight to her report if her judgment seemed swayed. "They're doing what comes naturally to them—which seems disjointed when we pick up only one thin slice of it through the translators. After all, look at their frame of reference. The Sli live in the flows and eddies of a gas giant. They sail for thousands of miles, letting emotions flow through them like the wind, carried from one to the next. The emotions are subtly altered and echoed along the way, but they always continue."

"If that's true, then the interconnecting reactions could extend to millions of Sli," Picard said.

"Yes. Entire planets could be encompassed." She tilted her head, gesturing fluidly with one hand. "Think how strange it must be for them to feel our crude reactions to one another's emotions. None of us are coordinated together like they are, and few of us are even fully aware of our own emotional swings. Not only that—there's an end to infinity for them in the shuttlebay. It's all sharp corners and straight lines."

"I thought they didn't have eyes," Picard commented. He seemed unduly suspicious.

"The computer analysis indicates that their skin itself is a sensory organ—absorbing both visual and emotional waves. The translator is now programmed to flash colors to the Sli to help them understand what our intentions are. It's already started. See the pink lights?" She pointed to a triple row of incandescent lights that were attached to the top of the window. "The computer decoded the colors that the Sli display with the translation of their thoughts. The program now judges the emotional intent of what I say and flashes the corresponding colors. Apparently the lighter the tones, the more contemplative and nonaggressive the emotion is. The darker it is, the more desire comes in, and what we would call greed. So pink, for instance, is a sympathizing emotion, while red seems to deal more with shame or guilt. A lime color is melancholy, while dark green is close to despair."

"Fascinating," Picard murmured, examining the Sli with a new interest. "The Sli are almost black right now."

"Apparently they want something very badly. See, the dominant color right now is that slate gray. The computer identifies that with pride, since it is a strange combination of reflection and greed. That seems logical enough, doesn't it?"

"Have you been able to find out what they want?"

"Here, look at this." Deanna reran the dialogue she had tried to establish. From the Sli's side, it was again seemingly random words and phrases strung together. This time, however, the tone was defensive—words like "no" and "stop" and the repetition of words like "protect" and "guilt" until it almost seemed as if they were frustrated. Deanna had asked, "Stop what?" And while the Sli hadn't responded directly, there had followed a dozen repeats of "protect," and then "Why is this?"

"I tried," she told Picard. "I wanted to let them know

Susan Wright

that we don't mean them any harm. But I still don't know if they're picking up the emotions of the assassin, or if they're just frightened out of their wits."

"Will the lights be enough to convey our message of goodwill?"

"There's no possible way to replicate emotional waves except naturally. And while I can feel them anywhere on the ship, I can't be sure they're listening unless I'm very close. Only when they're open will I be able to direct a precise emotional message back."

"How long before the next interval?"

She queried the computer, which took a few moments. "The average is once every twenty-six minutes. But that ranges from intervals of sixty seconds up to one stretch that was four hours long without any attempts at communication. Some intervals last only seconds. I felt one of those during this very conversation, but it was over before I could react."

"Are you the only one qualified to send this emotive message?"

"I am the only one who has been trained to control and direct my emotions. The colors are just a reflection of the feelings without the nuances."

"So you'd have to spend a good deal of time with the Sli, which could be detrimental to your judgment." Deanna prepared herself, ready to have to try to convince him, but the captain surprised her by lightly shrugging. "Very well, then. Spend as much time as you have to."

"Th-Thank you, sir," she managed, feeling as if she'd somehow gotten turned around.

"Perhaps you should change your outfit," Picard added.

Deanna quickly looked down at herself. She was wearing a plum-colored jumper—nothing unusual about it. "Sir?"

"The color is rather dark, you know," he told her. "I bet our two security guards have contributed more to our appearance of aggression with their red and black uniforms than the presence of a murderer on board."

"I didn't even think of that, sir."

"I know," he said, seeming to relish her reaction. He motioned to the guards. "Go change into something that's a lighter color. Tell them what would be best, Counselor."

"Aye, sir," she told him, blinking a little faster.

He started for the door. "And send me a copy of that report. Colors corresponding with emotions . . . I'd certainly like to see that."

"Aye, sir," she repeated faintly.

Picard was halfway back to the bridge when Mon Hartog paged him, requesting that he come to his quarters immediately. Picard suppressed a sigh and acknowledged.

When he got there, the Ferengi didn't even wait for the door to close behind him before he drawled out, "Soooo, the mighty *Enterprise* could not do what a single Ferengi manages in one morning."

"What is it, Hartog?" Picard demanded flatly.

"Oh, you should be nicer to me, Pi-card." Hartog's words slipped one over the other, sly and knowing. "It can almost be considered criminal neglect, the way you've run this investigation."

"I can assure you, my security chief is handling the investigation more than adequately."

"Your security chief has purple blood, Captain!" Hartog emphasized each word. "You put a Klingon in charge of discovering who murdered a Sli. Of course a Klingon wouldn't care who killed a Sli—a Klingon would be happy to see any number of Sli die."

Picard took one step forward, feeling his temper rise

sharply. "Do you have a specific allegation to make? Because if you don't, Mon Hartog, you will refrain from slandering my crew."

"Specific? Here's specific, Picard. Why was everyone on board the *Prospector* investigated—including me!—except for one man?" Hartog made a show of licking his lips, his hands moving in small rubbing motions against each other. "Who is it, you may ask? None other than our friend and partner—Captain Walch."

Picard deliberately showed no reaction. "Are you certain the captain wasn't included in the background checks?"

"Perhaps he was—I find it strange myself to think he could have been left out. But this information was obviously meant to be kept hidden."

"What information?" Picard insisted.

Hartog met his eyes quite firmly. "It seems Captain Walch had a younger brother serving on board the *Crockett* when it was destroyed. And considering how Starfleet blames the Sli for that, I'd say we've found the perfect motive."

"How do you know this?" It seemed unlikely that Hartog could discover something his crew had overlooked.

"It was in your own data banks—oh, I had to make some pretty peculiar links to, ah, 'dig it up,' as you say. Apparently Walch's brother used his mother's surname, and had been born on Talont Colony, while Captain Walch was born on Setti Alpha III. But the information is there, crystal clear. Your security chief"—Hartog sneered out the title—"apparently isn't capable of doing a simple background check on his old friend. Or perhaps it was more than that."

"What are you suggesting?" Picard asked, his tone warning.

Hartog shrugged one shoulder, slyly tilting his head to one side. "Oh, not much, not much. But perhaps, just perhaps, your Mr. Worf knew about Walch's brother and decided to protect his old friend who killed the Sli. Perhaps, just perhaps, he even helped his old friend—after all, who better to deceive the *Enterprise* sensors than your own security chief?"

"You are mistaken, Hartog. Mr. Worf would not aid an assassination attempt."

"Sometimes instinct wins out. Klingons will be Klingons at times."

Picard shifted, suddenly remembering how Worf had killed Duras, K'Ehleyr's murderer, in a cold-blooded rage. But the Klingons hadn't protested because it had been done in complete accordance with tradition.

"No," he told Hartog. "An anonymous missile is not the Klingon method of assassination. Honor would dictate they do it openly, letting the victim know who struck the killing blow."

Hartog raised his chin, grinning smugly. "Yes, *if* a Klingon was assassinating a sentient life-form, he would do it that way. But Klingons believe the Sli are less than animals. Killing a Sli would be considered extermination by them. That wouldn't limit them quite so strictly by dictates of honor."

Picard couldn't deny that, and it bothered him. Still, he didn't believe Worf had anything to do with this—except perhaps for negligence while performing his investigation. Even that was a strong allegation that would have to be dealt with.

"Thank you for this information, Mon Hartog. I'll talk to Lieutenant Worf—"

"Please, Captain Picard! You don't tip off a suspect so he has a chance to cover his tracks. Investigate him first, then talk to him." Hartog's tone became amazingly cold. "If you don't treat your security chief in the same way you'd treat any suspect, I'll have to assume this entire situation is a Starfleet cover-up and will immediately take the matter before the Federation Council."

Picard's lips hardly moved. "Very well."

"And that starliner captain—Walch. He's the murderer. He came to me, you know. He was planning this right from the start. He has that shifty look to his eyes—"

"Please, Hartog!" Picard held up a hand. "Don't start making assumptions. This is an investigation, not a trial. I'll turn the information over to my second officer, Lieutenant Commander Data. He's been unaffected by the Sli's presence and is the best choice for an unbiased opinion on this matter. Will that satisfy you?"

"The android? Certainly," Hartog agreed, making soft snickering noises, almost gloating. He made a movement toward the door, as if he was done and now expected Picard to go.

Picard stayed where he was, crossing his arms and gazing down at the Ferengi. "One other thing, Mon Hartog. This is a closed investigation. You will not repeat what we've discussed here to anyone. Do you understand?"

"Me? Talk?" He flapped his hand dismissively to one side. "I never talk."

"I see. I believe otherwise. In this matter, I will know you discussed this if anyone else finds out about it." Picard started for the door, feeling as if the whole interview had been conducted in tainted air.

Chapter Eighteen

LIEUTENANT CHRYSO DUCKED into her quarters as if she were being chased. She hugged the wall, breathing deeply, as the door slid shut. She knew she was overreacting, but she couldn't help it. She needed to get away from the bridge, away from the constant requests for updates from Commander Riker. She'd just given him her team's first summation, and he was after her for the results of the second round of inquiry. Didn't he know she was working as fast as she could? She hadn't been able to make him understand how delicate this analysis was.

Why, just an hour ago, she had caught an incorrect calibration estimation by Ensign Puckee. The measurement was off by three degrees, but during the simulations of theoretical solutions, even a small variation could mean a drastic difference in the outcome.

She shuddered to think what else had slipped by her, and was tempted to order a complete review of the current calculations. Remembering the sight of all those sick and dying people huddled on the ground was a goad to greater caution. One mistake on her part would doom them forever. The ecology hovered on the brink of no return at this moment, and it would take very little to completely devastate it. Those people who didn't die in the last convulsions of their world would eventually end up as homeless, reluctant colonists on another planet, under a vastly different culture. The essence of life as it had developed on Lessenar would be extinguished.

She blamed the Sli for interfering with her work. If a mistake was made, it would be entirely due to their disruptive influence. Much as she revered life, what were four beings placed against the survival of an entire world? She would tell no one her secret belief, but she envied Worf his ability to bluntly state that the Sli should be sacrificed for the safety of the ship and planet.

Still breathing shallowly, she walked toward her viewport. Lessenar slowly turned below. Circling it like a doomsday machine, the *Tampanium* silently mocked all of her efforts to save the planet.

Data walked into Ten-Forward, glancing at the scattered patrons who were mostly positioned near the large viewport. Then he saw Geordi.

La Forge was slumped in his chair at a table in the far corner, with his back to the planet. He was running his fingers slowly over his forehead as he absently stared at the iridescent synthehol in his glass, tilting it first one way, then the other, as if he couldn't take his eyes from the rippling patterns.

Data quickly crossed the floor to his side. "How are you feeling, Geordi?" he asked courteously. He remained standing beside his friend's table, waiting to be asked before he joined him.

"What? Oh, it's you, Data." Geordi relaxed back in his seat again. "I suppose you came to tell me I'm relieved of duty. I don't blame the captain after I walked out of the meeting like that."

"You are mistaken." Data paused for a second, but

Geordi didn't seem to understand. "It was not deemed necessary to relieve you of duty."

"No? Really? Maybe I should get back to Engineering then." But Geordi stayed seated, fixing his eyes on his glass again.

"If you wish," Data told him politely. When Geordi didn't say anything, he asked, "May I sit down?"

Geordi nodded, sighing and pushing himself up a little. "Sure. But I don't know why you'd want to, Data. I know it's the Sli and I'm trying to fight it, but I'm not exactly the nicest person to be around right now."

Data sat down, his movements precise. The soft lighting cast shadows around them, isolating them from the rest of the room. "I do not mind."

Geordi let out a soft sigh of irritation. "You wouldn't."

Data had to analyze that comment. "Ah, you intended that sarcastically, did you not?"

"Data, if you've got something to say, then say it." Geordi's tone was warning. "Otherwise, I'd rather be alone right now."

Imperturbable, Data said, "I wish to offer my assistance on erecting a forcefield around the Sli."

"Go to it. You don't need my help." Geordi held up his glass, as if toasting Data. "I gave it my best shot, but it wasn't good enough. Not that I see anyone else doing anything. Counselor Troi just sits there staring at them, and Worf's got enough security guards standing around —like he expects those giant squid to walk right out and start attacking people. Nope—nobody else is doing anything, but I bust myself and just get grief for it."

"Nevertheless," Data said, "I would appreciate your help."

"Not this time. Not unless the captain orders it," Geordi said, briefly meeting Data's eyes as he glanced up. The light from the wall lamp above him caught on the tiny bars of his VISOR. "You're on your own, Data. Go on—save the day. That's your specialty, isn't it?"

"Geordi, I do not understand your current attitude." Data had never seen his friend like this before. But before he could determine his next course of action, Guinan appeared beside their table. She was wearing a remarkable reflective fabric of Sabratic origin.

"Would you like anything, Mr. Data?" she asked, her hands clasped in front of her.

"No, Data's leaving," Geordi answered for him.

Data tilted his head. "I am?"

"Yes." Geordi turned to stare at the wall next to him, slumping down farther in his seat.

Guinan shrugged, briefly meeting Data's eyes. "Not exactly sociable. But at the very least, Geordi's the one human in here who's not fixated on that planet."

Geordi suddenly shifted uneasily. "It hurts."

Guinan smiled. "I knew you were an unusually sensitive person. It's only when we look beyond appearances that we truly see."

"Guinan, it hurts my head." Geordi tapped his VISOR with an exaggerated gesture. "This stupid thing makes me dizzy every time I look at the planet. I almost fell over walking across the room, and I'd like to not have to do it again right now. So if you'd both just leave me alone, I'll be fine."

Data raised one brow at Guinan. "The Sli are affecting Geordi in a most unusual manner."

Geordi let out his breath, a loud hint. "Will you just get out—"

"Commander Data, this is the captain."

Data glanced away from Geordi without hesitation, replying, "Data, here."

"Report to my ready room, please."

"Aye, sir." He rose to his feet, switching effortlessly from the matter at hand.

"Deus ex machina," Geordi muttered under his breath.

Guinan shot Geordi an amused look as she gently drew Data away. When they were out of earshot, she told Data, "I always knew Geordi wasn't merely stoical. Apparently your friend there not only endures his frustrations, but he controls them, channeling them into a productive goal. I suppose that's how he's come so far for one so young."

"Are you saying Geordi's behavior is the result of his irritation, and normally would not be expressed in a direct manner?"

"Isn't that what the Sli do?" She gazed fondly back at their friend. "Geordi's situation is unique, not only in the way he sees but because his VISOR gives him so much pain. But you never hear him complain. You've experienced difficulties yourself, Data, in being different from everyone else. Who better than you can understand how Geordi feels?"

"But I cannot," Data responded literally. "I can only consider emotions from an abstract position. I cannot apply them to myself."

"I don't believe that." Guinan shook her head at him. She seemed to be hiding something, but that wasn't unusual.

Data filed the contradiction for later consideration. "Nevertheless, it was my understanding that Geordi's condition would stabilize between the intervals of stronger emanations."

"Well, resentment's like that," Guinan said. "It feeds on itself. Right now Geordi's probably upset because he was rude to both of us—not because of anything the Sli are doing."

"I see. The emotional swings themselves perpetuate his condition."

Guinan pressed her lips together, nodding. "It's Geordi's way to accept things as they are, but that takes a certain mental effort. The Sli tap that very irritation he's trying to transform, causing it to surface again and wiping out all his efforts. Eventually the Sli stop, but then he's left trying to endure the results of his own actions. There is a timeless beauty in a struggle such as his."

Data glanced back at his friend, fully aware that the captain was waiting for him. "I will return as soon as possible to speak with Geordi again."

"You do that," Guinan told him. "I'm sure he'll be here."

Captain Picard gave Data the information on Captain Walch that Mon Hartog had uncovered, then he left the android to his station at Ops to verify the data.

Worf stood at Tactical, so when Data finally notified the captain that he had completed his research, Picard asked him to come into his ready room.

He looked up from Riker's report on the first summation of the scientific investigation as Data came to stand in front of his desk.

"Well, Mr. Data?"

"Mon Hartog's information is essentially correct, sir," Data informed him. "Worf cross-checked the passengers and crew for possible motives against both the Sli and Captain Jacob Walch. He neglected to determine if there was a direct connection between the Sli and Captain Walch."

"I see," Picard said, nodding. "Worf considered both of them the most likely targets, not suspects."

"It would seem so, sir." Data sounded so regretfully polite that Picard had a hard time believing the android didn't truly feel bad. "However, Captain Walch did indeed have a younger brother, Ensign Benjamin Marley, serving on board the *Crockett* at the time of its destruction."

"Worf!" Picard said under his breath, shaking his head.

"In addition, according to their own statements, Captain Walch instigated the arrangement which led to the Sli performing on board the *Prospector*. When Mon Hartog subsequently demanded a higher percentage of the gross, Captain Walch agreed to the proposed changes in a revised contract."

"Hum, that doesn't look too good. But it's circumstantial evidence at best."

"Agreed, sir. However, there are additional correlations involving Lieutenant Worf."

"Such as?" Picard braced himself.

"Almost simultaneous to the agreement made between Mon Hartog and Captain Walch, Worf began receiving subspace messages from Earth on the *Prospector* relay code. He has received six such calls during the past year. In addition, the *Prospector*'s computer was instructed to give Captain Walch continuous updates on the location of the *Enterprise* when it was in this quadrant."

"Perhaps Worf and Captain Walch are closer friends than we realized."

"Perhaps," Data conceded. "Yet, if you remember, Captain Walch expressed surprise when he first noticed Worf on the bridge, while the log indicates he had been informed that the *Enterprise* was in this star system. Indeed, shortly after the computer notified him as to our location, Captain Walch ordered the *Prospector* to proceed directly to Lessenar, bypassing both the Organi III comet and the Bolton shell star, which are usually included in the ship's tour."

"I don't like the sound of this." Picard tapped his fingers against the edge of his desk. "Many would agree with Hartog that there are too many connections between the two men to simply pass the situation off as coincidence."

"Sir, the subspace messages are still stored in the computer's encryption/decryption data banks. The contents of the messages can be retrieved through Ops with your clearance, bypassing Security."

Picard looked up quickly, not liking the implications of that. "I won't jump to conclusions based solely on these facts, Mr. Data. First I'm going to have Counselor Troi probe Captain Walch—as he should have been during the investigation."

Chapter Nineteen

COUNSELOR TROI ACKNOWLEDGED a message from sickbay informing her that Simon Tarses was awake and capable of talking to her. She told the two security guards—now wearing jumpers in the creamiest yellow and orange tones she could get from the replicator—where she was going and asked them to alert her if the new indicator light on the translator came on.

The captain's call caught her almost at the door of sickbay. She paused in an alcove to acknowledge it. "Yes, sir?"

"I'd like you to probe Captain Walch in relation to the Sli, Counselor. I've sent the pertinent data to the terminal in your office. I know I don't have to remind you to keep this confidential."

"Aye, sir." She hesitated. "I was just on my way to speak with Simon Tarses. I believe Mon Hartog was lying about what happened in his room, and I'd like to confirm that."

There was a pause, then the captain said, "Very well, it could be useful information. But I want your opinion on Captain Walch as soon as you can get to it."

"I won't be long with this," Deanna agreed.

"Picard out."

Deanna ordered her thoughts, wondering why the captain had developed a sudden interest in probing Captain Walch. He couldn't believe Walch had damaged his own ship. She distinctly remembered his deep anguish when he beamed aboard yesterday, the last evacuee to arrive. He had been carrying a silver cylinder with his ship's logs and registration documents under one arm, and he had clutched it tightly to his chest the entire time she had spoken to him. She hadn't seen him since.

She slowly made her way past the occupied beds. Injuries were increasing in frequency as more of the crew became disoriented by the emotional pull of the Sli. Most of the incidents were accidental, yet there had been a disturbing number of fights as well, even under yellow alert. The problem was, there was no way to force nonessential personnel to stay in their quarters while discipline was eroding throughout the entire ship. She had argued with Worf, and finally made it an order, that crew members be allowed to go wherever they felt the most comfortable. Geordi was a good example. Guinan had told her he'd been in Ten-Forward all day, and he wasn't likely to move anytime soon.

Deanna stopped to speak to the closest patient. She felt guilty, as if she should be in sickbay helping these crew members instead of waiting in the shuttlebay for the Sli to communicate. Many of these people were suffering emotional traumas that, if properly guided, could serve as breakthroughs in their personal lives. She couldn't help lingering with each person, listening, feeling their special turmoil and giving them a word or two of advice on which attitude would be most positive in their current state of mind. Her empathic senses felt heightened to a degree she'd never experienced before, and she could almost detect the source of the problem in each person before he or she spoke.

Then she saw Alyssa, Beverly's most trusted nurse. The dark-haired woman was leaning over a man, his hand clasped in hers as she looked down into his eyes. She seemed to challenge him, and as Deanna opened her senses, she felt the man relax under Alyssa's gaze, nodding up at the slender nurse as if in acceptance.

She straightened and looked directly at Deanna, her dark, slanted eyes more than eloquent. Then she smiled briefly, and went to the next bed.

Deanna swallowed, and behind her, Beverly said, "I don't know what I would have done without Alyssa. She's become a tigress, protecting everyone as if they were her own children. I never knew she had it in her."

"I'm glad they're in such good hands," Deanna said.

"Well, you're here to talk to Tarses, aren't you?" Beverly said briskly. "I'm glad. He's in a state of complete self-absorption. Worf got to him before I could, wanting to bring Mon Hartog up on charges, but Tarses wouldn't speak to him. After that, I tried, but I couldn't seem to get through."

Deanna drew in her breath. Trust Worf to try to bully his way through the man. Poor Simon. "Where is he?"

"In here," the doctor said, leading her toward a small, isolated room. As she gestured Deanna in, she commented with a slight raise of a brow, "Um . . . unusual color for you, Deanna. A little young, but I like it."

The doctor turned and was already striding off before Deanna could explain the reason for her light pink dress. It was a color she usually avoided—as pink as the pale blush enamel on the inside of a seashell. To the Sli, she would be sending a message of sympathy. Beverly probably thought it was frivolous in such a strained situation. But then Beverly herself had certainly been acting on the silly side ever since the Sli had arrived. Deanna thought that was a rather telling quality to be released by the Sli, and she reminded herself to point that out to the doctor once everything was back under control again.

Still, she was glad Beverly hadn't mentioned the rose-colored ribbons she'd put in her hair. It had seemed like the dress needed something extra, but now she wondered if it was too much.

Deanna abruptly shook herself—what was she doing? Simon Tarses was suffering in there, and all she could think about was her hair?

She grimly fought to get hold of herself, pressing down on the Sli-induced euphoria. After a few deep breaths, she felt more under control. Whenever her shields slipped, their emanations crashed in on her before she realized it.

Straightening her shoulders, she marched inside the dimly lit nook.

Tarses was sitting up in bed, staring off to one side. A silver embossed blanket covered his legs, and the medical readout glowed softly on the wall. He didn't move as she approached him.

"Simon?" she said softly. "It's me, Deanna Troi. How are you feeling?"

He stirred slightly, but he didn't look at her.

"Simon, don't hide yourself away from me. I want to talk to you." Beverly was right. Simon had withdrawn to a dangerous degree. She wondered what Worf had said to him. The last thing Simon needed was a verbal attack from the Klingon.

Deanna slowly reached out and let her fingers trail along the faint line of the sealed cut on the side of his head. He flinched, but she maintained contact. Her voice was low. "Dr. Crusher did a good job. You can hardly see any marks."

Tarses drew a deep breath, but he finally looked up at her.

"Mon Hartog tried to tell me what happened, but I don't believe him." She wanted to reassure those frightened eyes. No one should ever be that hurt and alone. "Tell me, Simon, why did you insist on going there?"

"I had t-to know if I was . . ." He trailed off, glumly staring down at his hands.

"You still thought you were a suspect? But you weren't —Worf and I told you that."

He shrugged, unable to meet her eyes. "After I crashed the bridge, I thought you might."

"I wondered if that was why you went to Hartog," Deanna said, mostly to herself. "But what happened? Hartog pulled his knife; we know that much. Why?"

"H-He wanted me to give him information. In exchange, he wouldn't tell y-you I came to him."

"What information did he want?" Deanna asked eagerly, certain this would be the answer they were looking for.

"He asked me if you knew what caused the explosion. I—I refused to help him."

"Did he say anything else?"

"No. Nothing. Honestly," he said in a stronger voice, seeing her draw back. "I didn't tell him anything. He called me a R-Romulan. When I said no, he got hold of his knife to threaten me."

With difficulty, Deanna swallowed her disappointment. She would have liked to have more detailed information as to what Hartog was looking for. "How did he manage to cut you?"

Simon twisted his hands together, his jaw clenching. After a couple seconds, he shook his head, unable to speak.

"Simon," she breathed, hearing the tremor in her own voice. "You didn't cut yourself, did you?"

He briefly met her eyes, understanding flashing between them.

"Oh, no." Deanna wanted to cry. Hartog's awful story had been true. The Ferengi hadn't been lying. "Simon. Why?"

"I couldn't stand it anymore!" he burst out. "I don't want to be Romulan. I thought if my ears weren't like this, maybe no one would know. They wouldn't think I was a traitor by just looking at me. Maybe then I could have a normal life—"

"Your ears aren't your problem," Deanna protested. Her temples throbbed, the effect of his intense turmoil. "Even if you had them surgically altered, you'd still be who you are. That's what you have to come to terms with."

Simon blinked rapidly, clenching his hands into fists as he deliberately broke away from her eyes. "Lying here like this—I can see that! But I don't want to be anything like a Romulan."

Deanna thought of the Romulans she had encountered. They were all so cold and sure of themselves. "Simon, calm down. Let's look at this from the other side. In what ways do you think you are like a Romulan?"

"I—I lied on my Starfleet application. And I manipulate things. Even this," he said, with a brutal gesture to his healed ear. "I guess I was trying to hide what I am."

"That's just the way you are, Simon. It's not Romulan and it's not human. It's you."

"I know that. I do now, I think. But it was like a fit of madness came on me—like some sort of instinctive cunning. I kept trying to push it away as if it weren't really me thinking those thoughts or doing those things."

Deanna nodded, understanding his withdrawal. "That's why you didn't tell Worf that you cut yourself."

"I couldn't admit that to him." Simon shook his head at himself, pushing the blanket off his legs. "Just the thought of telling him paralyzed me. But ever since he was here, I've been thinking and thinking about it, going over it in my mind. I keep fighting what I am—and look what happened! I got so crazy that I drew a knife across my ear."

"Someday you'll have to stop denying who you are."

He squarely met her gaze. "It has to be now. I have no place else to go. I can't keep ignoring these impulses I have. If I can just accept it, then maybe my Romulan part will only be one quarter of what I am instead of controlling my life like it does now. It can't get any worse than this."

His words danced in her ears, making a connection that she hadn't seen before. Deanna slowly sat down on the edge of the bed. "I've been telling everyone to resist these feelings the Sli bring out."

"I've been resisting them for a year. It hasn't done me any good."

"No, it hasn't," she agreed.

"I still don't feel so great right now," Simon told her honestly. "But I'm not desperate anymore. And I think I understand what's been happening."

"That's all you need," Deanna agreed, wondering— could it be true? She'd been resisting the Sli, too, despite her instinct to let herself go with the emotional waves. She had suspected that instinct—believing it was a consequence of her unleashed sensuality. But what if that was the key to lessening the effects of the Sli? Simon certainly seemed calmer now that he was facing his problem and acknowledging it.

Yet her judgment was not to be trusted right now. She hated to admit it, but she'd been terribly wrong about Mon Hartog. She had been sure he was lying, and hadn't considered the possibility that Simon had actually hurt himself. But of course, hearing what he had to say, now it made sense.

She managed a smile for him. "There's a lot to admire about Romulans, Simon. To be shrewd is not entirely bad—and it may have actually helped you with this very problem."

His eyes widened as he considered that, and a new resolve brightened his face. "You think so?"

"I do think so. You figured it out, didn't you?" She stood up, determined not to let him see her doubts. For Simon, at least, this was the right direction. "I'll come see you again soon."

"Can't I get out of bed?" He swung his legs over the side and carefully stood up. "I'm feeling much better, and I'd rather be helping all those people out there. And there're still medical supplies being sent down to the planet."

She hesitated, examining him closely. His medical readings were normal and his injury was healed. Her empathic senses told her that he was more stable than he'd been since she had refused his transfer request. She could see no reason for him to stay in bed. "All right, Simon. But if you start to feel bad again, it could be the Sli. I want you to contact me right away."

"Yes, Counselor."

"Good. Then I'll tell Dr. Crusher you can go back to work."

Deanna immediately returned to her office to read the information Captain Picard had transferred to her terminal. When she saw the implications of Worf's negligence in light of his friendship with Captain Walch, she didn't need to be told how important her judgment would be in probing Walch.

After a moment, she raised her head and asked, "Computer, where is Captain Walch?"

"Captain Walch is in Holodeck 3."

"Is he alone?"

"There are currently twenty-two people in Holodeck 3."

"Wonderful," Deanna murmured to herself.

She wasted no time getting to the holodeck. When she walked in, Captain Walch was just changing the program from the endless void of Tyken's Rift to a sunset on Earth's Siberian steppes, complete with a vast expanse of sky tinted flashy orange and dotted on the western horizon with fluffy, gold-rimmed clouds.

With the ground much darker than the sky, Deanna had to pick her way carefully through the thick grass toward the captain. Slim black silhouettes of the tourists rose against the sky, and she realized the erratic smudges that darted through the dry, crisp air were bats.

One of the figures gestured broadly to a vast pit just to the north. ". . . the gypsum mines were worked by exportees from Eastern Europe as well as exiled Russians brought out by trains—"

"Captain Walch!" Deanna called out. She felt a wash of disappointment as the tourists shifted and turned to see who was interrupting. She hurried closer. "Captain Walch, it's Counselor Troi. I need to speak with you."

"You act like you're in a hurry, little lady. Something I can help you with?"

She glanced at the dim forms of people around them. "Not here. Can you step outside with me a moment?"

Walch hesitated, but seemed ready enough to oblige her. "Give us a sunrise, computer." As the west fell black and the eastern sky began to brighten, Walch joined her. The spicy dryness of late afternoon disappeared as the slight breeze took on a moist tinge. "Just enjoy yourselves, everyone. I'll be back in no time." In a low voice meant just for her ears, he added, "Can't have them stumbling around in the dark. Tourii are as bad as a litter of puppies for getting into trouble."

Deanna felt her stomach sink, wondering if it was true that this exuberant man was responsible for the death of one of the Sli, and their current situation. Then she firmly marshaled her feelings back onto an impartial line for questioning.

She ushered Walch through the corridor and into a small lounge. "I just need to ask you some questions," she told him, gesturing to the couch underneath the window. "Sit down for a minute."

"What can I do you for?" Walch asked, settling himself heavily on the soft cushions and kicking his booted feet out.

She didn't want to put him on the defensive, making him more difficult to read, so she decided to work up to it. "That holodeck program you're showing the tourists, that's near your home, isn't it?"

"Near enough. That's the Kulunda steppes, south of Lake Chany, where my wife's family hails from. They have a nice spread out there."

"That's where Worf's foster parents are from, too."

"Aye," he said, his blue eyes narrowing somewhat. "Did you want to talk to me about Worf?"

"Well, you two are close, aren't you?"

"You bet. I knew him while he was growing up."

Deanna shifted slightly. "You've kept in contact since then. About how often have you spoken with Worf in the past couple years?"

Walch shrugged one shoulder, rubbing one of his eyes as he thought. "Last time was right after the Borg came to Earth. I was in port and gave him a hail on subspace jus' before Sergy and Helena came on up to see him."

She blinked a couple of times. "Nothing since?"

"No," Walch said, meeting her eyes. "I got to know his son pretty well on Earth, but I don't mess with Worf's business—he's a mite touchy 'bout that. Always has been. So, if it'd please you, I'd ruther not talk about Worf."

Walch was hiding something; Deanna was certain about that. She also knew about the six messages for Worf via Walch's relay, proving that Walch was lying. But she hadn't been able to sense outright deceit in him, only a vague reluctance. She felt as if she were trying to fly a shuttlecraft without sensors, having to second-guess her own intuition.

"I have a few questions about the Sli," she told Walch with a reassuring smile. "It was your idea to have them on board your ship, wasn't it?"

"Our main attraction," Walch claimed, grinning right back at her.

"But was it *your* idea?" she repeated.

"You bet it was," he agreed.

Deanna didn't know what to say. Walch was lying—she could feel it beyond a doubt—but Hartog had also said that Walch had contacted him about bringing the Sli on board his starliner.

Feeling as if it were hopeless, she plunged right in. "Captain Walch, you had a brother on board the *Crockett* when it was destroyed, didn't you?"

Walch sat up. "Benji?"

Deanna nodded, watching carefully to see what his reaction would be.

"You're talking about Benji," Walch repeated, mostly saddened, yet also surprised that she would bring him up.

"Were you close to your brother?" she pressed.

He sharply met her gaze, and she had to draw herself in quickly. But his voice was calm and his hands were steady. "Benji ran the *Prospector* with Pa and me until he went into Starfleet Academy. Yup, we were tight."

"Tell me about him," she urged.

"Not much to tell. The three of us went everywhere with the *Prospector*. But Pa and me managed to get along when he went into the Academy—it'd always been a dream for Benji." Walch smiled, remembering. "His first assignment was the *Intrepid*. He was in Engineering 'long with Sergy Rhoshenko, Worf's father. That's how I met my wife, Miriah. Benji was on shore leave at Sergy's home, and they invited me and Pa to come visit. Miriah's an old friend of Helena's, and she was in and out the whole time." Jake slowly got to his feet, pacing along the shadows of the room.

213

"That's how your families became such good friends," Deanna said softly.

Walch nodded. "Later, Benji transferred to the *Crockett* and was killed along with the rest of his crew. I sometimes think—if he'd stayed on board the *Intrepid*, he would have been alive when the ship responded to the Khitomer massacre. It's likely he'd've adopted Worf instead of the Rhoshenkos. He, Pa, and I had some good dealing with Klingons before the Federation ever did. Benji was always drawn to their ways."

Deanna felt his sorrow, mellowed into resignation by the passing of so many years. Yet his emotions were also lightly laced by the old memory of camaraderie and adventure, still very special to a man who'd managed to see almost everything since.

She firmly brought herself back to the main subject. "I wonder that you wanted to bring the Sli on board your ship. It's said they were responsible for the destruction of the *Crockett.*"

"Oh, I get it now." He stepped forward, letting the light fall square on his weathered face. His voice was rough, but he held himself with dignity. "I never believed those Sli could make people do what they didn't have in them to do. Benji may have been accepting of Klingons, but the rest of the Federation didn't trust 'em then. I talked to Sergy after, and he also figured it was our own fears that caused those two ships to be destroyed. I think that's one reason Sergy was so eager to do right by Worf when he had the chance."

Deanna believed him—she sensed no animosity toward the Sli. Still, she had to ask directly, "Did you have anything to do with the explosion that damaged your ship?"

His surprise slapped into her, quickly followed by guilt. Walch tried to suppress his reaction, covering it with a coughing spell. "'Scuse me, gets me this way sometimes," he managed to get out.

Deanna was stunned at the sudden reversal. Captain Walch had her believing his every word, and she was genuinely touched by the tragedy of his story, but now he was clearly trying to hide something. She'd caught him off guard with that question.

Walch straightened his shirt, clearing his throat. "Sorry 'bout that." His voice got stronger. "Of course I didn't blow up my own ship! I was sick over the whole thing; you know that."

"Yes, I do," Deanna said thoughtfully. Walch had indeed been upset.

"I mean, well, yeah, I'm feeling better now that we'll be getting another starliner. I mean, I put the past behind me, you know? Gotta get on," he added, a little nervously. "Hey, is this all you were wanting to ask me? I should be getting on back to the tourii. They can get antsy if I leave them dangling too long."

Deanna thought it was interesting the way Walch fell defensively back into his tour-guide mode, complete with folksy language and cagey grin.

She stood up. "Thank you, Captain Walch. I appreciate your cooperation."

She silently watched him leave the little lounge. The entire interview was a mass of contradictions, and she didn't know how she was going to unravel it for Captain Picard. She'd also have to warn him that her judgment might not be reliable—and yet she wanted to tell everyone on board to stop resisting the emotions provoked by the Sli. But then again, remembering how the *Crockett* and a Klingon vessel had fought and destroyed each other, she just couldn't trust that option.

Chapter Twenty

WORF CAME TO A STOP a few steps in front of Captain Picard, who stood in front of his desk. Worf clasped his hands tightly behind his back, not certain why he'd been called to the ready room. He'd been preoccupied since his confrontation with Alexander in the morning. Why had he never considered that aspect of K'Ehleyr's death? When Worf had been orphaned, he'd had a clear enemy in mind—one with pointed ears and shrewd eyes. An enemy on whom to focus his anger, to defeat by right of his honor. What did Alexander have? His enemy had the same face as Worf's. Alexander's face had humanity in it, like K'Ehleyr's. And Duras had killed K'Ehleyr in some pathetic bid for an honor of his own definition. What faith could Alexander place in honor? What was the PuqloD to him?

With effort, Worf struggled against his own thoughts. For the peace offered by pure concentration, for relief from all the doubts, he would have pledged any service. But it was not within reach.

Picard had been watching him, his face tilted up

slightly, eyes steady. When he spoke, his voice was cool, though tinged with regret. "Lieutenant Worf, why did you neglect to consider Captain Walch a suspect in your investigation?"

Worf broke from his stance slightly. "Sir?"

"Captain Walch. Every other person on the *Prospector* as well as the *Enterprise* was checked for possible motives regarding the Sli."

Worf shook his head. "Captain Walch was the most logical *target,* sir. It was his vessel that was damaged."

"He will be receiving a more than ample recompense. Another starliner, I believe."

Worf was focused now. The captain was still remote, as if conducting this inquiry for the record. "If I may ask, sir?" he requested. "What is the reason for suspecting Captain Walch?"

Picard nodded briefly. "There seems to be a strong motive for Captain Walch to want revenge on the Sli. Do you know about the death of his younger brother?"

Worf frowned, remembering vague references to Jake's brother Benji among the adults. He shook his head.

"He was serving on the *Crockett* when it was destroyed," said Picard.

For a strange moment, Worf was stuck. Despite living so long in the Federation, he'd always persisted in viewing the Sli disaster from the Klingon side, sparing little thought for those on the Starfleet vessel. "I did not know. They did not speak of this brother often."

"Well, Mr. Worf, perhaps it's unfortunate that they didn't. This places you in a rather compromising position. The one person you neglected to investigate appears to have a strong incentive to destroy the Sli. And this person is an old friend of yours."

"Sir! You don't believe I would subvert an investigation?"

"At the very least, it appears to be a serious breach of

duty. And while I can follow your reasoning, others might not. Mon Hartog does not. He is eager to take this straight to the Federation Council."

Worf flinched under the captain's seemingly nonchalant summary. The idea that he had committed a "serious breach of duty" made him grind his teeth together. "I cannot believe Captain Walch is responsible for the explosion!"

"Counselor Troi just questioned Captain Walch, and he is most definitely hiding something." Picard seemed to take in every flicker of Worf's face, but his own expression never wavered. "You should be aware that there are additional connections. You have received six calls that are imprinted with Walch's relay code since the Sli boarded the *Prospector*. In addition, you recently received a message directly from the council adjunct on the Klingon home world. Hartog is using this to conjure up a conspiracy theory, using you as the link to the Klingons. If you disclose the contents of these calls, that would allay any suspicion of your direct involvement. We would still have to deal with the charge of negligence that Hartog will surely bring on you."

"Messages!" Worf repeated, stunned. It took a moment, then he protested, "My foster parents have occasionally used Walch's relay code since their business acquired it."

"I see. Then it is a simple matter of releasing these messages so that it can be proven they don't contain any conspiracy plans."

Worf flashed vividly on the last message—his parents discussing Alexander's nightmares. And others before. Alexander wetting his bed, and the awful, stilted conversations about his son's terrible habit of stealing. All for other people to look at, examine for hidden nuances, perhaps even to discuss among themselves later. His son . . .

Picard was saying, "I'm sure there's just as reasonable an explanation for the message from the Adjunct Chamber on the Klingon home planet."

The PuqloD. Worf threw back his head, unable to bear the thought of that message of dishonor exposed. "I will not allow it!"

"Worf, if you won't cooperate, you could be charged as a direct accessory to murder." Picard was dead serious. "According to the *Prospector*'s logs, Captain Walch has been keeping track of the *Enterprise*. He broke from his itinerary when he found we were here. It could be that he's planned this from the start. He might have known you wouldn't consider him a suspect, based on your old friendship. Under these circumstances, it will be difficult enough to counter the charge of negligence, which is quite serious in itself. You can't leave yourself open to the possibility of direct involvement."

Worf was trembling with barely contained fury. Fire coursed through his veins, igniting responses he hadn't felt since . . . Duras. He suddenly let out a strangled cry, harsh as that of a bird of prey swooping down on its victim.

"Lieutenant Worf, what does this mean?" Picard demanded, his own eyes lighting with reckless gleam. He moved one step closer, his voice lower in warning. "You don't consent to release the messages that were relayed to you through Walch's code?"

Worf bared his teeth, unable to control himself. "Never!"

Without thinking, he backed up, crouching slightly as if seeking a better position for attack.

Captain Picard slowly raised one brow, coolly meeting Worf's gaze. Suddenly Worf heard how his breathing was loudly rasping in the confines of the small room. Picard was in complete control, unconcerned, yet fully prepared to meet his challenge.

Worf wavered, only now realizing how sharply his Klingon instinct had risen in defiance of his captain.

"You're temporarily relieved of duty, Lieutenant Worf," Picard ordered. "Return to your quarters immediately."

Worf's world couldn't have collapsed more completely. Stunned, he stayed exactly as he was, staring at the captain.

Picard's voice was harder. "Do not disobey a direct order, Lieutenant."

Worf had no choice. He turned and left, stalking blindly through the bridge, with his hands clenched into fists. The doors of the turbolift were closing when he saw the captain standing on the threshold of his ready room. The last thing he heard was the captain ordering Ensign de Groodt to take over as acting security chief.

Worf had not noticed how long the turbolift ride was, but when he stepped into the corridor, he knew by the shape that he was on one of the lower engineering decks. Instinct had brought him here.

He touched an access panel. "Computer, location of Captain Walch."

"Captain Walch is currently in his quarters, Deck 33."

In only moments, Worf was at Walch's door.

The older man was smiling through his bushy gray beard as he came forward to greet Worf. His utilitarian room was almost buried beneath a lifetime's worth of accumulated objects that he must have collected from dozens of different planets. Round containers were placed on top of steel boxes, while statues, figurines, masks, and models were piled on every surface and filled every crevice. Apparently the salvage of the *Prospector* was moving along rapidly. The color, the smell, the riot of shapes were like an exotic explosion in the room, unfamiliar to Worf, keeping him sharply on edge.

"Hold on there, son. What's wrong?" Walch demanded, stopping a few steps away. The door slid quietly closed behind Worf.

Worf lowered his head, glaring at Walch. "You have betrayed me!"

"Worf. I wouldn't do anything like that," Walch said, with something like relief as he started forward again. "The counselor was asking about Alex, but I didn't tell her a thing! I swear."

"Alexander!" Worf repeated, feeling the two things twist inside of him—honor and betrayal—producing Klingon impulses to destroy without control.

"She was asking all kinds of things, but you know me, Worf!" Walch put his finger to the side of his mouth. "I know enough to keep quiet. Believe you me, I told Helena and Sergy enough times, you can trust me with anything, you can. Worf's like a son to me, I always says."

Worf stared without seeing, fuzzy blackness taking his vision. And in that darkness he saw his foster mother talking to Jacob Walch—a long time ago, when Helena's hair was still jet black and the flesh of her face was firmly pink and white. Jacob was also younger, with a darker beard and sharp eyes that young Worf always admired. But his mother was telling Jacob about a fight Worf had started, and how she was afraid for the Klingon, seeming so pointlessly aggressive that she was sure he would be badly hurt someday. Yet with a quiver in her voice, she also admitted that sometimes she was afraid of her foster son. Worf could be so quick to anger the older he got, and she couldn't help shrinking back from him when he was in a barely controlled rage, though she did everything she could to hide it.

Worf had overheard this, home early one afternoon without his foster mother knowing it. He could still feel the shock, as if someone had knocked him into the icy winter waters of Chany lake. His mother was frightened of him? She was telling Captain Walch? Before he could recover, Jake told Helena that she wasn't imagining things—Klingons were naturally aggressive beings. That she shouldn't try to delude herself or Worf, but give him reasons to learn to control himself. Worf had run away, unable to listen to any more. He came home after dark to upset parents, but he couldn't bring himself to tell them what he'd heard.

What was worse—after that, whenever Helena was uneasy around Worf, she frankly told him. It had the effect she was looking for, though for different reasons. Worf couldn't bear the humiliation of remembering how she'd discussed her fears with Captain Walch, and would rather have swallowed his spiked burning rage and suffer silently than be reminded of that conversation when he'd been reduced to the level of a mindless, instinctive creature needing lessons on how to be civilized.

"Betrayed!" he barely whispered. He wanted to strike out and destroy, but all the walls and traps he'd carefully built to keep his aggression under control were triggered by this memory. He kept hearing the worry in his mother's voice. "Then and now, betrayed!"

"Worf, what's going on?" Jake was staring at him in concern, but he didn't come closer. "I didn't betray you. I always say even the Sli can't make you do what's not in you to do."

Lances of white-hot pain went through Worf's eyes. He wanted to kill—but he wasn't a barbarian. He made himself turn and staggered to the door, catching his shoulder against the frame.

"You used me," he growled out. With a sudden movement, he slammed his hand into the steel edge. The skin Dr. Crusher had bonded burst open, sending a splatter of blood against the wall. He gripped his wrist with his other hand, the pain steadying him. "You've destroyed my career! I had nothing to do with the explosion. The negligence is mine—but the blood is on your hands."

From the corner of his eye, he saw Walch reel back, his eyes wide with shock. "Worf, I didn't—"

Worf pushed himself through the door, leaving a smear of purple against the smooth surface.

Chapter Twenty-one

"THIS DELAY IS COSTING ME a great deal!" Daimon Brund protested to Captain Picard. "We'll both be stuck here until you get rid of those Sli."

Commander Riker was sitting forward in his chair, watching the tense exchange. Counselor Troi was standing slightly behind Captain Picard. She crossed her arms at the daimon's words and gave Riker a quick glance that conveyed her disbelief.

She ignored Brund, addressing the captain. "Killing the four Sli on board would stop the boomerang effect between the two groups. But it would be just as effective if Daimon Brund took the colonists away from this system."

"I told you, the Sli won't let me leave," Brund insisted, looking from one to the other. "Be reasonable, Captain. It's better to have four Sli dead than your crew in danger." His eyes narrowed. "The Sli are causing you problems, aren't they? Irritating your people, making them careless."

"Since you feel such concern for our welfare, why

don't you help us communicate with the Sli? Perhaps something could be worked out—"

"They're mad at you. They won't talk," Brund said, as if it were final. "You've only got one choice." He turned to one of his officers, hissing a command in Ferengi.

The interior of the Ferengi ship melted back into the starfield. Riker caught sight of the *Tampanium,* just moving past them in its orbit. The curved stern of the Marauder was enormous, vastly outmassing the defenseless *Prospector,* which was hanging just off their port.

"I don't believe him," Picard was saying thoughtfully.

"I don't either," Counselor Troi agreed.

"But what can we do about it?" Riker asked, joining them.

"Do?" Picard repeated. "Daimon Brund contacted us. Apparently something is being accomplished—he's becoming impatient. We will use that to our advantage." He nodded to them both. "I'll be in my ready room. You have the bridge, Number One."

Riker watched the captain leave, fighting back a sigh of frustration. "More waiting," he said under his breath.

"Try not to worry, Will," Deanna said.

Behind them, Ensign de Groodt announced, "Shuttlecraft *Voltaire* docking in the main shuttlebay."

Lieutenant Chryso turned from her science station at the news. They had discovered a glitch in one of the readings from the ground module a few hours ago and had sent Ensign Puckee down to investigate. The problem had grown worse as time passed, and just before Daimon Brund called, Puckee had informed them over the garbled communication line that she was returning to give them her assessment.

Riker ordered, "Tell Ensign Puckee to report to the bridge observation lounge immediately."

"Aye, sir."

With a sharp gesture to Lieutenant Chryso, Riker

turned away from Counselor Troi and strode toward the lounge. Inside, he hardly listened as Chryso began repeating an anxious summary of solutions her team had eliminated as possibilities. Riker already knew everything she was saying, and he answered her questions in monosyllables, knowing that she was also preoccupied with waiting for Ensign Puckee to arrive.

Puckee bounded into the room, her face alight with eager confidence. "Lieutenant Chryso, I found our problem!"

"Report, Ensign," Riker ordered.

"Sir," she said in belated acknowledgment. She held up her tricorder. "I ran a Level One diagnostic on the ground-based relay module. A fine layer of silty dust, slightly magnetized, has collected around some of the contact points. Apparently the high-speed winds that kick up around sunrise and sunset penetrated the few ventilation sites on the module. The damage is worse in those areas."

"Dirt?" Riker repeated incredulously. "How can that be?"

"Conditions are not normal down there," Puckee reminded him.

Riker remembered the amount of dust and particulates in the air and the condition of the soil. "Why weren't precautions taken?" he demanded.

"Precautions were taken," Puckee immediately replied, her tone absolutely certain without being disrespectful. "The situation on Lessenar is unique. However, I determined that a low-level static field would screen most of the dust without interfering with our research."

"Did you consider the effects on moisture readings?" Chryso asked.

"I've already thought of that," Puckee said. "We can run a remote link through the static field to relay any information that may be affected by the disruption."

Chryso frowned as she considered the implications. "This means we'll have to rerun all our calculations."

"Is it that serious?" Riker quickly asked.

"Every reading needn't be discounted," Puckee protested. "That's unwarranted."

"Caution in these matters is never unwarranted," Chryso insisted. "Everything we've collected for at least the past eight hours must be suspect."

"That would invalidate the first summation of the situation," Riker pointed out.

Chryso nodded. "Yes, it would."

"Isn't that overcompensating, Lieutenant?" Riker asked.

"I think so," Puckee burst in. "It's just not necessary. Until the contact was blocked, creating that glitch we noticed, the readings were correct. This isn't a situation that slowly deteriorated. Check the tricorder readings, if you'd like."

"There is no way to be absolutely certain of that," Chryso said. "This isn't an Academy science project, Ensign. It's essential that we arrive at a precise analysis, or we could be accessories to destroying an entire planet."

Chryso apparently took her decision as final. Riker silently considered both of them, wondering if he should overrule the Lieutenant. It was obvious that Chryso had become overly cautious due to the Sli, yet Ensign Puckee could be reacting hastily. Then there was the pressure from the Advisory Council for results.

"Discount the readings back to the first summation," he ordered. "Have your team start the next series of calculations as soon as the module is repaired."

Chryso looked up at him, her eyes wide in surprise. "Sir, I protest!"

"Noted." Riker turned to Puckee. "How long will it take to set up the static field?"

"Just as long as it takes to get a generator and get back

down there." Puckee clasped her hands behind her back. "The difficult part is cleaning the module. That will take at least an hour with a rarefaction unit."

"Damn," Riker muttered. La Forge was the man he'd usually send on a mission of this sort. But he was still down in Ten-Forward, deep in the sulks. Data had left not long ago to try to snap him out of it, but Riker didn't want to delay the repairs. "I'll send Ensign Barclay to perform the rarefaction. How was your pilot? Is he still functional?"

"I believe so, sir."

Riker wanted nothing more than to go with them down to the planet, but he had his orders from the captain to stay on board. "You'll leave immediately."

"Aye, sir." Puckee nodded to them both before rushing from the lounge.

Chryso rounded on Riker as soon as Puckee was gone. "I know you're in charge of coordinating this mission, but it's my duty to perform the scientific research. I cannot accept data from faulty equipment."

"Ensign Puckee is a technician as well as a scientist. She examined the unit. I can't entirely discount her recommendation." Riker held both hands up slightly, warning of what he was about to say. "You're being affected by the Sli, Lieutenant. You seem to feel a pervasive fear that something is going to go wrong, and you're overcompensating. It's paralyzing your entire research team."

Chryso drew herself up straighter, silenced for a moment. But she gazed steadily back at Riker. "Perhaps. But you know as well as I do that Ensign Puckee is reacting rather loosely and fast to this situation. Her judgment is not to be trusted." Chryso's eyes narrowed. "I also wonder about your judgment, Commander. You seem to feel that any course of action is better than none. Yet rather than commit yourself to either one of our recommendations, you've vacillated into a foolish compromise."

"Lieutenant," Riker said warningly, "return to your station, or I won't be able to ignore that remark."

She hesitated just long enough to make her point. "Aye, sir," she finally said in a light, falsely deferential tone.

Riker glared after her, his fists clenched. It didn't help that her shoulders were obviously drawn tight with tension.

The noise was getting louder in Ten-Forward as crew members arrived at the end of first shift despite yellow alert.

"I'm telling you, Data—go away."

Data gazed impassively down at La Forge. He considered acknowledging defeat and retreating at the stern rebuff, but Guinan had approved when he informed her that he intended to resolve the matter between himself and Geordi. Guinan was currently on the other side of the room, tending the customers at the counter, but when he glanced over, she was watching them. The faint smile on her face was sympathetic but unsurprised by Geordi's reaction. Data deduced that the reconciliation was proceeding normally.

He sat down stiffly, pulling his chair in close to the table. Usually he conformed to the behavior of humans, copying their actions depending upon the environment. But in his eagerness to speak with Geordi, he neglected to access his most treasured files.

"I am not offended by your behavior, Geordi."

La Forge clenched his hand around his glass. Data was forced to quickly assess the probability that his friend would throw the contents at him. Under the current conditions, it did not look favorable. He slid his chair back slightly.

"'Scuse me," a man drawled from behind him. "Mr. Data? You're the second officer, ain't you?"

Data turned to see the captain of the *Prospector*. Captain Walch appeared to be disturbed, shifting back and forth and raking his hand repeatedly through his straggling beard.

Data shifted his attention effortlessly. "Yes, sir, I am."

"Androids don't have emotions, do they?" Walch asked with narrowed eyes, as if seizing on something.

"No, sir," Data said patiently. Geordi managed to turn away from them both, staring into the wall.

"Good, I can talk to you," Walch told him. "Everyone else is crazy from the Sli. Him, too," Walch said, gesturing to Geordi. "Don't make no nevermind to me. *I* know you just gotta go with the flow in these things, but no one else seems to understand that. You sure you're not affected by them?"

"No, sir, I am not."

"It's all in the mind anyway," Walch confided. "But the mind is a powerful thing to tamper with."

Data considered the possibility that Captain Walch was being influenced by the Sli, yet according to his previous encounters, Walch's behavior fell well within set parameters.

"Is there something you wish to discuss?" Data asked.

"He's pretty far gone," Walch said about Geordi. But he glanced from side to side, checking to see if anyone else was near enough to hear him. He bent closer. "I got to tell someone. I'm in deep, but I can't be dragging in a good man like Worf."

"This concerns Lieutenant Worf?"

Walch nodded, easing off on the nervous clawing of his beard as he spoke. "Sergy and I did our part with the Klingons. I can't risk anything happening to hurt Worf. I don't care if I don't get my new ship—you can't blame Worf. He's an old friend, sure, but that don't mean he knew."

"What exactly is Lieutenant Worf unaware of?"

"That counselor of yours has been after me, asking all kinds of questions. Now, I don't hold no grudge against them Sli," Walch insisted, holding both hands up. "Don't get me wrong. But something's been bothering me about this whole thing. You see, I did sort of eject stuff from the ship—just like I always do when I dump the trash."

Geordi slowly turned his head, his mouth opening. "You're not supposed to do that! You were in orbit."

Walch grimaced in Geordi's direction, defensive. "Everyone does it! And this planet's so bad anyways, it's not the worst place I could dump the stuff."

"That's not the point," Geordi insisted. "You can't just leave your waste for others to clean up."

"If it's so important, why ain't the fine bigger?" Walch countered. "I never heard of any harm coming from a little trash disposal."

"Gentlemen, if I may interrupt," Data put in. "It is quite possible an explosive device was planted among the discarded refuse, thereby causing the damage to the *Prospector*. If we could determine what material was discarded," he finished, "we could then attempt to track the device to the being who planted it."

"Yeah, but how do we figure that out?" Geordi asked glumly.

Data thought about it a moment. "Captain, how did you dispose of the material?"

"An old intake airlock. What we used to bring samples in through."

Geordi was starting to nod. "Aren't those the type of cycling bins that scan the material as it's processed?"

Walch shuffled his feet. "I, ah, sorta cut the link to the computer logs."

"Well," Geordi asked, "was it the core memory you blocked or the subprocessor?"

"Core memory," Walch admitted. "I cut the link from the cycling bin to the optical data network."

Geordi smiled. "Then the memory chips in the control panel would still have the data from the scan. All we have to do is download the subprocessor."

Walch nodded, his blue eyes serious. "I was afraid the dumping had something to do with this mess. If you can get me a pressure suit, I'll show you which airlock I used."

Data stood up, tapping his communicator. "Commander Data to Captain Picard. I believe we may have the means to determine the origin of the explosion. However, Captain Walch and I would need to beam over to the *Prospector.*"

Picard's answer was quick. "Meet me in Transporter Room 2."

Data acknowledged as Geordi pushed himself up from his chair, carefully keeping his back to the view window. "If you're going to do a subprocessor download, you might need my help."

Data nodded. "Agreed." He gestured to Walch. "Come with us, please, Captain."

As they passed Guinan, Geordi said under his breath, "By the way, Data. Thanks."

Data nodded briefly to Guinan, then turned to his friend. "I do not wish for you to feel pain, Geordi." His voice was wistful. "Yet I have found the discovery of this aspect of your character to be most . . . exhilarating."

Deanna was sitting in the flight control booth, resting her chin on one hand and gazing at the moving colors of the Sli with what she knew must be a sappy smile pasted on her face. Her other hand was stroking the silky texture of her dress, letting the filmy fabric slip through her fingers as she savored its cool weight. She also kept sighing, then stretching long and hard like Data's cat after a warm nap.

She wanted to resist these feelings, but she had realized that blocking the emanations of the Sli made it harder to tell when the intervals of communication were coming. She had to force herself to relax and open her emotions to them, and even then she could only partially drop her shields. Still, she believed that the Sli were aware of what she was doing, because the frequency with which they were attempting to listen to her had risen sharply in the past few hours.

She frowned thinking of that, as she watched the colors of the Sli go through their intricate, slow-moving patterns. It was odd that their intent had not become any clearer despite their exchanges. She felt as if understanding was just within reach, yet her own inability to release the sensuality she usually restrained was somehow interfering with her concentration and focus.

"Counselor Troi, this is Captain Picard. Please meet me in Transporter Room 2."

Deanna's elbow slipped out from under her and she thrust her hands onto the panel, just catching herself from collapsing face-first into it. She'd been that deep in a trance over the Sli. Scrambling to her feet, feeling as if she had just woken up, she adjusted her dress and hair with small, swift movements. Ensign Saart was watching her carefully. Ensign Hassett wasn't paying any attention, as usual.

Picard's voice repeated, "Counselor Troi. Please respond."

"Yes, sir!" She gave her head a quick shake, trying to clear it. "I'm on my way, sir."

As she hurried toward the transporter room, she tried to reassemble her shields. It was almost impossible. The effects of the Sli seemed to form a wedge, keeping her from completely blocking the projections.

Captain Picard was standing in front of Captain Walch as the man completed the last fastenings on a gray and black low-pressure suit. Picard's arms were crossed, and he was examining the older man's reaction as he listened to Data's summary.

"—simple interface with the subprocessor using a tricorder. The computer system of the *Prospector* is compatible."

Geordi added, "Then we'd know exactly what objects were ejected and could compare the readings to known explosives."

Picard nodded in acknowledgment, then turned to Deanna to explain. "Captain Walch has confessed to ejecting a number of items from his ship in the form of refuse. Data believes that the explosive may have been among them."

From Picard's tone, Deanna immediately understood the reason he had called for her. He didn't know if he should trust Captain Walch or not. She turned her empathic concentration on Walch. "Why didn't you tell us about this earlier?"

The big man pushed his hood back as he slowly shook his head from side to side. "Honestly, folks, I didn't think of it right away. We always dumped out that lock. It weren't till the Federation started frowning on it that Pa cut the link to the computer logs." His magnetic boots clinked against the floor of the transporter room. "I only figured it out when you asked me, Counselor, if I'd had anything to do with the explosion—then it sorta hit me all at once. I dumped the garbage jus' after we went into orbit, and not more 'n an hour later came the explosion."

Deanna nodded. She remembered Walch had been surprised when she had asked him. Now it made sense. "Why didn't you say something then?"

Walch pursed his lips and shrugged, as if the answer was obvious. "Had to think on it a bit. Starfleet's against dumping, you know."

Deanna ducked her head to hide her expression. She wanted to remain professional. "Excuse me, Captain Walch, but frankly, there was something else you lied about during that conversation. When you said it was *your* idea to bring the Sli on board the starliner."

Walch squirmed a little, as if settling his suit. The delay grew noticeable before he finally looked up, squarely meeting her eyes. "Well, yep, Counselor. Sorry 'bout that. Really, I am." He struggled for a moment before bursting out with "But it jus' makes a better story that way!"

"Better story than what?"

"Than the truth," Walch admitted. Then he laughed shortly at himself. "Truth is, Hartog came to us. Oh, it didn't take much to convince me. Miriah looked into everything real good, and when she gave the go-ahead, I had them Sli installed in the cargo hold quicker than you can snap your fingers. Did wonders for the business. And Hartog's always given me the credit! He's that way, you know," Walch said, as if in an aside. "Sucking-up little frog, you ask me. But we always got along jus' fine."

Deanna was nodding. "So now you want to go over to the *Prospector* to find out what was in the trash?"

"We can pull it from the subprocessor memory," Walch told her.

Picard took a step forward, and without a trace of discomfort, directly asked, "Your opinion, Counselor?"

Deanna quickly checked Walch's reaction, but he didn't seemed bothered by the captain's abruptness. "I believe Captain Walch is telling the truth, sir."

Picard must have agreed, because he turned to Data. "Very well, then—make it so."

Data nodded briefly and stepped onto the transporter. Lieutenant La Forge and Captain Walch followed. Deanna held up her hand, saying, "Wait a moment, please." That was probably the quickest decision she'd ever seen the captain make. "Geordi, are you fit for an away team?"

She could tell Geordi didn't like suddenly being the center of attention, and his irritation rose sharply. But he just shrugged. "I don't see why not. I haven't been very easy to get along with, but Data said he likes it."

"You like it?" she asked Data, puzzled by the degree of Geordi's improvement.

The android's head was turned, partly obscuring one side of his face. "I cannot consider any emotion negative, Counselor."

From an android's point of view, it certainly made sense. Anyway, Geordi seemed satisfied, so Deanna went ahead and nodded to the transporter chief. She silently watched as they dematerialized.

Picard waited until he and Deanna were in the corridor before speaking again. "I'll delay Mon Hartog's request for the release of Worf's messages until this matter has been resolved. I'd like you to go update Lieutenant Worf. Determine if he can be returned to duty."

Deanna took a deep breath. "Yes, sir."

The away team materialized in the *Prospector*'s main transporter room. As the two men composed themselves, Data initiated a subprogram in his memory banks. Since this was his second visit to the *Prospector*, the program would make a running comparison between his original analysis and the data he was currently gathering. Any deviations would be noted and immediately shunted to a process node for action.

His tricorder reading was consistent with the first contact, and Data repeated his earlier warning word for word. "The fluctuations in the gravity field vary from 1.23g to 0.74g. The microgyros in your suits will compensate, but there could be a delay of up to two milliseconds."

Geordi grimaced at Data, then shook his head silently. Data quickly concluded that Geordi's reaction was deviant and chose to ignore it. But he carefully filed the incident for later study.

"This way!" Walch called, already walking past the fountain. "It's on Deck 6, all the way t' the fore."

During the turbolift ride, Data again observed the adverse reactions both Geordi and Captain Walch experienced due to the gravity fluctuations. However, he refrained from comment.

The ejection port that Walch used for disposal was in a maintenance access corridor adjacent to the bridge. The long, narrow room was lined with racks that were filled with equipment and spare parts in various stages of decay. The ancient airlock was in the end wall, with a scarred metal table in front. It was about one meter square with molded edges that jutted from the bulkhead.

"There she is, boys." Walch made his way through the debris with practiced ease. "This here's the controls."

Geordi was none too steady yet, and he stumbled into a condenser unit while following Data to the airlock. Data offered assistance, which Geordi brushed aside, so he began performing a routine sensor sweep with his tricorder, leaving the computer interface to Geordi.

"Don't access the files yet," Geordi told Walch, preparing his equipment. He inserted a remote device into the input slot. It only took a few moments before the link was ready. "All right. Now you can."

Captain Walch entered the command on a small, slanted keyboard. There was a significant pause before the information appeared on the tiny screen.

"Recording," Geordi announced, monitoring the phase tracking. "There, that should be it."

Suddenly Data's tricorder picked up unusual transmission activity in the area. He established a remote link to Geordi's tricorder, circuitously patching himself through to the computer subprocessor of the *Prospector*.

Analyzing the information, Data announced, "Junction link to the ship's optical data network is transmitting data across the subspace boundary layer."

237

"What?" Geordi quickly glanced at Walch. "I thought you said you cut the link to the ODN."

"I did." Walch immediately brushed Geordi aside, and with a hand probe he pried open the panel. "Let's see here . . ." With the probe, he poked inside. Data was about to offer his assistance when Walch said, "Wait a gosh darn—this ain't my work! The link's been reconnected. And there's a transmitter chip here in between—"

Data rapidly drew several conclusions. "To the bridge!" he ordered.

With the ODN now connected, Data had direct access to the ship's computer through his tricorder. By the time he reached the *Prospector*'s Ops station, he had intercepted the command series that was being rapidly transmitted to the computer. He quickly confirmed his findings, even as Walch and Geordi finally arrived on the bridge, left behind him in his dash.

"Data!" Geordi exclaimed, out of breath. "What's going on?"

"The accelerator/generator of the impulse engine has been instructed to power up," Data informed them without looking up. "I am attempting to override."

Geordi immediately went to the engineering station. "We're in trouble. Impulse reaction chambers are already powered up, providing partial energy to the ship's distribution net."

"The initial command is write-protected. I am unable to override," Data informed them. "Impulse power in thirty-seven seconds."

Walch was sweating, gasping for air. "Without structural integrity, the ship'll be crushed."

Data was already determining the status of the structural integrity field. "I am unable to establish a coherent network of forcefield segments." He hit his comm badge. *"Enterprise,* this is Commander Data."

The captain immediately replied, "Picard here."

"Sir, the *Prospector*'s impulse engines are set on an automatic engage sequence. We will enter impulse propulsion in thirty-one seconds. Structural integrity is compromised."

Through the communicator, they heard Captain Picard issue an order to the transporter chief to beam them back on board the *Enterprise*.

Data was aware of what would happen if the *Prospector* engaged impulse power under current conditions. Without the structural integrity field, the human body could not withstand accelerations in excess of 3g. Impulse drive would immediately take them to 500g and beyond. His own skeletal mainframe might survive such acceleration; however, the resulting compression explosion of the *Prospector* would undoubtedly disintegrate his components.

Data waited a moment, but when they didn't dematerialize, he checked his deduction with the computer. "Irregular gravity bleed is interfering with transporter functions. The *Enterprise* is unable to lock on."

"We'll never get out in time," Walch shouted.

Geordi was still working at the engineering station. "I'm trying to shut off the deuterium to the reaction chambers."

Data shook his head. "There is a sufficient pulsed fusion shock front already built up in the reaction chamber. High-energy plasma will be exhausted into the accelerator in twenty-two seconds."

Geordi hit the control panel with the palm of his hand. "Damn! Are you sure the command can't be overridden?"

Walch quickly cleared his throat. "Computer, this is Alpha clearance, code Peristroika Walch, 079–2867."

The computer responded, "Voice verification confirmed."

"Deactivate impulse accelerator," Walch ordered.

"Working," the computer said in a monotone female

voice. "Unable to comply. Activation of impulse engine generator in sixteen seconds."

Geordi hit the panel again, this time harder.

"Mr. Data," Captain Picard informed them. "The radiation is preventing us from getting a positive transporter lock. What is your status?"

"Situation unchanged, sir. Impulse power in twelve seconds."

"I've got it!" Geordi suddenly swung toward him. "Data, initiate the secondary mode in the matter-antimatter reaction core! That'll begin the power-up sequence to create a warp field."

"Geordi, entering warp will also create intolerable stress on the structural framework."

"But," Geordi said, quickly closing the few steps between them, "warp is the default choice in the software routines. The computer will have to shut the impulse engines down to keep them from conflicting with warp fields. There's no command blocking the matter-antimatter reaction chamber, so we'll be able to shut that down."

Data understood even before Geordi had finished and began entering the command. "Power-up sequence engaged. Engine pressure in the reaction chamber is rising to forty-five thousand kilopascals. The MRI and ARI nozzles are open."

"Come on," Geordi murmured.

Data checked the countdown. "Three seconds to impulse generator activation. Two seconds—"

Geordi leaned forward. Walch was holding his breath.

"Impulse accelerator/generator off-line," Data calmly announced. "Diverting energetic plasma to the EPS taps. Deactivating secondary reaction mode of the warp core."

Geordi pushed away from the control panel, reeling back. He almost didn't make it to a chair in time to sit down.

As Data completed the power-down sequence of the

warp power generation and set a lock on the impulse accelerator/generator, he noted that both Captain Walch and Geordi were experiencing severe reactions. Data had observed similar agitation in humans before, following incidents of extreme danger, and he didn't allow their behavior to interfere with securing the *Prospector*. However, he did gather a great deal of empirical data regarding their physiological responses, and routed the information to his personal files. He knew Geordi wouldn't mind.

Chapter Twenty-two

DEANNA HESITATED outside Worf's door. The dull orange surface was exactly the same as the other doors spaced along the corridor—but behind this one lay Worf's quarters. The few times she had entered, the ruddy lamps and the rich smell of leather had always brought to mind ancient times of flashing swords and torchlight, despite the curved bulkheads and familiar shape of the rooms.

She sighed out loud, knowing that she was here under captain's orders rather than her own decision. She'd been avoiding a direct confrontation with Worf, but now she had no choice.

The only thing that made her feel better was the ease with which she'd been able to read Captain Walch in the transporter room. That interview tended to confirm she was much less disoriented than before.

Still, she had left the captain without telling him about the possibility that the crew should stop resisting the Sli. She wasn't certain yet, and she couldn't ask him to trust her unless she was confident her theory was on target.

242

Abruptly the door slid aside and Worf filled the opening. He was glaring down at her.

She hadn't touched the panel for access. "Worf!"

"Why do you lay in wait at my door?" he demanded.

Flustered, she gestured to the panel. "I was about to call." She waited, but he didn't move aside. "May I come in, Worf?"

Worf stepped aside, shaking his head at himself and putting a hand briefly to the waistband of his uniform.

"Everyone's being affected, Worf." Deanna didn't sit down, because Worf made it clear he would remain standing. "Where's Alexander?"

"He is with a friend. I believed since I had been relieved of duty . . ." Worf started formally, but he had to break off. He didn't meet her eyes, and there was a faint sheen of sweat on his face. The muscles of his jaw were twitching even though he was obviously trying to remain calm.

"Worf." Her voice was kind. "I came to tell you that we believe we know how the explosive was launched. Captain Walch ejected refuse from the *Prospector*. He, Data, and Geordi have gone over to find out if the explosive was among the items."

Worf drew in his breath, a long hiss. "Walch did cause the explosion!"

Deanna quickly shook her head. "He didn't know what he was doing—I can tell. Someone may have planted a bomb among the trash, but Captain Walch didn't have anything to do with it other than inadvertently putting it into space. I'm sure of that."

Worf's fist tightened and he stiffly took a few steps away. "I cannot trust him." Then he winced, placing his hand to his stomach.

Deanna reached after him in concern, but he quickly dropped his hands to his sides and straightened up. Raising his chin with a slight jerk revealed the effort behind his stance.

"Worf, what's wrong with you?"

"Nothing." When she came right to his side, he added insistently, "I am in control, Counselor."

"I don't care about control." She noted the strain around his eyes, the difficulty he had standing up, and the way his eyes seemed to glaze over, then clear, as if waves of pain were going through him. "It's physical, isn't it?"

"It will pass." He was trying not to move.

"For pity's sake, Worf!" She distantly recognized her words as an expression of Lwaxana's, but they seemed particularly apt right now. "Why didn't you call sickbay? You're in pain, aren't you? It's from the turmoil the Sli are causing in you."

"Emotions!" Worf ground out, as if he were shaking off a slime nit.

"Come lie down," Deanna told him, trying to take his arm.

He resisted. "I cannot give in. Response must be controlled. Desire must be resisted. Aggression harnessed—" He clenched his teeth together, silently trying to withstand another surge of pain.

She pushed him toward the couch, using more force when he tried to hold back. "There is a physical reason for this pain," she tried to tell him. When he didn't seem to hear, she raised her voice, pulling on him harder. "Listen to me, Worf! It's a medical fact that digestion is directly linked to emotions. You've got spasms in your muscles—this is not the time to tough it out! Lying down slows your intestinal activity."

She pushed him onto the couch, where he lay glaring up at her. But after a few moments his face eased slightly.

She pulled up a chair. "Did you take anything for it?"

Sullenly he nodded.

"Then just relax." She sighed and leaned back. "I've told you you're too hard on yourself. You can't always be in control."

"I struggled for my honor." He sounded much better.

"We all have our weaknesses we grapple with." Her own was hanging rather vividly before her eyes right now. It was the image of Lwaxana and the late-blooming Betazoid sexuality. Deanna feared that she would lose all sense of propriety and begin indulging herself as shamelessly as her mother when she grew older. She shook off the thought, smiling reassuringly at Worf. "But don't you feel better lying down?"

She didn't hear Worf's reply—her own words seemed to echo inside of her. That was the key to the Sli. Worf was resisting with everything he had, and it was actually affecting him physically. Tarses had been resisting and he'd cut his own ear—but once he dealt with what he was feeling, he was able to start helping everyone else down in sickbay. And Data, too. He had accepted Geordi's behavior and thereby allowed Geordi to accept it himself.

"That's it!" She herself had been resisting the specter of Lwaxana in herself, and that was the last bit of static that was interfering with her understanding of the Sli. "I've got it, Worf!"

He shook his head slightly, not understanding.

"The Sli," she told him. "Don't you see? We have to stop resisting them. If we allow ourselves to feel the emotion that their projections bring out, then it will pass away quickly. Resisting them sets up a sort of feedback loop inside of us, triggering the emotion over and over."

Worf pushed himself up. "We cannot give in to them!"

"Don't you see, that's the only way to beat them."

Worf swung his legs over the couch, grimacing as he moved. His voice was low and grim. "The barbarian will not be released."

"Worf." She tried to stop him from getting up. "You have to stay lying down. You've got to accept that you're feeling this way. Own it, don't fight it."

"Am I still relieved of duty?" he asked, abruptly meeting her eyes.

She blinked a couple of times, not liking what she saw in his closed expression. "Yes. I want you to lie back down."

He tightened his lips, his eyes blazing as if he were going to challenge her authority.

Her communicator chittered, then Captain Picard's voice said, "Counselor Troi, please come to the lounge. The away team has brought back evidence to suggest that Mon Hartog was responsible for the explosion. I need your input on breaking this to the Sli."

Worf was on his feet, a growl rumbling deep in his throat. "Hartog accused me!"

"Hartog!" Deanna repeated to Picard in complete disbelief. "Are you sure?"

"We are attempting to determine that," the captain replied curtly.

She realized she was discussing this over the channel. "I'll be right there."

"And Lieutenant Worf . . . ?" asked the captain.

"Counselor—" Worf demanded.

"Worf is still relieved of duty," she interrupted flatly. She glanced up at him, standing there quivering in rage and pain. "Medical reasons."

"Very well," Picard acknowledged.

Worf glared at her. "Hartog attacked a crew member—"

Deanna held out her hands. "No, Tarses cut himself with the knife. He admitted it to me. Mon Hartog is no longer under guard."

Worf seemed to swell with anger. But Deanna just pointed to the couch. "Lie down, Worf. We'll deal with Mon Hartog."

Picard signed off with the counselor, returning his attention to Data and Geordi, who were standing just inside the doorway. Commander Riker was slumped silently in one of the chairs, his chin near his chest and his feet out. Picard chose to pace at the head of the table, from the window back to Data and Geordi, as he considered the new information.

Data held out a transmitter chip. "This chip created the link between the subprocessor and the optical data network. It also contained the command to proceed to impulse power."

"Origin?" Picard inquired.

"It is Ferengi hardware," Data told him.

"And we got a record of the software command, sir," Geordi told him. "That also looks Ferengi, but the computer's not done analyzing it yet."

Picard nodded, trying to cover every angle. "Did you retrieve the scan of the ejected material?"

"Aye, sir," Geordi told him, glancing down at his tricorder. "That's the most interesting of all. Each item was compared to known bomb configurations—from the empty atmospheric supply modules to half a dozen cracked copper-yttrium hard lines. The only thing that could possibly have contained an explosive was a power cell for the Sli's life support unit."

"The Sli?" Picard broke off his pacing. "They only use Ferengi equipment."

"That's right," Geordi told him. "And isn't it a coincidence that a scan of the power cell reads very similar to a Ferengi-style explosive?"

"Apparently all avenues of inquiry lead straight back to Mon Hartog."

Data nodded agreement, his brows raised. "In addition, planting an explosive device among refuse to be illegally ejected could also be considered typical of Ferengi practices—"

He broke off as Counselor Troi came in behind them. She had to slip between Data and Geordi to get into the lounge. "So it was Mon Hartog himself who tried to kill the Sli?"

Picard flared one hand. "There seems to be a cascade of evidence against him."

"Well, I don't think Captain Walch did it." Troi shook back her hair. "But Hartog lives off the Sli. Why would he want to hurt them? He has nothing to gain by causing all this."

"However, if Hartog is involved in something much larger than a concert tour, that would explain a great deal." The current status of Federation/Sli/Ferengi inter-relations was uppermost in Picard's mind. "Perhaps his true goal is to perpetuate hostilities between the Federation and the Sli."

Geordi nodded. "The Ferengi do depend on the fuel the Sli colonies produce. And they do believe it's best to hold a monopoly on the market."

"This would explain the deceit I keep sensing in Mon Hartog," Troi agreed. "It could also be the reason why he's been spreading rumors and instigating discord among the crew."

"If Mon Hartog is attempting to provoke a negative reaction on the *Enterprise,* he is achieving his goal," Data informed the captain. "Currently, eight percent of the crew has been relieved of duty. An additional eleven percent did not report to their duty shift."

"That's one fifth of my crew."

"I wonder if it was the last diplomatic team Starfleet sent to Qizan Qal'at that worried the Ferengi," the counselor put in.

"Perhaps," the captain agreed. "The Ferengi Alliance thought they were losing their monopoly of the Sli, so they sent a few groups out simply in order to create as disagreeable a situation as they could. They might have hoped the Federation would reclassify the Sli as dangerous, perhaps even nonsentient, and give up attempts at contact."

"The alliance would have the means to do something on this scale," said Geordi.

Troi glanced around the group. "If that's true, then Daimon Brund must also be a part of it. I'm sure he brought that Sli colony here deliberately, and it makes sense if he did it just to make the situation worse for us."

Picard looked at her sharply. "He claims that the Sli forced him to come here."

"I don't believe the Ferengi can communicate with the Sli any better than we can, sir. I've seen no evidence of it." She shook her head to show what she felt about that. "After working with the Sli, I find it hard to believe that they could give Daimon Brund these coordinates and insist on being brought here. That isn't the way the Sli think."

Riker slowly sat forward, his brow furrowed. "Maybe telling the Sli about Hartog will direct their attention back where it belongs—on the Ferengi instead of us."

"That's just it," Troi protested. "I don't think the Sli *can* direct their emanations, whether they're angry or not. From what I've seen, their projections are releasing suppressed emotions in everyone on board—including Mon Hartog! Only he isn't being bothered as much because he allows himself to express his feelings. The crew members who are being affected the most are the ones who are working the hardest to deny their impulses."

"Intriguing," Data said. "That would explain the wide range of intensity in the reactions of the crew."

Troi was nodding. "That's also why the children aren't being affected like the adults—they naturally have less control over their reactions anyway. Inner turbulence, especially in the teenagers, is fairly natural for them. They just absorb what the Sli are projecting, never really noticing or fighting it." She took a step closer to Picard, as if wanting to convince him. "But when we resist certain impulses, as we've all learned to do, it sets up a boomerang effect, whipping the emotion back to the Sli, who amplify it and return it."

Picard said thoughtfully, "The harder you fight, the worse it gets."

"The ones who aren't resisting—like Captain Walch—seem to be able to ride the emotional swings without much difficulty."

Picard took in her flushed face and ruffled hair, and he couldn't help wondering if her judgment was sound. Just as he'd wondered about Guinan—who had claimed there was no reasoning with the Sli.

"May I point out, sir," Data said, almost echoing his thoughts, "the Sli are currently affecting both yourself and Counselor Troi. The degree of those effects is unknown."

"I'm right about this," Troi insisted.

"If I am correct, Counselor," Data demurred, "the area in which you are experiencing emotional imbalance involves the release of . . . inhibitions?"

The counselor swallowed, nervously glancing around. Picard kept his expression quite still.

Data continued smoothly. "If so, then you would naturally conclude that the crew should indulge themselves in the emotional stimulus provided by the Sli. Is that not true, Counselor?"

Troi stared at Data, not moving. All eyes were on her, and she knew it.

The silence drew out for several heartbeats, then Troi drew herself up, lifting her chin to directly meet the captain's gaze. "I'm quite certain my recommendation is correct, sir. Data's concern is the very reason I distrusted this solution, and instead suggested that we resist. But every indication points to acceptance as the way to cope with the Sli's projections."

Geordi softly added, "I can agree with that, Counselor."

She nodded back at him. "Not just Geordi. Look at

what's been happening. The concerts were usually a success because the people expected to be moved by the Sli and welcomed it. Since there were only five Sli, they weren't very powerful, and besides, there were mostly pleasurable emotions on the starliner. Not until the explosion, when the tourists and crew became frightened, with their lives completely disrupted, did the Sli react. Then they simply amplified that initial emotional surge back to us, and our resistance made the return wave even stronger, back and forth. The arrival of the colonists escalated everything out of control." Her voice was firm. "Sir, for some people it will be very difficult to accept the feelings the Sli have awakened in them, but it's our only option to try."

Picard felt an answering accord that did more to alert him than reassure him. He knew full well that Data's argument could be used for him as well. He had become more reckless under the influence of the Sli, quicker to take action based on intuitive feeling rather than waiting for facts. It could be this same urge for abandon that pressed him to agree with Troi.

But before he could respond, the computer signaled a communication. "Captain Picard, this is Simon Tarses. We have a problem down here outside of Shuttlebay 3."

"What is it?" Picard demanded.

"Sir, Mon Hartog's been strangled."

Chapter Twenty-three

WORF PACED UP AND DOWN the length of the room several times. His anger was strong enough to supplant the pain in his gut. Mon Hartog, assassin, left unguarded! The idea was unendurable. Orders or no, his primary duty to the safety of the *Enterprise* and her crew would not allow him to sit idly by as a known assassin freely roamed the ship.

"Computer, location of Mon Hartog!"

The impassive voice of the computer answered, "Mon Hartog is currently in the flight control booth of Shuttlebay 3."

Worf snarled quietly. The Ferengi was provoking the Sli, worsening the situation on board. He would not allow that.

He moved through the corridors with single-minded purpose, ignoring the chaotic activity of crew members. But as he approached the shuttlebay, he noticed Technician Tarses in the doorway of the access tube. The part-Romulan nervously looked both ways before quickly ducking inside.

Tarses hadn't seen him. Worf silently made his way to

the access tube, alerted by the technician's furtive manner.

Inside the tube, Tarses was crouched in front of a control interface. Worf barely had time to note that it was the manual release of the exterior space doors as Tarses disconnected the safety and quickly manipulated the locking mechanism.

Worf threw himself forward.

He slammed Tarses into the side of the tube and was jolted away. With one easy motion, Worf grabbed the technician and flipped him away from the control panel. Tarses let out a loud cry as he hit the floor of the tube, twisting to get away from Worf's reach.

Worf looked down at the panel. Only one more command was left to open the exterior doors of the shuttlebay containing the four Sli. The annular forcefield was disengaged, so the bay would immediately depressurize.

"They have to die!" Tarses insisted, breathless. "We're being destroyed!"

Blowing the doors had been Worf's suggestion. His hand hesitated over the panel.

"Do it!" Tarses urged.

Worf drew his hand back, shaking. Suddenly he felt the pain shooting through his stomach. "No. The captain would not allow it."

Frantic, Tarses stared up at him. "You have to! Sickbay is in turmoil. The crew is suffering—in terrible pain. And what about those people on the planet! They have no hope except for us. You can't let this continue!"

Keeping tight control of his own hands, Worf carefully engaged the safety, clearing the command sequence from the panel. "It is not our decision."

With a drawn-out moan, Tarses collapsed back. Worf rechecked the control panel, and when he was certain it was normal, he took hold of Tarses' arm and hauled him along after him. "Come with me," he ordered.

At the round opening of the tube, Worf paused when he heard voices. Motioning Tarses to keep quiet, he carefully looked out.

"Please, Captain Walch, you must be mistaken." The Ferengi was backing away from the big captain, holding his palms up as he whined his innocence.

"I'd shove you out an airlock, but that's too quick for my taste." Walch's tone was deadly, and he advanced on Hartog, slowly closing the distance. "You destroyed my pa's ship, you little maggot. You thought to kill me, too, rigging that impulse command! Well, you missed. Now you get what you deserve."

"I don't understand!" Hartog wailed, trying to fight off Walch, hitting at him with his open hands and trying to wrench away.

"Save your breath," Walch hissed.

He snatched up the Ferengi with both hands around his scrawny neck and lifted him until his feet kicked at the air. Hartog let out an astonished chocking sound, his face immediately turning red as he grabbed ineffectually at Walch's hands.

Worf was motionless, mesmerized by the attack. Every instinct was in complete agreement with Walch's actions. Hartog had killed. Hartog had also seriously disrupted the crew and attacked Worf's very honor. The Ferengi should die slowly for his crimes . . .

Hartog's struggles were lessening. His eyes were bugged out whitely and he reached forward to try to scratch Walch's face.

"He's killing him!" Tarses exclaimed, peering under Worf's arm.

Snapped out of his fierce gratification at the sight, Worf gave Tarses a startled look.

"You're letting him?" Tarses asked, his tone more admiring than doubtful.

Convulsions rolled through Worf's stomach, making

him want to double over. Sweat broke out on his palms. He struggled deeply with his own desires.

"Stop!"

The word burst out of him, releasing him. He stumbled out of the access tube toward Walch.

"Die!" Walch spit at Hartog, giving him a hard shake.

"No!" Worf ordered, grabbing hold of Walch's wrists. Walch wouldn't let go. Worf had to use most of his strength to separate the older man's arms. Finally the Ferengi dropped to the floor, disregarded.

Worf kept hold of Walch's arms as the captain glared at him. "What are you doing, Worf! Let me go!"

"You cannot kill him!"

"Watch me!" He struggled against Worf. "He deserves to die."

"You almost did it," Tarses said, kneeling beside the Ferengi. But Hartog's horrible, rasping gasps were enough to tell Worf that he would survive.

Reluctant to let go of the incensed man, Worf told Tarses, "Contact Captain Picard."

Deanna was trembling. She wanted to stop, but she knew the Sli emanations were strengthening. If she fought it, her reaction would intensify.

"Is he alive?" Picard demanded.

"Barely, sir."

"Who's there with you?" Picard asked.

"Sir," came Tarses's hesitant voice, "Captain Walch, the Ferengi, and Lieutenant Worf."

Deanna suddenly had the most terrifying thought. Klingons preferred the hands-on method of assassination. Had Worf tried to kill Mon Hartog because of his attempt to dishonor him? Or was it Tarses himself? For a moment, she truly believed that under the influence of the Sli, Tarses had become more Romulan than she'd ever dreamed possible and had tried to kill Mon Hartog.

Picard tilted his head. "Mr. Worf is supposed to be confined to quarters. Did he understand that order?"

Deanna slowly nodded. "I believe so, sir." She didn't like it. Here she was recommending to the captain that the crew accept the Sli's emotional prodding, when the last two people she'd advised to do so were now involved in an attempted murder.

"Lieutenant Worf, is your situation under control?"

There was a slight pause before Worf answered. "Aye, sir. We will proceed to sickbay. Hartog requires immediate medical attention."

"Very well," Picard acknowledged. "Picard out."

He turned and gazed out the window to where the Ferengi Marauder was lurking. The others silently waited, all looking to him.

When he turned back, there was a gleam in his eye. "That ship has to go."

Without another word, Picard strode through his senior officers and stepped onto the bridge. Peripherally he saw them scatter to their stations, while he took up a stance in the middle of the floor, facing the main viewer.

"Sir, I have Daimon Brund," Ensign de Groodt announced.

Picard drew a deep breath, smiling slightly without meaning to. "On screen."

"Picard!" Brund spat out, thrusting his face closer.

"Daimon Brund, we have new information regarding our investigation."

Picard saw that he'd caught the Ferengi's attention, but the daimon merely shrugged. "What do I care about investigations?"

"I believe you will be interested in this." Picard paused, knowing how it tantalized the Ferengi when someone else knew more than they did. It was almost a compulsion for them to drag out secrets.

He didn't misjudge the daimon. The Ferengi waited as long as he could, actually turning away at one point as he took care of some task. Picard stood silently with his hands behind his back.

Gradually the daimon let out a few impatient grumbles and sighs, finally demanding, "Yes? Yes? What is it? If you're going to tell me, get on with it!"

Picard smiled slightly. "You appear to be agitated, Daimon. Perhaps you're experiencing some effects from the Sli?"

"No!" Brund immediately denied. His head swayed, and he licked his lips carefully. "The Sli have no reason to be angry with us."

"I say you are being affected." Picard was satisfied. The daimon's denial had the ring of a rehearsed line. "You claim the Sli can direct their emanations—so perhaps they are already aware of my news."

Brund glared at him. "What is it already!"

"It does appear more likely, however," Picard said, ignoring his question, "that the Sli affect everyone, the degree being determined by how much resistance one puts up. Wouldn't you agree, Daimon? Perhaps you've sensed the escalations of the Sli's projections yourself?"

The daimon didn't want to commit himself, but his eyes were squinting almost closed and he opened his mouth several times as if about to speak, then closed it again.

"Yes, Daimon Brund, I do believe you are under pressure from the Sli." Picard nodded to himself.

Brund was almost ready to explode. "So what! What does it matter? Did you find out anything or not?"

As if he'd just been waiting for Brund to ask, Picard said smoothly, "We have discovered that the explosion was caused by a bomb disguised as a power cell for a life support unit. A Ferengi life support unit, made especially for the Sli. It was this explosive that homed in on the Sli when it was ejected from the ship, causing the damage to the *Prospector.*"

"Who ejected it?" Brund quickly asked.

257

Picard raised one brow. "Who ejected it? Who brought it on board the ship? Who had it made in the first place with this intent in mind?" He stepped forward. "I do believe the last question is the most important, Daimon Brund."

The daimon's eyes suddenly began to shift back and forth. "Where is Mon Hartog? I want to speak to him."

"It's interesting that Hartog's name should come up at this moment."

"He should be here!" Brund insisted.

"Even if it was he who engineered this entire situation?"

Brund was stuck for a couple of beats, then he gave a barking, sneering laugh. "Hartog? I think not. Let me speak with him!"

"With him?" Picard repeated, catching that nuance of familiarity. "I've wondered what incentive Hartog could possibly have to destroy his own profit-making ensemble. Yet if the Ferengi Alliance was backing him, he'd be amply rewarded for his efforts—"

"Baseless accusations!" Brund burst out. "I will not discuss this further until Mon Hartog is present!"

"That won't be possible," he told Brund. "Mon Hartog has been seriously injured."

"What?" The daimon seemed dumbstruck. "How?"

This was the question Picard had hoped to receive. "Random violence, provoked by the Sli."

Brund nervously licked his lips, glancing at the yellow lights flashing over Picard. "You're all going insane over there, aren't you?"

Counselor Troi shifted as if to alert him. Picard held out a hand, silently watching Brund.

The daimon grabbed the back of a chair with one hand, pointing the other to Picard. "I have an idea!" he said desperately. "Transport those four Sli to my ship. Maybe then the Sli colony will let me go."

Picard glanced at Troi. "Abandoning the original

request." His tone was speculative. "It appears that Mon Hartog also preferred these Sli were destroyed rather than fall into Starfleet's hands. Now, why is it both of you want that?"

"I don't know anything about a bomb!" Brund denied. "Or Hartog. What is he to me?" Brund looked from one to the other before tossing them another tidbit. "You're right about one thing—we're being affected as much as you are." A hand sneaked up to wipe the moisture from his neck. "Be reasonable, Captain. Maybe if we unite the Sli, we'll both be free to leave here."

"That's unacceptable," Picard told him.

"The suffering of both our crews is on your hands, Picard." Brund turned to one of his officers, hissing a command in Ferengi. The view abruptly returned to the derelict *Prospector* with the green-swathed planet beyond.

Picard immediately turned to the counselor. "I don't believe Brund can communicate with the Sli."

"I don't either, Captain."

"Yet you've managed to make preliminary contact?"

"It's just that I have to get beyond the emotions they provoke in me. I will have to open myself completely."

"Can you do that?"

"It's difficult to tell where that will take me. You see, the basis for their language isn't made up of word-symbols like ours, but is comparable to being dragged along in an emotional torrent, with the meanings emerging and submerging in the patterns."

"Do you think you could convey what we discovered about the explosion, letting them know the Ferengi may have betrayed them?"

She looked doubtful, chewing her lip for a moment. "They don't operate under the law of cause and effect. Emotions are simply emotions to them, nothing negative, nothing logical."

Frustrated, Picard paced back to his chair, tapping the

fingers of one hand against his thigh. Guinan had told him it was impossible to reason with the Sli.

"What do the Sli want?" Riker suddenly spoke up, sitting heavily in his chair.

"I believe they're stimulated by us," Troi told him. "From what I've learned so far, it's the only thing the Sli are getting from all this. Humans seem to be a strong and constant source of emotional fuel."

Riker frowned. "If fresh emotional stimulus is all they want, then the Sli on the Ferengi vessel won't want to leave no matter what we do."

There was a tense pause after his words. Then Picard slowly looked up, realizing the error in their reasoning. "But it's not really important what the Sli want, is it? What matters is what the Ferengi want."

"Sir?" Troi asked.

"Daimon Brund could leave anytime he wishes. If he can't communicate with the Sli, how are they keeping him here? He's staying here until we relinquish control of the Sli—either by killing them or turning them over to him. The last thing the alliance would want is Sli left on board the *Enterprise.*"

"The daimon is very worried about the situation," Troi said doubtfully. "He is afraid things are escalating out of control."

That was exactly what he was looking for. Picard smacked his hands together, making both Riker and La Forge start at the sharp sound. "As long as Daimon Brund believes we're able to talk to the Sli, that's all we need. Ensign," he said to the tactical officer, "be ready to patch Daimon Brund into the viewer in Shuttlebay 3."

"Sir?" Riker asked, standing up. "You're going to try to talk to the Sli?"

"The Sli are just my messengers, Number One. Right now it's Daimon Brund I'm trying to reach. That Sli colony has to leave before everyone on board the *Enterprise* goes mad."

On their way down to the shuttlebay, Deanna suggested that the captain change out of his dark red and black uniform. "It indicates intense greed or desire, sir. And I think the red has something to do with envy or shame."

Picard gave her a tight grin. "Perhaps the Ferengi are also aware of the significance of color to the Sli, Counselor. If so, then Daimon Brund will think that's exactly the message I'm trying to give them."

"Captain, I thought Starfleet wanted us to establish diplomatic ties with the Sli."

Picard paused in front of the access door to the flight control room, looking at her for a moment. "We'll be able to do that once that colony group is gone and these four Sli are safe."

When they walked in, Deanna could tell the security guards were uncomfortable wearing their pastel garb in front of the captain. Both stared straight at the wall.

The Sli were breathtaking. She'd never seen them like this before. The muddy smears were gone, leaving brightly colored flakes swirling and tumbling across the surface of their skin. Ruby red, glowing aqua, and sapphire facets churned together, along with brighter yellow, rose, and powder blue chips. Their tentacles were gold, opaque and shining. Deanna wondered whether her many attempts to reach them had somehow brought them to this state.

Picard gave the Sli a searching look. "What was their reaction to the explosion?"

Deanna tightened her fingers in her skirt. "That's just it—they feel everything! Any emotion you can imagine, they experience it and emanate it. Which in turn stimulates that emotion inside anyone who's susceptible to it.

Our translator gives us the humanoid reasons we assign to our emotional responses—we're upset because we'll miss the person that died, we're indifferent because we didn't care about that person—but there's no real way of knowing why the Sli feel the way they do."

Picard pressed the point. "Are they trying to communicate with us right now?"

"No," she said reluctantly.

The captain raised his head slightly. "No matter. Perhaps I'll get their attention as I go along. The stronger emanations would serve to convince Brund."

Deanna silently shook her head, not sure what the captain had in mind.

"Ensign de Groodt, this is Captain Picard. Put me through to Daimon Brund."

"Daimon Brund, sir," the ensign immediately announced. The small screen in the side wall flickered on. Daimon Brund took one look at the captain and reached forward as if about to disconnect the link when he saw the Sli behind them.

"What are you doing to them?" He stared open-mouthed, then quickly glanced down at a monitor.

"I've been informing the Sli of your betrayal," Picard announced, sweeping an arm toward the floating aliens.

"You can't talk to them—" Brund realized what he was saying and abruptly cut off his protest.

"You say that because you believe no one can communicate with the Sli."

"That's absurd!" Brund denied. "I meant the Sli are mad at you people; that's why you can't talk to them. They told me that," he added with a righteous nod.

"He's lying," Deanna said, not bothering to keep her voice down.

"You!" Brund sputtered. "You, shut up!"

"Please, Daimon Brund. You're speaking to the person who achieved this remarkable breakthrough. Counselor Troi has brilliantly combined her empathic abilities with a spectral translator programmed to respond to the Sli's colors." Brund flinched at that. Picard smoothly added, "As you know, the Sli react negatively to darker tones."

"Oh, really," Brund said nonchalantly. "I've heard that might be possible."

"I was in the middle of informing the Sli that their own partners—no, more than that—their own friends have slaughtered one of them in the name of greed. I thought it only fair that you hear my accusation as well."

"You aren't really telling them that," Brund denied.

"It's a sad duty I must perform, but the Sli have a right to know."

"What are you talking about?" Brund demanded. "You got no proof." He yelled directly at the Sli, "He's got no proof!" He gestured to the captain. "Go on, tell them you've got no proof."

"If you can communicate with them, I suggest you do it yourself."

Brund's upper lip was twitching. "Did you tell them someone tried to kill Hartog? Who do they think is going to protect them?"

"I appreciate your concern," Picard said softly. "Such a short while ago, you wanted to kill these four Sli."

Brund blinked at him, then tried to sneer. "I don't need to talk to you, Picard—"

Deanna suddenly realized the emanations were increasing in strength. She nudged the captain.

Picard barely acknowledged her. "That's fine, Daimon Brund. The Sli appreciate it when you struggle against yourself. I'm sure you must be feeling quite battered upon right now." He turned to the Sli, giving them a fond smile. "I'll just keep talking to the Sli. I'll keep telling them different ways they could feel about this betrayal of yours. There are dozens of possibilities. I suppose they could be flippant about it—after all, with friends like the Ferengi, who needs enemies? Or they could be naive," he said in a mocking voice. "I know you were just trying to help the Sli with that bomb, not hurt them. Or they might even feel contempt for your pitiful attempt to destroy them."

The words echoed in Deanna's head. It was the speech from *Cyrano de Bergerac*. The captain was throwing himself into the words, acting them, feeling what he was saying. She followed his lead, copying his emotion and focusing it for the Sli.

"Of course," Picard said, tapping a finger lightly to his chin, "the Sli could feel a bit uneasy about so many Ferengi being around—you would like to kill them; isn't that what you were asking me to do?"

In the Sli, the bright colors were splintering into even smaller fragments, whirling faster as she concentrated.

"Now, hold on, Picard!"

Picard directly addressed the Sli, ignoring the daimon's attempts to interrupt. "I'd understand it if you're feeling ashamed for having trusted the Ferengi all this time. Still, you also seem to be a rather quick-tempered lot; perhaps you've been thinking of retaliation. It would be difficult to blame you for that as well. I also know you like to brood on things, so I guess you'll be spending a fair amount of time worrying about whether you'll want to associate with the Ferengi anymore—"

"Stop it, Picard!" the daimon was shouting. "You'll get us all in trouble agitating them like that!"

"I?" Picard asked, rounding on the daimon, his eyes blazing. "I am in no trouble, Daimon. However, you are."

The Sli flickered with brilliant color, four burning fires coalescing into a single blaze, a vibrant inferno. Their tentacles dangled below, ebony, dense and wet.

Picard gestured toward them with flare and drama. "You've betrayed these Sli, Brund, and there are more reactions than stars in the sky to the sort of behavior you Ferengi have indulged in. Oh, yes! I've only just begun!"

The voice of Commander Riker suddenly cut in.

"Captain Picard, should we arm photon torpedoes? I suggest we forcibly repel the *Tampanium* from our vicinity."

Picard lifted one brow at Brund. "An excellent idea, Number One. Hold your fire until I finish my suggestions to the Sli." He turned back to the quartet as if it were perfectly reasonable to destroy the Ferengi Marauder. "Now, where was I? Oh, yes, hysteria is always expected in cases of this sort—blind, uncontrolled abandonment of all senses. Once you're through with that, you'll probably be quite sad for a while." He frowned thoughtfully at them. "Perhaps even depressed. I wouldn't worry; the vindictiveness that follows can be quite an enlivening experience—"

Brund leaned forward, sharply cutting off the subspace link.

Riker requested, "Captain, shall I fire across their bow?"

"Hold your fire." Picard lifted his hand. "What is the position of the Ferengi vessel?"

There was a pause, then Data's voice evenly announced, "The *Tampanium* is leaving orbit, sir, heading 03 mark 25, at warp three."

"It worked!" Deanna exclaimed. "Brund really believed we were communicating with them."

Picard snapped his hand shut in the air as if capturing something. "All we needed was a little panache."

The captain's smile spread across his face, and she felt herself laughing in response. He so rarely allowed himself to show such strong emotion, and she was caught right up in it with him. When she realized their quartet of Sli were still listening, she focused the good feeling right at them, this time not holding anything back.

Chapter Twenty-four

CAPTAIN PICARD immediately gave the order for the crew to stop resisting the effects of the remaining Sli. As Deanna said, "With only four Sli, the projections won't be nearly as strong. There may be a short burst of activity among the crew, then things should quickly settle back down to normal once everyone stops fighting it."

They went to sickbay, where Dr. Crusher gave Deanna and Captain Picard the results of her examination of Mon Hartog. Deanna caught a glimpse of him, restrained by a blue security forcefield. His headpiece was ripped, revealing paler skin on the base of his skull. His neck was red and swollen.

"According to Lieutenant Worf and Technician Tarses," the doctor said, "they observed Captain Walch strangling Mon Hartog. Worf intervened to save the Ferengi's life."

"Where is Captain Walch now?" Picard kept glancing over at Hartog's motionless form.

"Worf called Security. He ordered the guards to escort Walch back to his quarters and remain on duty there."

She pulled her coat around her more securely. "Tarses had a strained ligament in his right arm, and Worf's hand was bleeding again. I bonded it, and he supervised the erection of the forcefield around Hartog. Then he said he was returning to his quarters. Apparently he was supposed to be confined there."

"And Tarses?" Deanna asked.

"He's helping Alyssa in the other room. He seems jittery, but everyone's calming down now that the Ferengi are gone."

Deanna suppressed a sigh. She was relieved that neither Worf nor Tarses had anything to do with this attempted murder.

Beverly tightened her lips. "I hate to think of that sweet old man trying to kill someone. But I know it was because of those Sli."

"I agree," Deanna said. "Captain, I'd like our inquiry to be strictly confidential for the time being. One thing we do know—the circumstances were extremely unusual and provoking. Now that the Sli are gone, there's little chance Walch will try something like this again."

Picard considered her suggestion for a moment. "Agreed, Counselor. Meanwhile, I'll find out what Starfleet's position is regarding this situation."

Deanna returned to check on the Sli, but was eventually called back to her office by crew members who were feeling more normal now, but who were also wondering what it was they'd just gone through. It was as if everyone on board decided to have an emotional crisis at once, and were now trying to discuss their insights with her.

During a brief lull, Deanna sat down, putting her hand to her head and trying to subdue the ache that seemed to have settled there after her heightened emotions had drained away.

She was almost too tired to get up again. Her office was so serene, with its cool, pastel lighting and soft couch. She closed her eyes for a moment, breathing in the faint, crisp scent she programmed into the air freshener.

The door chime startled her. She called out, "Come in," as she struggled to get up. When she saw it was Worf, she sat back down.

"Counselor Troi," he said by way of greeting. He stepped inside awkwardly, glancing around suspiciously as he usually did. He'd once told her the delicate decor of her office made him . . . edgy.

"Worf, what are you doing here?"

"I wish to be returned to duty. The situation on board is not yet stabilized and I am needed at my post."

She leaned back, folding her hands in her lap. "How are you feeling?"

"I am well."

"Your stomach?" she pressed.

"I am well," Worf insisted, clasping his hands behind his back.

"Come on, Worf. I need more than that." She sat back, calmly looking up at him. "I haven't seen a report from you regarding Captain Walch's attack on Mon Hartog."

He looked down at her with something like surprise. "I informed Dr. Crusher and Captain Picard what happened."

"I have Captain Walch's statement. Based on my earlier assessment, I believe it was due to the Sli's influence that he tried to kill the Ferengi."

"I would agree."

"There may be a full investigation, especially if Mon Hartog files charges," she said, carefully watching his reaction.

There wasn't a flicker on his face. "Hartog is an assassin. He is not in a position to file charges."

Deanna shrugged uneasily. "It all makes sense to you, doesn't it?"

"Yes," he said simply.

Deanna thought for a moment. "What was Tarses doing with you on Deck 13? That's nowhere near sickbay."

Worf hesitated for the first time during the interview. His hands tightened their hold on each other behind his back. "The Sli were affecting Tarses."

"You mean they drew him to the shuttlebay?"

"I believe that is true."

"So," she said, "Tarses just happened to be there, and you both saw Captain Walch try to strangle Hartog. Then you stopped him."

Worf met her eyes, his face expressionless. "That is correct."

Deanna stopped, stymied by his monosyllabic approach. His report lacked substance. "Is there something you're not telling me, Worf?"

"Do not pursue the matter," he said evenly. "The emanations of the Sli caused temporary insanity. No one can be held accountable for crimes committed during this situation."

Deanna was tempted to pursue the matter, but the things that happened under the Sli's emanations were so deeply buried that she didn't know if she could get to it without doing more harm than good.

After a moment, she asked, "Are you still angry with Captain Walch?"

Worf actually relaxed. "No."

"You're sure?" she pressed.

"I erred when I believed he had betrayed me. Captain Walch was instrumental in the development of my sense of honor. For that, I owe the man a great debt."

She put her finger to her lips, thinking fast. "Did it

have something to do with why you've been upset about Alexander lately?"

His eyes widened, but he didn't answer.

"Come on, Worf. You know I'm not going to return you to duty with just that." She almost wanted to smile, this was so perfect. "Sit down and talk to me."

Worf seemed about to refuse, but he dropped into the chair she gestured toward and glared at her.

"I do not need to discuss this. I understand my error."

"Oh, really." She leaned forward. "That being . . . ?"

Worf let out his breath almost in a growl. She had him. "Very well. I have been proceeding under the assumption that Alexander would not develop a sense of honor unless he confronted his Klingon nature."

"But Alexander's no more aggressive than other boys his age," Deanna protested.

"Yes, that concerned me. I grappled with my aggressive urges when I was young. I developed a creed of honor to guide my actions."

"Worf, your son follows a very different path to his honor."

He gave her a sidelong look of surprise. "That was my conclusion."

"Perhaps you identified with Alexander too much. His situation is easier than yours was, Worf, in many ways. He has you, his own father and a Klingon role model. Don't be so concerned with how he gets there, just *be* what you want Alexander to be. Let him see what can be his. And then let him make his own choice—to be human or Klingon, or both."

Again, Worf seemed uncomfortable. "It did not occur to me until today that Alexander's mother was killed by a Klingon's hand."

"Well, that's something you and Alexander do have in common. You both had parents killed in Klingon plots for power."

"The Duras family! The curse on our clan." Worf

turned his head away. "But I did not know that when I was young. I believed my enemy was Romulan. It served to strengthen me."

"Romulan or Klingon, what does it matter? You know that honor isn't gained by fighting individuals but by taking a stand on your ideals. In that area, I have no doubts about Alexander."

"Kurn does." Worf seemed to wish those words unsaid as soon as he uttered them.

"What do you mean?"

"He has challenged Alexander and me to the Dobatlh PuqloD. A test of a son's honor to his clan."

"What does Kurn want?"

A simple question, but Worf considered it carefully. "Alexander has never been to Qo'noS, the Klingon home world. He has never met my brother."

"Perhaps Kurn is offended by your distance and is expressing it this way," Deanna offered.

Worf seemed struck by her words. He frowned in thought. "It is true that Alexander is to be the next head of the clan. Kurn may feel . . . slighted."

Deanna was glad to see that Worf was actually reflecting on his problem. "Why don't you find out what your brother really wants?"

Worf nodded. "I will speak to Kurn. Perhaps he will withdraw the challenge if I agree to return with Alexander for a visit." He stood up, his eyes slightly creased at the corners. "Thank you, Counselor." He held her gaze for one more moment, then turned and started for the door. When it opened he glanced back. "May I return to duty?"

She hesitated. "You do like to work things out on your own, don't you, Worf?" He nodded, his faint smile gone. She threw up her hands, a mock gesture of defeat. She couldn't get away from it. "Yes, you may return to duty."

* * *

It was late by the time she got to Captain Picard's ready room. Deanna headed straight for the sofa, comfortably tucking one leg under her as she sat down.

The captain got up from his chair and came around to lean against the front of his desk. "Well, Counselor?"

"Jacob Walch confessed to the assault on Mon Hartog. Both Worf and Tarses witnessed it. Worf made the point that under the conditions of the past two days, no one could legally be held accountable."

"Starfleet Command seems to agree. We're to turn Mon Hartog over to Starbase 81." He rubbed his chin. "I believe our investigation has been more than thorough."

"I agree. But I'm glad you're back to being cautious again," she told him.

Picard straightened his uniform. "The Sli were an exhilarating experience, I must admit. I haven't reacted with as much abandon in a very long while."

"Some of the crew have requested access to Decks 9, 10, and 11 so they can experience the four Sli again. Captain Walch put in an official request from his tourists."

"Surely you're joking, Counselor." Picard couldn't seem to believe it. "After everything that's happened?"

"You said it yourself—it's exhilarating."

Picard shook his head. "Deny their requests, Counselor. More study needs to be done regarding the effects of the Sli." He consulted his padd. "We've also notified the other two commercial vessels carrying Sli 'artists' about the Ferengi bombing. Scans will be performed on every power cell for the Sli's life support units."

"Daimon Brund has probably alerted them to dispose of any bombs." Deanna shook her head. "I don't know which of them was worse. Brund left Hartog behind without a second thought."

"Starfleet won't deal lightly with Mon Hartog. He not only killed the Sli and destroyed the *Prospector,* but he endangered everyone on board."

"I wouldn't doubt it if he was hovering around the Sli just so he could project terrible thoughts to them in those brief moments they were actually listening. I'm sure that's what he was doing with Alexander in the flight booth—provoking the boy's emotions to disturb the Sli."

"Hartog always wore black," Picard said thoughtfully.

"Well, this is exactly what the Ferengi were trying to prevent," Deanna said with certainty. "For the first time the Federation has unlimited access to the Sli. Our diplomats will finally have the chance to establish communications with them."

"Guinan still laughs when I suggest that to her."

Deanna smiled and looked down, remembering her own stimulated enthusiasm over the Sli. "Guinan may be right. At best, the Sli will be difficult to understand. But I do know they're much more willing to listen to me now that I've stopped resisting their efforts."

"Your discovery of the fractal basis for the Sli's language has also been commented on. Starfleet's diplomatic corps believes that may be the key they needed."

"They have some interesting work ahead of them."

"Whether or not they will succeed, they are eager to start. And the Federation Council is very pleased that we have the four Sli on board as our guests. We're to drop them off at Starbase 81 when we tow in the *Prospector.*" Picard glanced back toward the window. "They won't have to wait long."

Deanna shook her head, confused. "What about the Lessenar mission?"

"Our participation appears to have been terminated." He frowned slightly. "Commander Riker has reported a possible violation of the Prime Directive."

"Sir?" she asked, completely taken by surprise.

The door opened as Picard said, "Here he is now. Just back from the capital city. Commander."

Riker nodded to Deanna, and she was glad to see his old casual confidence had returned. "Sir, I didn't see Council Head Wiccy. The council was . . . forcibly recalled this afternoon. Something called a 'People's Coalition' is now in charge."

"That sounds like a coup, Number One."

"It was." Riker's answer was dry, reminding Deanna of his battles with Council Head Wiccy. "Apparently the outlying populace finally caught on that the government wasn't doing anything about the problem. I saw the people in the more remote regions. They were desperate."

Picard nodded thoughtfully. "The primary concern of the council did appear superficial."

"Yes, sir." Riker squarely met his gaze. "I spoke with one of the new leaders of the coalition, a man named Reeves. Chryso and I met him while we were delivering relief supplies. Sir, he told us that they formed the coalition and organized the takeover with the communication tranceivers we included in the supplies. The tranceivers were meant to help the outlying areas coordinate distribution."

"Instead, they used them to plan a coup," Deanna said.

"I see, Number One. You're right—this could be interpreted as a violation of the Prime Directive."

"Giving the inhabitants tranceivers is standard procedure in coordinating a long-term relief effort. It's supposed to prompt the inhabitants to help themselves." Riker couldn't hold back the pleased light in his eyes. "They learned quickly in this case."

"Our intervention caused the destruction of the very government that requested our aid," Picard reminded him.

"Sir, that Advisory Council would have paid lip service to our suggestions and gone on with exactly what they were doing." Riker tried to control his anger. "Council Head Wiccy was engaged in trade talks with Daimon Brund when the People's Coalition took over."

"Trade talks!" Deanna exclaimed.

"Yes. The agreement with the Advisory Council was natural resources for barastatic filters and atmospheric ion generators. A Ferengi Alliance supply ship was scheduled to be here within hours."

Deanna couldn't believe it. "The Ferengi would steal that planet breathless."

"So we told them." Riker flicked a glance through the viewport. "Lieutenant Chryso was right. Their problem is too complex for simple repairs. Their atmosphere and water require eco-regeneration, and that takes a coordinated application of dozens of procedures over the next few generations."

"Lieutenant Chryso believes the Ferengi measures wouldn't be enough?" Picard asked.

"With the research her team has done, Chryso had the data to prove ion generators would only aggravate the situation." Riker shifted, the only sign of his discomfort over his battles with the scientist. "She was very thorough. She convinced the coalition, and they immediately ordered the implementation of her recommendations. They also rescinded their agreement with the Ferengi and formally requested the aid of a science ship from Starfleet to guide them through the first stage of regeneration."

Picard nodded. "We just received notification that the *Von Neumann* has been assigned to this system."

"That's why we were late. We waited in the council chambers for confirmation. Starfleet informed the new government that the science ship should be here by tomorrow to begin work on the regeneration. Now it's up to them."

"Well done, Commander," Picard acknowledged. "However, the use of the tranceivers to instigate the coup is unfortunate."

"But, sir, the needs of the inhabitants are being served now."

"We will never know that for certain, Number One." Picard's voice was flat. "That's the danger with violating the Prime Directive, even if indirectly. The repercussions reach far beyond what we can see." He held up a hand, stopping Riker from comment. "However, I won't recommend a change in the standard procedure. In planetary relief efforts, the inhabitants must be an integral part of the solution."

"I agree. I believe they took a positive step."

Picard nodded shortly. "Very well. The planet is stabilized pending the *Von Neumann*'s arrival?"

"Aye, sir. My report will be ready shortly."

"First, see to securing the tractor beam for the *Prospector*. Starbase 81 is waiting for those Sli."

"Aye, sir."

The captain waited until Riker left, then he was drawn toward the viewport. He gazed thoughtfully down at the planet. "If you want to see the borealis again, you should come look now, Counselor."

She shook her head. "I never much liked it, sir."

Simon Tarses paused outside the holodeck. There was a swelling inside his chest, an anticipation that surprised him with its sharp clarity. A hole was yearning to be filled, an open wound ready to be bathed in a warm and healing sight.

"Computer, begin program."

Tarses took a deep breath as the doors hissed open. Clouds of low-lying fog swirled up and around him as he slowly stepped forward.

He was standing on a low dirt butte overlooking a vast

and fertile valley. It was bounded on all sides by tall, jagged mountains at impossible distances. The sun was low, coolly tinting the mist at his knees. On the slopes just in front of him was the city, a gracefully spired, towered cluster that soared to sparkling heights.

Tarses raised both hands, smiling. Romulus.

THE INCREDIBLE STORY BEHIND ONE OF STAR TREK'S BEST-LOVED CHARACTERS

STAR TREK®

SAREK

A.C. CRISPIN

Pocket Books is proud to present SAREK, the sweeping story of the life of Spock's full-Vulcan father. Since his introduction, the coolly logical Sarek has been the subject of endless speculation. Now, finally, comes a book that spans Sarek's life and illustrious career as one of the Federation's premiere ambassadors as well as his unpredecented marriage to a human woman, and conflict with his son, Spock, that lead to an eighteen-year estrangement between the two men.

POCKET
BOOKS

**Available in hardcover
from Pocket Books**

934